Shirley Shea left school at 15 to earn a living. After the war she joined a local radio station as women's editor and continued to work in radio and TV until the late 70's when she retired to take up full-time writing.

Although this is her first novel, she has written several documentaries, two of them award winning. She lives in Toronto.

Already published in the
Pandora Women Crime Writers Series are:

Pandora Contemporary Crime

Amateur City and Murder at the Nightwood Bar
by Katherine Forrest
Stoner McTavish and Something Shady by Sarah Dreher
Fieldwork by Maureen Moore
Vanishing Act by Joy Magezis
The Monarchs are Flying by Marion Foster
Study in Lilac by Maria Antonia Oliver.
The Always Anonymous Beast by Lauren Wright Douglas

Pandora Classic Crime

Green for Danger and London Particular
by Christianna Brand
Death of a Doll and Blood Upon the Snow and Duet of Death
by Hilda Lawrence
Murder in Pastiche by Marion Mainwaring
Bring the Monkey by Miles Franklin
The Port of London Murders and Easy Prey
by Josephine Bell
The Spinster's Secret by Anthony Gilbert (Lucy Malleson)
Mischief by Charlotte Armstrong
The Hours Before Dawn by Celia Fremlin
Murder's Little Sister by Pamela Branch

Victims
SHIRLEY SHEA

PANDORA

London   New York   Sydney

First published in Canada in 1985 by Simon and Pierre Publishing Co
Ltd.
This edition first published in Great Britain in 1989 by Pandora Press,
an imprint of the trade division of Unwin Hyman Limited.

© Shirley Shea 1985

All rights reserved. No part of this publication may be reproduced,
stored in a retrieval system, or transmitted in any form or by any
means, electronic, mechanical, photocopying, recording or otherwise,
without the prior permission of Unwin Hyman Limited.

This book is sold subject to the condition that it shall not, by way of
trade or otherwise, be lent, resold, hired out or otherwise circulated,
without the publishers' prior consent in any form of binding or cover
other than that in which it is published, and without a similar condition
including this condition being imposed on the purchaser.

Pandora Press
Unwin Hyman Limited
15–17 Broadwick Street, London W1V 1FP

Allen and Unwin Australia Pty Ltd
8 Napier Street, North Sydney, NSW 2060, Australia

Allen and Unwin New Zealand Pty Ltd with the Port Nicholson Press
60 Cambridge Terrace, Wellington, New Zealand

British Library Cataloguing in Publication Data
Shea, Shirley
Victims.
I. Title
813'.54[F]
ISBN: 0-04-440291-0

Printed in
Great Britain by Cox and Wyman Ltd, Reading

*To my aunt Stella
who believed
but couldn't wait.*

Pandora Women Crime Writers

Series Editors: Rosalind Coward and Linda Semple

In introducing the *Pandora Women Crime Writers* series we have two aims: to reprint the best of women crime writers who have disappeared from print and to introduce a new generation of women crime writers to all devotees of the genre. We also hope to seduce new readers to the pleasures of detective fiction.

Women have used the tradition of crime writing inventively since the end of the last century. Indeed, in many periods women have dominated crime writing, as in the so-called golden age of detective fiction, usually defined as between the first novel of Agatha Christie and the last of Dorothy L. Sayers. Often the most popular novels of the day, and those thought to be the best in their genre, were written by women. But as in so many areas of women's writing, many of these have been allowed to go out of print. Few people know the names of Josephine Bell, Pamela Branch, Hilda Lawrence, Marion Mainwaring or Anthony Gilbert (whose real name was Lucy Malleson). Their novels are just as good and entertaining as when they were first written.

Women's importance in the field of crime writing is just as vital today. P. D. James, Ruth Rendell and Patricia Highsmith have all ensured that crime writing is treated seriously. Not so well known, but equally flourishing, is a new branch of feminist crime writers. We plan to introduce many new writers from this area, from England and other countries.

The integration of reprints and new novels is sometimes uneasy. Some writers do make snobbish, even racist remarks. However, it is a popular misconception that all earlier novels are always snobbish and racist. Many of our chosen and favourite authors managed to avoid, sometimes deliberately, the prevailing views. Others are more rooted in the ideologies of their time but when their remarks jar, it does serve to remind us that any novel must be understood by reference to the historical context in which it is written.

Some of the best writers who will be appearing in this series are: Josephine Bell, Ina Bouman, Christianna Brand, Pamela Branch, Sarah Dreher, Katherine V. Forrest, Miles Franklin, Anthony Gilbert (Lucy Malleson), Hilda Lawrence, Marion Mainwaring, Nancy Spain ...

Linda Semple
Rosalind Coward

December 1984

The Ford pickup turned off the side road and pulled in between the slightly run-down buildings with practiced precision. The young man at the wheel stepped out into the frosty not-yet-light morning and glanced over his shoulder before stepping away from the truck. The gesture was more habit than precaution, so deeply ingrained that it came frequently and without conscious thought. His friends teased him about it occasionally, and he suffered their good-natured joshing without rancor.

His co-workers at the paint factory called him Mac, and this, too, he tolerated without comment. It had taken some time to become accustomed to the nickname. There were still times when he failed to respond to it, but they had become the exception rather than the norm. So, too, were the dark moods of depression that in the past had engulfed him with bio-rhythm regularity.

A light fall of snow covered the ground, marred only by his tire tracks and footprints. Gusts of wind swirled the fine white powder into drifts, a shifting mosaic of mini moguls.

A blizzard was forecast for later in the day. The morning news had carried a storm warning followed by the suggestion that listeners stay home if at all possible. Mac, who had long since lost his faith in weathermen, ignored the warning.

The buildings, clustered on an acre of ground on the factory edge of town, were empty. The plant was closed for the Christmas season and Mac, who had volunteered as skeleton staff, enjoyed being on his own with no one else around. He had a phobic need for privacy that led him at times to lock himself in the bathroom at home, remaining cloistered until routed by someone with a need more immediate. The Christmas shutdown was ideal. It provided a legitimate excuse to get away for a few hours each day, with the spin-off advantage of enhancing his reputation as a good Joe-on-the-job.

After unlocking the door of the main building he stepped

inside, stamping his feet on the worn sisal mat in the hall. Switching on the fluorescent lights in the general office, he hung his parka on the coat-tree next to old Mrs. Brown's desk. Later he would check the buildings to make sure nothing was amiss, but his first priority was a cup of coffee along with the copy of yesterday's newspaper he had brought from home.

He plugged in the electric kettle, and spooned some instant coffee into the mug kept in his drawer. There was no creamer so he drank it black, sipping slowly as he worked his way through the paper, reading each item with equal interest. There was another layoff at the local auto plant, a rumored Cabinet switch in Ottawa, a thank you to readers who had supported the community Christmas drive for toys and used clothing.

After-Christmas sale ads outpercentaged the news and editorial content. He read sizes, colors, price comparisons, with the same meticulous care expended on the front section. One of the shops had a special on children's snow-suits. He made a mental note to stop there on his way home.

The stern boyish face relaxed in a smile. Whenever he thought of his young family a gentle, spring-like warmth spread through his body. In spite of the times when he had to shut himself off, to feel nothing around him but empty space, he knew he couldn't have survived without them. They were his reason for being, his silver cord to the future.

Once he would have welcomed death. Now he had everything in the world to live for. Every day he offered born-again thanks to the Saviour who had brought him out of the wilderness into the promised land.

Folding the newspaper, he dropped it in the waste-paper basket, then rinsed his mug and replaced it. Compulsively neat, his friends said. A pain in the ass, some of them thought privately, when he was held up as a model by their wives.

The ancient clock above the filing cabinets showed eight a.m., time enough to check the outbuildings and be back in the office to answer the phones by nine. Not that he expected a barrage of calls. Orders had fallen off sharply during the last few months. Word had it they wouldn't pick up until spring. On Monday there was one call that turned out to be a wrong number. Tuesday morning his mother called to ask if he was lonely. Tuesday afternoon there was a call from home asking him to pick up some milk. It wasn't exactly business as usual, which was all the more reason to be on hand, just in case.

Nu Colour Paints was a family business, started half a century before by a farmer who discovered he could make more money mixing paint for his neighbors than by selling milk to the local dairy. The original farmhouse still stood on the site, half-hidden at the rear of the property by a tangled screen of mature cedars. The narrow lane that led to the abandoned house had grown over through lack of use, branches laced above what was now little more than a trail.

The plant at the front of the property consisted of one large and two smaller buildings, with an adjacent parking lot for visitors and staff. The surrounding area, once grazing land for cows, was a maze of factories and industrial units. During the uptempo seventies the manufacturing plants had run three shifts a day, holidays included. This year all had closed down, taking advantage of the season to cut operating costs and trim overhead.

Mac pulled on his parka and walked through the warehouse and shipping area toward the back entrance. The varnish department was just a few yards away, housed in a shed-like structure that afforded an unobstructed view of the interior from the doorway.

Everything seemed normal, yet he sensed something was out of kilter. Mac's animal instinct, mothballed for years, flashed a warning signal to his brain. There was just enough heat in the small building to keep the pipes from freezing, but his shiver was a reaction to more than the temperature.

Cautiously, body tense and at the ready, he stepped inside. The windows and back door were locked, bolts in place as he had left them the day before. Satisfied the building was undisturbed he stepped out into the fresh air, pushing against the door after he heard the lock catch to make certain it was secure.

Frowning, he cut across to the powder building where colors were mixed and blended into a chemical rainbow of pastels and solids.

This building, too, was empty, but the feeling of a recent presence was even stronger. Whether it was déjà vu, osmosis or gut instinct, Mac knew, without knowing how he knew, that he was walking in someone else's footsteps.

There were no signs of forced entry or tampering, either inside or out. The windows had not been jimmied, the door had not been sprung. Nor was there a sign of loitering in the snow. He shrugged, telling himself whoever had been there had long since gone, with no harm done.

He glanced over his shoulder as he started back to the main building, thinking once everyone was back on the job he'd bring up the idea of a watchdog one more time. Not that he worried about a break and enter. There was nothing in the plant worth stealing. But ever since his promotion to foreman he had been obsessed by the thought of vandalism. The danger of fire was so great that a rock through the window, a kid with a match, and the whole place could blow sky-high. He had seen a paint plant on Toronto's lakeshore blow up, steel drums soaring through the air like champagne corks, rising effortlessly through rolling clouds of black smoke. It was a terrifying sight, visible for miles. He had no desire for a repeat performance.

Back in the warehouse he locked the door and dropped the heavy holding-bar in place before checking the main floor offices and storage areas. He saw nothing, sensed nothing.

The caustic department was last on the list. He had never been comfortable in the small, dark basement room with its twin acid tanks and rough concrete floor sloping into a bucket-centered drain. The windowless brick walls were sinister reminders of another time and place. It was a room he avoided whenever he could, sending others to clean the drums and check the bucket for overflow each night. Escaping the caustic room was one of the advantages gained by his promotion.

Treading slowly, he descended the narrow staircase one step at a time, fearful of its imminent collapse. The wood was old and creaked under his weight. He was almost at the bottom before he noticed that the door at the foot of the stairs was open. It, too, was old, and the latch had a habit of not holding, but he was sure he had closed it the day before. One more thing to have maintenance check when the plant was back on schedule.

He pressed the light switch and the wire-caged bulb in the ceiling blinked on, casting an orange glow over the tanks and stacks of steel drums. The stale air was still and motionless as a tomb.

As he stepped into the room he felt it. He knew that this time it was more than a feeling, more than the whisper of a presence come and gone. This time there was a living breathing body. The body was there, and it was in wait.

His skin prickled as the hair on the nape of his neck and backs of his hands rose. Rooted to the spot, upper body swiveling like a heat-sensitive monitor, he scanned the close quarters with eyes narrowed and ears fine-tuned. His body was on full alert, but he was not frightened. His superb physical condition, the result of years of daily workouts with weights and pulleys, gave him confidence in the face of danger.

There was no movement, no shadow out of context, no sound of breathing but his own.

'Is there anybody here?' His voice bounced off the walls, the words ricocheting like bullets.

He waited for a moment, not really expecting an answer, then started toward the platform beside the large vat.

As he neared the side of the tank he glanced back over his shoulder. As though coordinated to the turn of his head, the light went out and the door slammed shut.

Mac dropped into a half crouch, tensed for contact. The room was still. 'Who are you? What do you want?' He spoke with clear, sharp authority.

Seconds passed. The silence continued. Mac felt the old, half-forgotten rage welling up, the hot rush of adrenalin flowing through his veins. He wanted the light on, an explanation from whoever was there, the game to be over and done with.

He inched toward the door, groping along the wall for the light switch. When he was just one step short, the light came on as suddenly as it had gone off. He blinked, his eyes trying to refocus after the inky blackness.

Like the jumbled images of a television set just turned on, the room came into slow perspective, bringing the form of the intruder with it. Tall. Slim. Standing at ease with feet apart and hands clasped behind.

Incredulous, Mac stared at the figure before him. Then, feeling the walls closing in, the suffocating pressure of this room he hated, the anger at being played with and mocked, he lunged forward.

The activated response was lightning swift, slow-motion slow. Time slipped into another dimension, undisciplined as in a nightmare when events stream by but their parts remain static.

It happened too fast for Mac to counter, yet he saw the entire scene in minute detail. He saw the arm swing up in a graceful arc, the can of spray with nozzle aimed, recognized the familiar brand name of a household insecticide that his wife had used to get rid of roaches; he saw himself riding his bicycle home from school, skinny dipping in the river, on his wedding day, eating breakfast that morning.

The last thing he saw was the fine, mist-like spray as it spurted from the nozzle. It struck him full in the face, blinding him, cutting off his breath, seeping into his pores. Eyes streaming, gasping for air, he doubled over, cradling his face in both hands. It was the perfect position. The iron bar smashed across the exposed neck, crushing the spine and flopping the head off-center. The curved end of the bar, used to hook the drain bucket, crashed against the floor, chipping the concrete. Bits of flesh clung to the metal. Mac lay in a crumpled heap. After a few moments his body stopped jerking and lay still.

It took almost an hour to remove the clothing, dismember the body, stuff the parts into garbage bags, label each with a shipping tag inscribed with a large black number 9, slip the bar into the acid tank and hose down the floor.

It took almost as long to walk up the farmhouse lane for the car, load the bags into the trunk, then lock up neatly as Mac would have done. The car pulled away slowly.

At the intersection, the driver braked and looked back. The snow, falling heavily, had turned the grubby buildings into a pristine picture post-card. Within minutes there would be no trail to follow, no tracks to trace. Nothing left behind but a Ford pickup humped with snow.

1

Late May 1984

It was a sunny, warm Sunday morning in Etobicoke. David was out of town, a weekend rarity. Sylvia had the whole day to herself. A pleasant thought. The air was still, the neighborhood country-quiet: the only sound the chatter of birds trying to drive a determined black squirrel from the peanut feeder.

She opened the morning paper. Glanced at the headline:

BATTERED BLONDE LATEST IN STRING OF APARTMENT MURDERS

The large black caps were a threatening reminder. No one was safe. Fear not only stalked the streets, it found its way behind locked doors and drawn shades.

Sylvia shrugged. It's getting worse, she thought. Still, it had never been a picnic for women. Moralists blamed the victims: *If they didn't flaunt it, men wouldn't want it.* A trite cop-out. Women were humped, thumped and ravished back in the days of high-necked dresses and button boots. So what else was new?

David and Sylvia Jenning lived ten minutes from downtown Toronto but their peaceful residential street was light years removed from the brooding inner core of Canada's largest city. The street was permanently foreshortened into a single block, bounded on the east by a main artery, on the west by an overgrown railroad yard inhabited by rabbits, skunks, redwinged blackbirds and shunting engines. The railyard was splendid dog-walking ground. It was also, judging by the empty wine and whiskey bottles, a favorite haunt of district winos. But that was a half block and several lifestyles removed. Here in a backyard made private by steel fencing and dense shrubbery, even the next door neighbors were comfortably distant.

Sylvia poured herself another cup of coffee and sipped it absentmindedly. Early morning was her favorite time of day.

The lawn, covered with dew, looked lush and rich. The water

in the pool was translucent. Masses of pale pink petunias and impatiens splashed gentle color against the green. Even Prinnie, the stray white Persian, harmonized, her pink pads and ears a perfect match for the white planters filled with pink geraniums set at intervals around the pool.

The white Persian was just one of a half dozen neighborhood strays that Sylvia fed surreptitiously. She was not overly fond of cats, but she couldn't bear the thought of them starving in the midst of an overweight diet-conscious society. The strays Sylvia fed were as sleek and glossy as pampered house pets.

Coffee finished, she headed for the heated pool where she swam her routine fifteen minutes followed by the usual half hour of exercise in the gym set up in the basement. David no longer had time for the gym. Sylvia, on the other hand, had become a fitness buff. Growing up in the Northern Ontario mining town of Sudbury she had learned to swim in icy spring-fed lakes, handle a canoe in rough water, snowshoe along backwoods trails. With the coming of David her priorities had changed, as had her lifestyle. Over the years she had become sedentary. It was the week she spent with her parents at the family cabin, the week she discovered she could no longer swim the narrow inlet between their island and the mainland, that she decided to take herself in hand. David had both pool and gym installed at her request. As a result she found herself at thirty-nine years of age in better shape than at any time since the early days of her marriage.

She was attractive but not beautiful. Tall and slim, with sun-streaked hair and skin tanned to an even bronze, she had a healthy outdoor look that belied her life as suburban wife. Her eyes, large and smoky grey, framed by dark lashes that contrasted sharply with her sun-bleached hair, were her most striking

feature. She had been told they were lovely. She had also been told they were hypnotic and slightly disturbing. It amused her that the dreamy, far-off quality that unsettled even her closest friends was the result of nearsightedness. It appealed to her sense of humor that her most serious physical flaw should be perceived as her most appealing physical attribute. Typical, she felt, of a world more concerned with appearance than substance.

Ten minutes into her laps, the phone rang. She thought of not answering it, then raced to pick it up on the fifth ring because it might be David.

'Syl?'

She could have kicked herself for not letting it ring. The shrill, high-pitched voice belonged to Anne Campbell, a friend recently divorced and temporarily anti-male. There were times when Sylvia enjoyed her company but today she wasn't in the mood.

'Yes, Anne.'

'I was hoping I'd catch you. Got anything planned?'

'A nice quiet day doing nothing. David's out of town. I thought I'd just fiddle around. Maybe do some gardening.'

'Good. I'll come over and help.'

The line went dead before she had a chance to protest and Sylvia knew she would be spending part of the day with a newly-liberated female who saw life in terms of issues.

'At least David isn't around to fight with her,' she thought. The two of them together were too much. David had never been overly fond of Anne, and since her divorce his dislike had grown into barely concealed hostility. Not that Sylvia blamed him. Unlike many divorcées, Anne reveled in her new freedom. She was a born-again feminist, impatient with marriage, sex roles and male superiority. She was also very much into minority rights and the failure of the judicial system to protect the law-abiding citizen from harm.

It was her cynicism about the law that David couldn't accept. As one of Canada's most successful criminal lawyers, his life was devoted to justice and the law. Sylvia knew that in his place, she would react the same way. Even when she agreed with Anne and felt David was missing a point well put, she never sided against him. It would have surprised him had he known her tacit support was parented more by an aversion to confrontation than agreement with his views. She was too practical to expend time and energy in useless bickering.

Anne arrived just as the lakeshore carillon began its call to worship. Millie, Sylvia's overweight arthritic dog, tail-thumped a welcome.

'Jesus, Syl, I never get to hear church bells. They're beautiful.'

She came through the side gate like a small, dark whirlwind. The quiet serenity of the morning was replaced by a feeling of energy and tension. Alive. That's what Anne Campbell was. Vibrantly, electrically alive. She seemed to be moving even when she was sitting still. Her round dark eyes snapped and sparkled, her short dark hair bounced, her expression shifted in an endless mobility of mood. She had always been volatile. With Ken out of her life, she bordered on the frenetic. There were times when Sylvia relished her company. This was not one of them.

'God, it's hot downtown.' Cargo pants. Silk shirt. A diamond so big it looked fake. Anne's fashion sense was as eclectic as her conversation. She pulled a chair into the shade and dropped into it, ballooning the webbing under her trim bottom. 'How can you lie in the sun like that? You'll frazzle. Where's David? What's he up to? What have you been doing with yourself? You look terrific. When are you coming into town for lunch? Here,' — extending a bottle of gin in a no-name shopping bag — 'how about a drink?'

Sylvia set the bag down on the deck. 'It's pretty early. Wouldn't you rather have coffee? It's fresh.'

Anne shrugged. 'Coffee's fine. I just didn't want to put you to any trouble.' She lit a cigarette and offered the pack to Sylvia.

'No thanks. I stopped.'

'You? The world's leading smokestack? What brought that on?'

'It was getting to David. He stopped and it bothered him that I hadn't. So . . . I did.'

'Beautiful. You married women are a pain in the ass. I suppose if he told you to wear Granny corsets with steel stays you'd run right out and buy a pair. It's women like you who . . . '

Sylvia poured the coffee and handed a cup to Anne. 'Would you like some Chelsea bun?'

Monologue interrupted mid-stream, Anne stared at her for a moment then tilted her head back and broke into deep, throaty laughter. 'That's what I like about you, Syl. You never get mad. Never get upset. If it weren't for people like you, people like me would be in deep trouble.'

As she settled back in her chair, smiling affectionately at Sylvia, a rusty screech ripped the air. A moment later a black-and-white head appeared over the top step. A bloody gash ran from behind one ear halfway across the throat. A pair of baleful green eyes stared unblinkingly at Anne. Then, dismissing her as a threat, the body inched laboriously on to the deck.

Anne recoiled. 'What in God's name is *that*?'

'Good Heavens, it's just a poor old stray. I didn't know you were afraid of cats.'

Anne shuddered. 'I'm not. But that's no ordinary cat. He looks evil. My God, he's going to attack me.' She hunched back in the chair.

Sylvia, surprised, realized that she really was frightened. Out of consideration for Anne's feelings she picked the cat up and held him on her knee. He spat at her when she touched him, then settled across her legs and gazed steadily at Anne.

Fidgety, Anne stared back. 'If I were you I'd get rid of him, Syl. There's something not right about him.'

'There's something not right about all of us,' Sylvia said quietly. 'He's starved, torn up, he's been kicked from one end of the street to the other. Do you expect me to throw him back out there to die?' She reached for her coffee cup and the cat struck out, raking the back of her hand.

Anne screamed. 'I told you so. That animal is bloody dangerous. You could get blood poisoning and die.'

'He's just starting to get used to me,' Sylvia explained. 'I've been feeding him for a couple of weeks but he wouldn't let me touch him until just a few days ago.' She tapped him gently on the head and said mildly, 'That's bad, Ciba. Bad.'

He looked up at her, green eyes pale and menacing, body taut, ready to strike.

Sylvia stroked his head and he relaxed. She reached for her cup, picked it up; he didn't move. The marks on her hand were nothing more than white streaks against the tan. He had not drawn blood. The lethal claws had barely grazed her skin.

Unmollified, Anne muttered, 'I'm surprised David allows you to turn his home into a halfway house for these decrepit creatures. How in hell does he put up with it?'

'He doesn't. I don't let them in the house. All I do is feed them. It's not a problem.'

'It could be. You could get a disease . . .'

Something in Sylvia's eyes cut Anne short. They were flat, implacable, the gaze as cool and steady as that of the cat on her knee.

Anne had the eerie sensation of a bond shared, a link forged between the two. She felt awkward and uncomfortable. Glancing away, she noticed the newspaper with the battered-blonde headline. Eager to change the subject she asked, 'Did you read about that girl?'

Sylvia shook her head.

'Nineteen. Young. Beautiful. The sonofabitch beat her to a pulp and nobody in the whole goddamned building heard a thing. Right in her own apartment. Jesus Christ, how do these things happen?'

Sylvia watched a squirrel swinging in one of the hanging planters. He was digging up a geranium in his search for peanuts. She clapped her hands, hoping he'd run away.

'She was lying there naked. In a pool of blood. Her head caved in. The police,' she added drily, 'suspect foul play.'

Sylvia noticed that the usually dauntless Anne was shivering. 'These things happen,' she said softly. 'People die. People get killed. It's a fact of life.'

'Death may be a fact of life. But murder? Syl, do you really believe murder is a fact of life? Something we should let ourselves take for granted?'

'You know what I mean. The world is a violent place. People get killed. Some of them actually help. They want it to happen. They make it happen.'

Flushed and angry, Anne snapped, 'Balls. I don't believe you, Sylvia. Christ Almighty, are you saying a pretty nineteen-year-old, with her whole life ahead of her, invited someone to smash her head in and God knows what else?'

'Not consciously. But maybe she was out on the town, picked someone up, she could have asked for it. Who knows?'

Anne leaned forward as though she would strike her.

Ciba's head rose, cobra-like, with a hissed warning. His skinny hind legs tensed. Sylvia put her hand on his back to prevent him from springing.

The aborted impetus of Anne's body was reflected in her voice. 'Damn it, Sylvia, you're beginning to sound more like David every day. That's something he'd say. Something a lot of men would say. You should know better.'

'You said yourself she was very pretty.'

'Is that a crime? Because you look good you should walk around in sackcloth and ashes with a bag over your head? And what about the other one a couple of weeks ago. The grandmother in a wheelchair.'

'What grandmother?' Sylvia held up her hand, sorry she'd asked. 'No. Don't tell me. I don't want to know. You're obsessed with violence. It's unhealthy.'

'Unhealthy.' Anne was ready to explode. 'It's *violence* that's unhealthy. Not talking about it. Not recognizing that it exists. It's the existence itself that's unhealthy.'

Anne gazed over the garden, talking more to herself than to Sylvia. 'Three women have been murdered in the past three weeks. Brutally. All in their own apartments. All within a few yards of their neighbors. One was beaten to a pulp. One was stabbed. One was choked with her own pantyhose after being sexually mutilated. In the past three weeks, yet.

'Which does not take into account the woman killed at high noon in that busy west end shopping mall. The girl in the Beaches, stabbed in the hallway of her own apartment building. The child, that tiny wee child raped and mangled in the east end. Or the black ten-year-old found in the culvert at Marie Curtis Park.

'What is happening here? Just what the hell is going on? Is there some kind of mass movement underway to get rid of all things female? Doesn't anyone give a damn?'

The despair in Anne's voice prompted a quick rush of concern from Sylvia. 'Most of those cases are solved,' she said reassuringly. 'And the ones that aren't, will be. It's just a matter of time.'

'Just a matter of time,' Anne echoed. Then, wearily, 'So they catch one of the bastards. And some smart lawyer gets him off. Or maybe he's nailed. And the judge says it's one of the worst cases ever to come before his court and he's determined to make an example of him; the s.o.b. is sentenced to a couple of years and he's back on the street in a few months. The whole damn system is out of whack. And I don't see how it will ever get put right.'

'David says it may not be perfect but it's the best we've got.'

'David says shit.' Anne's eyes flashed with anger. The mood of depression was over.

Sylvia smiled with relief. 'How about a swim? And then I'll fix some breakfast.'

The rest of the day was relaxed and easy. Anne talked less than usual. When she did, Sylvia managed to steer her clear of causes and issues. They swam, had breakfast on the deck, floated in the pool chairs with tall glasses of gin and tonic. The real world seemed shadowy and not-so-real after all.

The Yonge Street bars and strip joints, the street people and shuffling bag women, the sub-culture that is part of the fabric of every large city, lay far beyond the quiet garden on the shaded street in the residential west end.

The only reminder of a hard, tough world where violence lay in wait for its next victim was the wasted body that dragged behind Sylvia like a whipped dog. 'Not a dog grown loyal through love,' Anne thought to herself, 'but a mangy cur that has finally found its own private bone and will never let go.'

She did not mention the animal aloud until late in the day, when she was getting ready to leave. Then, almost timidly, she said, 'Syl, please get rid of that cat. There's something abnormal about it. I wish you'd do something.'

'I have,' Sylvia answered. 'I've got an appointment with Wollmer for tomorrow.'

The veterinarian was a friend of Anne's. She looked relieved. 'You're going to put him down?'

Sylvia, annoyed by the assumption, said matter-of-factly, 'I am not going to put him down. I'm having him neutered. He'll have his shots. And have his neck tended to.'

Anne acknowledged defeat. 'Neutered? Castrating bitch,' she grinned. Sylvia grinned back. 'Now who sounds like David?' They hugged each other, promised to get together soon.

The cat watched, still as death. Only his eyes moved, following Anne as she crossed the lawn to the side gate. He continued to watch, long after her car had disappeared down the street.

He remained on the deck for the rest of the day. That evening, when he heard David's car pull into the driveway, he dragged himself off into the shrubbery beside the house. He did not reappear until David left for work the next morning.

David Jenning was six years old when he was beaten up by the neighborhood bully who was twice his age and double his size. The experience had a profound and lasting effect. David made up his mind that he would never again be on the losing end of a battle. Small for his age, he also realized that he would have to fight with something other than his fists. He decided to study law.

Life wasn't easy for the Jenning family. David's father was dead, his mother had an office job that paid just enough to feed and clothe her son and two daughters. The settlement she received, following her husband's fatal mining accident underground, paid off their modest bungalow, but there was nothing left over for the children's future. Once out of high school they were on their own.

David knew this and was occasionally resentful of his father's untimely exit. Years later he claimed gratitude for the past and the discipline it had imposed. By then he was successful, no longer remembering the missed football games and casual mingling for an after-school coke, the hours of pumping gas and working on summer road gangs while his classmates spent long, lazy days at camp or the family cottage. The kids he had envied, married, saddled with debt and trapped in dead-end jobs, now envied him.

David Jenning was a self-made man and like most self-made men, he was pleased with his handiwork.

It was a Sunday afternoon in late spring and David was on his way home after a successful meeting with a distinguished group of clients. The day had gone well; he would be sorry when it was over.

His mind, capable of formidable concentration under fire, slipped into alpha. Fragmented images flashed against his closed eyelids. The long, low-slung car traveling at high speed along the narrow road. Sylvia walking up the school steps on her first day of their last year in school, the new girl that he knew from the start he would marry some day. His father's funeral, the casket open and his face forever frozen in a smile. The small church where he and Sylvia were married. The day he was called to the bar and the celebration that followed, climaxed by a marathon bout of lovemaking that marked the high point of their physical relationship.

David opened his eyes and fixed on a roadside point of reference to accentuate the sensation of swift, sure movement. Submitting to the low throb of the Imperial's powerful engine he relished the luxury of playing passenger with an accomplished driver at the wheel. He stole a sideways glance at the man beside him, admiring the strong, clean-cut profile.

Craig Faron was the only person David allowed to drive his car. Even Sylvia was no exception. It was not that she lacked ability. She was actually a better driver than he. But he knew that to his wife, cars were nothing more than transportation.

The Imperial was more than a car to David, it was an extension of himself. He loved it. He was also *in* love with it, physically responsive to the elegant lines, the buttery softness of the leather upholstery, most of all to the power that surged through him when he pressed the accelerator. The car gave him the same rush he had felt with Sylvia in the early days before they lost interest in each other. He had never articulated the way he felt about the automobile but he knew it was a feeling both understood and shared by his companion.

Craig pulled out to pass a string of cars and whipped in at the head of the line just inches in front of oncoming traffic. He had gauged the distance to a hairsbreadth, executed the manoeuver with computer-like efficiency.

David looked out the window at the fresh green countryside, neatly divided by the ribbon of road. The highway from Niagara Falls to Toronto was not one of his favorites. The single lanes were narrow and the gravel shoulders were skimpy and ditch-edged. It was a dangerous drive. When alone he lost no time getting home. Today he was in no hurry. Like a man traveling through space, weightless, effortless, he felt he could go on forever.

'The Beacon's coming up. Feel like a stretch?'

Without waiting for an answer Craig swung on to the side road that ran along the water's edge to the Beacon Motel and Restaurant.

They arrived, got out, and walked toward the restaurant in silence; Craig tall and graceful, with the easy stride of a man accustomed to open air and space and physical action; David short and fleshy, expensively tailored, skin sauna-fresh. Completely unlike each other, they were at the same time fully complementary. Craig's piercing blue eyes, brilliant under arched brows and a heavy shock of blue-black hair, looked outward to far horizons; David's pedestrian dark eyes looked inward, concerned always with motive, attitudinal bias, hidden intent. One saw the forest, the other the trees. Together they formed a gestalt, a unified whole greater than the sum of their parts.

The last of the Sunday brunch crowd were on their way out so there was no problem finding a table by the window. The lake was a clear, sparkling blue enhanced by a drift of white sails and bright spinnakers.

'Sylvia and I used to stop here,' David said when they were seated. 'But it's been a couple of years now.'

'How is she?'

'Fine, I guess. We don't seem to spend that much time together. I'm busy. So is she, doing God knows what. We don't crowd each other.'

'She's an attractive woman.'

David nodded. 'She's fond of you, Craig. Now that you're back in town you'll have to make it over for dinner.'

'I'd like that. As long as you're sure she won't mind.'

'She'd be pleased. She asked about you just the other day. Wanted to know where you were this time, what you were up to, if you're still making a killing in the market and dishing it out in venture capital. You're one of the few people she shows any interest in these days.'

'I get like that. I enjoy people yet sometimes, I dunno. I get fed up. If I didn't take off by myself I'd explode.'

'Is that what you've been doing all winter? Hiding out on a desert island?'

'Close. One of my fundees got into the black and turned into a prime target. I had to head south to beat off a take-over bid. Hot 'n dirty. When it was over I headed back up here into the hinterland. Built myself a real down-home log cabin. With the help of some Indians. It's nature in the raw. You'd love it.'

'A cabin in the woods? That's kid stuff.'

Craig heard the wistful note in David's voice. 'You'll have to come spend the weekend some time. I know you'll like it.'

His voice was so gentle that David looked away, embarrassed. He covered with, 'I'm no Paul Bunyan, Craig. Where is this backwoods cabin of yours anyway?'

'Remember that island I told you about? With the ghost town on one end and the terrific beach on the other? Well I bought some shoreline last winter. We had to get the stuff across on the ice. So we just went ahead and did it. That's what I've been doing. Now what's happening with you?'

'Not much. It's been busy as hell, but nothing special. Pretty boring, actually.'

'Damn. I was hoping you'd have something interesting I could dig into.'

'I have an indecent assault coming up. Could use some help on that. If you'd like to see where the plaintiff is coming from . . . who she hangs out with, where she spends her free time, that kind of thing.'

A muscle twitched in Craig's cheek. 'You know how I feel about that, David. I wouldn't lift a finger to get one of those bastards off the hook. They should be put away for life.'

David, who waved the banner of 'innocent till proven guilty' at the slightest provocation, had learned early in their relationship to never press the premise with Craig. It was a subject Craig Faron could not discuss rationally. David did not know why, but he did know better than to try. He prized their friendship too highly to provoke a rupture.

Sensing the wisdom of a change of subject Craig asked, 'What's happening with Wynn and P?'

Happy to switch topics David said, 'We're appealing the appeal on that fraud charge. The manipulation of stock transactions. Remember it?'

'Wasn't that the multiple-count laid under one charge?'

David nodded.

'But you won an acquittal.'

'That's right. But the Crown appealed. There were found guilty on twenty separate counts.'

'Can they do that?'

'No. An appeal must be based on a ground of law, which was not at issue. So now we're back into it.'

'A lot of people lost money over that deal.'

'People lose money in the market every day. That's the risk they take.'

With the financial genius of an Adam Smith and the killer instinct of a Bengal tiger, Craig seldom lost money on anything he invested in. On the whole, he agreed with David. The risk was part of the game. But when the game involved big-time operators bilking small-time investors of their life savings, he drew the line.

What to Craig was a moral issue was, to David, nothing more than a matter of law. 'It should never have gone to Appeals in the first place,' he continued.

'Taylor and the board must be fit to be tied.'

'They're not too happy. It's dragged on for over two years. Messy as hell. But I think they feel better now. It was time well spent, Craig. Thanks for coming along. I really appreciate it.'

'That's okay. It worked out for me, too. Saw some friends I haven't seen for awhile. And by the way, I dropped in on the Henrys.'

David looked at him, the glance sharp and penetrating. 'How are they?'

'Older. But happy. It's finally come together for them. After all these years.'

'They're good people. It takes a hell of a lot of guts to come through what they've been through.'

Craig started to say something, changed his mind, asked instead what David thought his chances were with the Wynn and Pelham appeal.

'Good,' David assured him. 'You can't ever be certain of course. But we've got a better than even chance on this one.'

Craig looked out over the lake, lost in thought. The beer he had ordered sat untouched. David wondered, as he often did when they were together, what Craig was thinking about.

Finally, his gaze following a sailboat heeling in the wind, Craig said, 'It's all so Christly complicated.'

'Not if you know the rules.'

'The rules! Bugger the rules. When you get down to it, life is simple. You eat, sleep, try not to hurt people, try not to think about dying, forget that dying is really what it's all about.'

'I think we'd better go.' David finished his Scotch. 'You're working yourself into a mood.'

Craig drained his glass of beer. 'You're right.' He forced a smile. 'It's always hard to get back in the swing after being away for awhile. Up there on the island . . . well, I'd forgotten how much garbage there is.'

They walked back to the car in companionable silence. Craig got in on the driver's side and waited until David buckled his seat belt before starting the engine. Cutting smoothly into the traffic, he eased around slower cars until the road ahead was clear and unobstructed. David tuned in the all-news station. A smiling announcer cheerfully reported riots in Poland, a general strike in Britain, a street-bombing in Paris. The litany of disaster was followed by an upbeat promise of 'a sunny day tomorrow.' David switched to a program of oldies-and-goldies.

As they neared the city they were slowed to a crawl by the build-up of weekend traffic. Billboards that had streamed by in a blur on the highway came into focus, a welcome diversion from stop-and-go frustration. Something for everyone. One of the back-lit boards featured the photograph of a handsome middle-aged man with the reassuring slogan: HALLWORTH, A Name You Can Trust.

Craig glanced at the sign, then turned to David and asked, 'How's the Jenning Journal?'

'You know more about that than I do. You and Sylvia. I haven't even thought about it since the last time I saw you. I've just been too busy.'

The Jenning Journal. Craig's pet name for David's pet hobby: a private information bank containing comprehensive records of crimes and criminals. What had started as a simple scrapbook of his own cases, initiated by Sylvia when they were first married, had grown into a unique library of contemporary cross-referenced material. There were enforcement agencies that had as much information on crime. There was a reporter who had built up a catalogue of cases solved and unsolved. But nowhere, to David's knowledge, was there as much information about the perpetrators and their activities both past and present.

Interested in the psychology and motivation of law-breakers, David relied on Craig's more pragmatic nature to flesh out the legalese on file. Craig tracked selected subjects through incarceration, parole, release, life back on the street; Sylvia collated the information and kept the files in order. David did not understand Craig's dedication to the project, but he welcomed it. There was a book buried in the masses of information on hand. Someday, when he had time, he intended to write that book.

'Did I tell you I've got a computer?'

'God, no. What kind?'

'An Apple. It will cut down on the paper. Those damn files have taken over the den. There's hardly room in there for me.'

'It'll take months to program it. Can you do it?'

'No. I wouldn't have the time anyway. Sylvia's thinking about it, but she'd need some help. She's been doing house stuff on a Radio Shack TRS for a couple of years now and she seems to know what she's doing.'

'There's a slight difference, David.'

'I know. As I say, she'd need some help. Maybe a student. Some of them are pretty sharp.'

'Well, if you ever get it set up it'll be terrific. I have a friend who used to work for Wang. I'll talk to him if you like.'

'Not yet. I still haven't decided exactly what I want in there.'

'Motive. MO. Type of weapon. Typical victim. Stamping ground. . . .'

'Whoa,' David laughed. 'You're going too fast. I want to think about this and do it right.'

'Well I'd sure like to be around when it happens.'

The line of traffic inched forward slowly, bringing them abreast of the Highway 10 exit. Craig swung right and headed south toward the lake. He drove straight to the Jennings' house. When David remonstrated he said he would walk down to Lakeshore Boulevard and hail a cab; it was just a few blocks. He felt like stretching his legs.

'Not even one drink?' Craig was adamant. He was anxious to get home. David watched him stride off. Probably had a woman waiting. A sexy redhead in a black negligee. Satin sheets and a champagne on ice. He sighed. Sylvia did not expect him for dinner. The house looked cold. Unoccupied. What he needed was people, the sound of laughter and music.

Easing the car out of the drive he headed downtown, along the waterfront to Pier 4. The dinner crowd had reached the coffee-cum-liqueur stage; the air crackled with joie de vivre. Spirits revived with garlic-drenched escargots, Malaysian shrimp and a bottle of fine Chablis, David watched the boat people barbecuing on the decks of tall-masted craft docked along the wharf. When the waiter cleared the table he moved to the bar for coffee and a double brandy. Listening to the music, watching the faces in the crowd, he felt the loneliness seep back.

It was late when he arrived home. The house was dark, Sylvia obviously in bed. Just as well. He was not in the mood for small talk. The usual husband-wife exchange. What did you do all day? Did you have a successful meeting? Who all was there? Familiarity did not always breed contempt. Too often it bred nothing more than boredom. He felt it. He knew Sylvia did, too.

Mellowed by the wine, he undressed in the dark so as not to wake Sylvia and went straight to bed. Within minutes, he was sound asleep.

* * *

Craig Faron lived in a downtown highrise overlooking a small patch of park. His apartment was spacious, airy and starkly modern. The walls were white, the wall-to-wall broadloom was black. The over-sized bathroom had black marble fixtures and the major appliances in the functional kitchen were lacquered in a high black gloss. The upholstered furniture was white leather, the tables and lamps were glass and chrome. The only color was provided by a brilliant but disturbing Cahen abstract, hanging baskets of lush green foliage, and the occupant.

He had enjoyed the day with David, but it was good to be home. It was twilight, the time of day when the view from his balcony was at its best. The air was blue and lights were coming on slowly, sparkling below like fireflies. At this hour, from this height, the city took on a magical, mystic quality. The scars were invisible, the bumper-to-bumper traffic was a ribbon of light, the dot-sized pedestrians were happy, alert and well-fed. If only it were really so.

There was ham in the refrigerator, a loaf of rye in the bread box. He made himself a sandwich, opened a beer, went onto the balcony to eat. Stretched out on the padded chaise longue, sandwich and beer at his side, Craig Faron, unlike his friend David, was perfectly happy to be alone.

Handsome enough to have his pick of women, he had rarely been as interested in them as they were in him. He was, by nature and upbringing, a man's man. But there were times when male company paled as well, when the only company he wanted was his own.

In his teens he shipped out as a radio operator on a succession of tramp steamers. Later he opened a small electronics firm. When he sold it at a profit, he used the money to buy property. The income from his real-estate investments left him free to indulge his insatiable curiosity and zest for life.

He had sheared sheep in Australia, scuba'd off the Coral Reef, worked as an extra in a B-movie, climbed the Rockies.

Craig Faron had crammed more into his thirty-five years than most men experience in a lifetime, and during the process had learned that the things you enjoy most are the things you do best. He had seldom enjoyed anything more than his sleuthing assignments for David. Their intermittent relationship was one of the few long-term associations of his life.

They had met ten years earlier when David was defending a young man accused of robbing a corner milk store and shooting the elderly proprietor when he resisted. The evidence against the youth was overwhelming. There were three eyewitnesses plus a countertop print of the accused's middle finger, right hand. Listening to the Crown's opening address, Craig felt the trial would be little more than a formality, the outcome assured.

The case came up during a period when Craig's restless attention had come to rest on the law. It was chance that placed him in the courtroom where David was acting for the defense.

Like most laymen, Craig believed eyewitness testimony was irrefutable. Convinced the trial would be a boring recital of undisputed facts, he decided to leave at the first opportunity. Later he was glad he had changed his mind and stayed for the afternoon session. This was his introduction to David Jenning, and he was impressed.

David was slimmer then, and his cheap rack-suit fit him as well as the expensive tailor-mades he wore now. He was not an imposing figure; his lack of height cast him at a disadvantage. But as the trial progressed it became apparent that he was the principal player.

The first witness was the bereaved widow. David dismissed her without cross examination. She was followed by the fingerprint expert who spoke with an air of quiet authority. David limited himself to two questions, each of which might have been asked by the Crown rather than the defense. 'Are you positive the print was right middle finger?' 'Exactly where was it located?'

Feigning confusion over the answer to the latter question he produced a blow-up of the counter and asked the technician to indicate the location. The witness pointed to the edge of the counter, fronting a cardboard display of chocolate bars and chewing gum. David circled the spot and entered the photograph as evidence.

The next witness was a schoolgirl who had entered the store during the commission of the robbery. Bright and articulate, she gave her testimony in a straightforward, matter-of-fact voice. David approached her slowly, his manner benign.

'Where do you attend school? . . . What were your classes on the morning in question? . . . You had a written exam scheduled for that afternoon, were you concerned about it? . . . Were you thinking about it when you took your lunch-break? . . . What happened when you entered the store? . . . How far were you from the assailant? . . . Did you enter before or after the shots were fired? . . . If you entered before, the assailant must have had his back to you. . . . You saw the deceased stagger back, then slide to the floor. . . . You described the assailant as having long hair, blue eyes and a cut lip. . . . You were watching the deceased yet you also saw the face of the man on the other side of the counter. . . . Tell us again exactly what happened from the moment you stepped inside the door. . . . '

To the jury and spectators David seemed to be doing his methodical best to unravel the sequence of events. The girl, held by the steady gaze of his unblinking black eyes, was under no such misapprehension. Pressured to recall the scene in minute detail her confidence unraveled. She could not say how long she had the perpetrator under observation, at what point she saw his face, whether he had any distinguishing features aside from the cut lip that would set him apart from many other young men of similar build and dress.

When asked if the person she had seen in the store was present in the courtroom, she hesitated. The defendant's hair was neatly cut and the split lip had healed without a scar. He looked more like an innocent schoolboy than a wild-eyed gunman. Her moment of hesitation was noted by the jury. Shaken, she left the stand.

The remaining eyewitnesses, an elderly couple, were afforded the same treatment. David was polite, low-key, and relentless. He asked about the light in the store, the confusion leading up to and after the shooting, whether the accused was identified from a photograph or in a line-up, if they were relating the defendant to the original identification or to the man observed in the act.

The woman used reading glasses; her husband wore trifocals. David dwelled on the fact that neither had 20/20 vision. There was no doubt in the minds of the elderly couple that they had seen the defendant pull the trigger, but they left grave doubts in the minds of the jurors.

By the time David began his summation, Craig Faron was hooked. He watched, fascinated, as David addressed the jury, speaking to each in turn, reminding the panel that most cases of miscarriage of justice are due to mistaken identity, that for this reason there is a special need for caution when identification is at issue. He pointed out that human observation is notoriously unreliable, influenced by a host of unrelated factors; that when an eyewitness says 'I saw' he really means 'I believe I saw.' He talked about the schoolgirl worried about an exam; the elderly woman who couldn't read even the largest print without her spectacles; the man who wore trifocals and the blurring of vision that can occur beween close focus and intermediate, intermediate and distant.

Turning his back on the jury he walked toward the defense table and casually asked the defendant to hand him a notebook he had placed on the table earlier. The boy picked it up with his right hand and David took it from him, spun around and waved it triumphantly in the air. 'Ladies and gentlemen of the jury,' he exclaimed, 'as you have just seen, the defendant is right-handed. If he had held the gun, if he had pulled the trigger, he would have done so with his right hand. The hand we know was resting on the counter at the time of this unfortunate incident. The evidence produced by the Crown proves the innocence of the accused. I place his future in your hands.'

The jury deliberated for less than an hour and returned with a verdict of not guilty. Craig watched while the young man's family crowded round, laughing and boisterous. As they filed out into the hall one of the group offered the youth a cigarette. Craig wondered if anyone else noticed that he reached for it with his left hand.

David was one of the last to leave the courtroom. There was a police officer in the corridor and Craig, nodding toward David, asked, 'Who is that guy?'

'David Jenning,' the officer said coldly. It was obvious the young lawyer wasn't one of his favorite people.

The next day Craig phoned David's office and made an appointment to see him. David had assumed Craig was a new client. Instead, he found himself interviewing a would-be investigator. It was some months before he called on Craig for background information on a key witness he wanted to discredit. The dossier Craig presented contained everything from casual acquaintances and living habits to a psychological profile. It was the first of a number of assignments handled by Craig over the years.

Craig finished his sandwich and stored plate and cutlery in the dishwasher. Off and on throughout the evening, his thoughts returned to David. He still felt David Jenning was one of the finest lawyers in the country, but the admiration he felt for his skill was flawed by a growing unease over the way he manipulated the law to serve the ends of his clients.

Craig Faron did not believe the guilty should be set free, nor the innocent be made to suffer. When he first started working with David, he accepted assignments without question. During the last couple of years he had discriminated, refusing cases involving violence unless assured of the client's innocence. It had reached a point where most of the work he did for David involved civil cases and the upkeep of his personal records.

Craig went to bed early and lay awake, thinking about his cabin. The road crew, subsidized to build roads on a ghost island where the only vehicles were a pair of tractors and an ancient jeep, had offered to clear a landing strip for a light plane. He would be able to fly up on weekends, perhaps even live there and commute. It was a pleasant thought.

He drifted off to sleep thinking of the pines standing tall on the craggy shoreline, the crazy cry of loons in the twilight, the long stretch of beach untracked except by a single deer. Asleep, he dreamt about the island and the shadowy figure of a woman who shared it with him.

In the morning he remembered the dream, but he did not remember that the woman in his dream was Sylvia Jenning.

2

June 1984

The start of another week. How time flew by. Sylvia sat across from David as he ate his breakfast and thought how the two of them had changed over the years.

The slim young idealist had grown into a pinkishly plump member of the establishment. Once he had wanted to change the world. Instead, the world had changed him.

When they were first married she had worked to help him through law school; doubled as his secretary when he opened his first small office in Northern Ontario; never missed an opportunity to hear him in court. He fought like a tiger for his clients. That, at least, hadn't changed.

Occasionally, because she had worked as hard at his career as he had, she objected to the way a case was handled, or to his representation of someone who was obviously guilty and, in her eyes, deserved to be punished. When she realized he was no longer interested in her opinion, she withheld it. His career had assumed a momentum in which she had no part.

His first major case came within a year of moving to the city and setting up on his own. They had worked on it together. Looking back, it was the most satisfying period of their marriage.

The defendant was a tiny mouse of a woman from the backwoods north of Hearst. She was thirty going on sixty-plus. Worn to the nub through years of drudgery on scrub acreage miles from the nearest neighbor, she was accused of shooting her common-law husband in the back with a sawed-off shotgun. After the shooting she left her ten-year-old daughter in charge of the six smaller children and walked through four miles of drifting snow to turn herself in. Having made her initial statement to an RCMP constable she retreated into silence, saying nothing more to anyone until the day she broke down and told her story to Sylvia.

Sylvia had learned about Lucy Menard through a six-line item on one of the back pages of *The Toronto Star*. Edited down to the bare essentials the report, datelined Sudbury, mentioned the shooting but not how or why it had occurred. Sylvia knew the north. She also knew that no woman, living deep in northern bush and dependent upon her man for the most basic necessities of life, would take such drastic action unless there was no other way out. It was coincidental that the woman was being held, and would be tried, in Sudbury. It was not coincidental that Sylvia decided it was time for a long overdue visit with her family.

The week at home had gone by quickly. Her mother took her shopping and on a round of visits with old family friends. Her father took them out to dinner, proudly showing off the new Japanese restaurant (a rarity in the meat-and-potatoes mining community) that Sylvia predicted would fail. (Shortly thereafter the menu switched from rice cakes in eel-skin to chop suey and butterfly shrimp.) One day she spent the entire morning with David's mother, a shy little homebody who had never felt quite at ease with her poised young daughter-in-law. Every day there was something to do, but every day she managed to work in a visit to the local jail and Lucy Menard.

Conversation was not Mrs Menard's strong point. She did not open up until the last day of Sylvia's stay, and then only because Sylvia arrived with news of the Menard children. Her children were all that mattered to Lucy. They were, in fact, the only good thing that had happened to her from the day she was born. Ignored by an ill, overworked mother, sexually abused by a brutal stepfather, at the age of thirteen she was handed over to a shiftless thirty-year-old drunkard. The years that followed were a nightmare of misery. An isolated shack on inhospitable scrubland. Grubbing for enough to eat. Through it all pregnancies, miscarriages, beatings, heart-pounding terror.

She had never owned a store-bought dress, never had the convenience of running water, never known a peaceful night's sleep. Nor had she ever confided in anyone until the day she talked to Sylvia.

Quietly, eyes fixed on the table between them, she said, 'I ain't sorry. All our life he beat me. He was mean when he was sober. When he was drunk he were plain crazy. I blowed a hole right through him and I ain't sorry fer one minute.'

When she got back to Toronto she called David at the office and told him about the Menard case. 'I wish you'd handle it, David. She needs you.'

He told her it could wait until he got home and they would discuss it then. That evening she tried again, pointing out that it was self-defense, the family had been mistreated for years, the woman had no choice but to act as she had.

David was not convinced. He reminded her that 'there's nothing to do up there but drink. Some of those binges go on for days. Next thing you know there's a fight and somebody gets killed. It happens all the time. By now she's probably got herself a lawyer, anyway.'

Sylvia assured him Lucy Menard did not have a lawyer. Nor did she have any money, or a family to help her. She explained that Lucy didn't seem to care about what happened to her; her single concern was her children — five girls, two boys — now in the custody of Children's Aid.

It was not until she told him about the children that he agreed to take the case.

Menard had been having an incestuous relationship with his eldest daughter, Bella, since she was five years old. When Bella left home he took the next eldest. At the time of the shooting he was beginning to show the first signs of interest in the four-year-old. Lucy was not surprised, although she hoped he would confine his attention to the older girls and herself.

It had never occurred to her that he did not have the right to avail himself of his children's bodies. She had been used by her stepfather. She had watched while he beat and kicked her mother. She knew of no other life but the one she was living. It was not his treatment of the females in the family that brought about his death. They yielded to his abuse stoically. Menard was killed because of his son.

Sylvia could still hear the low, expressionless voice as she described the shooting. 'He come home and beat on me. He said as how some day he'd see me stone cold and the girls too. He was drinkin' moonshine and it made him crazy.

'I was fixin' supper cause when he et he most times passed out. I put the plate down and he banged me with his fist. I felled down and he kicked me. Here. In the stomach. Then he started beatin' on me with his fists.

'And then I seen Timothy with the gun and I knowed he'd kill him sure and it didn't seem right fer him to do it stead of me. So I say "don't do it, Timmy, don't do it," and he turned round and seen the gun and just grabbed Timmy and busted his face. I picked up the gun and I seen it was time and I pulled on the trigger.'

Of all the cases David had handled, the Menard case was the one Sylvia was most proud of. Lucy was found guilty of manslaughter but was released on probation due to 'extenuating circumstances.' Having Lucy free was all that mattered to Sylvia, but David never referred to the case and she knew that he considered the finding a defeat. Looking at him now she wondered if he ever thought of Lucy Menard and the role he had played in her life.

David finished his bacon and eggs and asked, 'What did you do yesterday?'

'Nothing much. Anne came over for awhile. We just sat around. How was your trip?'

'It worked out. Craig drove down with me. Spent the time visiting. He's good company.'

'How is he?' Her voice quickened with interest.

'Fine. He's been up in the bush building a log cabin on some island. He looks great.'

'He always looks great. Why don't you invite him over some evening? I'd like to see him.'

'I did. Asked him for dinner. He said to make sure it was all right with you.'

'David, I can't think of anyone I'd rather have. Do you want me to call him, or will you?'

'I'll talk to him. Will you have time to pick up my suit from the cleaners?'

'I'll make time if you need it.'

'Good. Grasski comes up tomorrow. I *will* need it.'

'Grasski. Is that the wife beater? Or the one that insured his partner just before he got burned up in the factory?'

'Good God, Sylvia, why do you talk like that? The woman wasn't beaten up. She tripped on the rug and fell down the stairs. And as for that fire. . . . '

Sylvia patted his arm. 'I'm sorry, David. It's just that I keep getting these people mixed up. Which one is Grasski?'

'Remember the break-in in New Toronto? Three years ago. The poor guy had a few drinks and decided to drop in on a friend. Trouble was, she'd moved. Instead of explaining she no longer lived there, the owners called the police. The whole thing never should have happened.'

Sylvia thought for a moment. 'I do remember. He was falling-down drunk. He forced his way in and said he'd wreck the place if she didn't come down and speak to him. There was no one there but two women who were scared to death. When they called the police he took off in his car, smashed through a road block, crippled two policemen for life and ran over a pedestrian.'

'That's right. If those women had used their heads everything would have been fine.'

'Isn't he the one who's never appeared before a courtroom jury, David?'

'There was no point in making him lose a day's pay when we knew we'd be postponed. Anyway, it's dragged on for three years. I'm glad it's finally settled.'

'You said it comes up tomorrow. How can it be settled?'

'We've worked out an agreement.'

Sylvia stared at him. 'What kind of agreement?'

'An equitable arrangement.' Aware of her disapproval he added, 'Don't be naive, Sylvia. You know as much about these things as I do.'

Sylvia stood up and began cleaning the table. 'I really don't, David. There's a lot of things lately that I don't understand at all.'

He brushed past her and stopped in the hall to pick up his briefcase.

As he opened the door and stepped into the driveway a shaggy black body moved from under his car to the safety of the hedge.

David slapped at the shrubs with his briefcase, then banged on the door until Sylvia appeared. 'I told you to get rid of that cat. I don't want him hanging around here. Either you do it or I'll call the Humane Society and let them look after it.'

His face was flushed, and the soft roll of flesh above his collar was crimson. For a man renowned for never losing his cool or raising his voice in a courtroom, the display of temper was completely out of character.

Face expressionless, voice calm, Sylvia said, 'David, what in the world is the matter with you? If you're not careful, you'll have a heart attack.'

David stared back, his mouth a thin straight line. 'I don't want to see that cat around here again. Do something about it. And do it today.'

Sylvia said nothing.

David got into the car and slammed the door.

Ciba lay under the hedge, his large green eyes fixed on Sylvia, his tail swishing back and fourth through the wet grass.

When the car was out of sight the cat crawled out of the hedge and walked purposefully toward Sylvia. His legs were as stiff as sticks and his tail continued to thrash from side to side. He looked so malevolent that Sylvia took a step backward as he flung himself at her feet. Front leg stretched across her foot, his claws hooked into the strap of her sandal. Carefully she leaned over and moved his paw. His head moved like lightning and powerful jaws closed around her wrist. He held her for a split second and then let go, rubbing his head against her ankle.

The only mark on her arm was a tiny indentation from one of his fangs. She stepped away from him carefully. Wasted though he was, the power in his jaws was lethal.

Sylvia felt no deep affection for the cat. She would have been happy to turn it over to a good Samaritan who would nurse it back to health. But she had no intention of having it destroyed. She did not know how she would deal with David's ultimatum.

She decided to think about it later.

It was mid-afternoon when David called and said not to expect him for dinner, he had an important business appointment and there was no need to wait up for him.

Sylvia put the partially thawed steaks in the refrigerator and checked the crisper to see if she had enough fresh greens for a salad. There was a quarter head of lettuce browning at the edges and a single tomato. A quick trip to the vegetable market was in order.

Ciba was lying on the porch. She almost tripped over the cat as she stepped outside. Yawning and stretching he rose to his feet. She ran her hand along his back and felt the knobs on his spine.

'Two cans a day and you're still skin-and-bone. How long is it going to take to get you filled out?'

Rearing up on his hind legs he pushed his head against her hand. She sat down on the step and he sat on his haunches, facing her.

'Listen to me. You can't stay here forever. David doesn't want you around.'

The cat stared back as though he understood every word.

'I'll make a bargain with you. Stay out of sight when David's around and I'll look after you till you can take care of yourself again. Okay?'

Should she cage him to make sure he was there when she returned for his trip to the vet? She decided against it; better to do her shopping and get home as quickly as possible. As she pulled out of the driveway she looked back and saw him, motionless as a figurine.

Her first stop was the veggie shop where she picked up tomatoes, fresh spinach and a head of lettuce. On her way past the freezer she noticed a carton of frozen liver and added it to her basket. Although liver was one of David's favorites she seldom bought it because she hated handling it. This wasn't for David — it was for Ciba. The sooner he shaped up and shipped out, the better.

She was bending over to stow her groceries in the back seat of the car when the scuffle broke out. She looked up in time to see a muscular teenager shoving an elderly woman up against one of the buildings. He was pulling at the woman's purse. She was clinging to the strap, crying for help. Sylvia saw the sharp glint of a knife, his angry, distorted features, the helplessness of the white-haired victim. Rage, white-hot, visceral, surged through her body.

Infuriated by her resistance, the boy released the strap and struck out with his fist. The old woman crumpled to the ground, moaning. Her attacker snatched the purse from her limp hand and started to run. No one moved. It had happened too quickly.

He ran in Sylvia's direction. The purse dangled from one hand, the unused knife jutted from the other. She waited. Like a movie still clicked into motion, pedestrians began moving back, clearing a path. Immersed in flight, the teenager looked straight ahead.

He came even with Sylvia. She made a half-turn. Her foot hooked his ankle in full stride. He went down with a heavy thud, breaking the fall with his elbows. Frantic, he scrambled back to his feet. Sylvia hit him across the cheekbone with the sharp edge of her hand. He went down again.

In the distance she could hear the woman whimpering, excited voices calling for an ambulance, the sound of running feet and bodies moving. He struggled half upright. Sylvia brought her knee up under his chin. His head snapped back. He screamed. She grabbed a handful of hair and pulled his head up, slapped him across the face, open-handed. Blood poured from his nose. A purple lump formed, egg-shaped, on his cheek. The purse and knife lay where they had fallen.

She continued slashing at him until they pulled her away, pinioning both arms at her sides. Voices, muffled like a station off-tune, grew louder, gradually, as though being tuned in, the volume turned up. 'Holy Mary, Mother of God, lady, you're killing him.'

The scene came into focus with the voices. Sylvia saw it, out-of-body, as though looking down from one of the windows above. She saw the crowd milling; the arrival of the ambulance; the woman placed on a stretcher and taken away; the body of the boy, unconscious at her feet, and standing over him an attractive, well-dressed woman held in the vice-like grip of two agitated men in blue. It was like waking from a dream. 'What happened?' she asked.

The policeman on her right said, 'Lady, you're dangerous. You damn near killed the guy. I'm going to have to book you.'

'Book me?' Then slowly, coming into focus, she said, 'He attacked that woman. He knocked her down and stole her purse.'

'You almost killed him,' the officer said. He was angry, incredulous. 'You can't go around acting like that.'

'He could have killed *her*,' Sylvia answered.

'I don't care what he did. You can't take the law into your own hands. You'll have to come down to the station.'

'You mean you're going to lay a charge?'

'Yes,' he snapped, bulldog-determined.

'What charge, Officer?'

Nonplussed, he groped for an answer. She could almost see the wheels turning. A long pause, then, with evident relief, 'Excessive force!'

It was Sylvia's turn to be incredulous. 'Officer,' she said calmly, 'he had a knife. He was armed.' She held out both hands, palms up. 'Excessive force? You can't be serious.'

He glared at her. The bystanders shuffled, murmuring. The policeman looked down at the crumpled heap on the pavement.

'If that isn't excessive force. . . . ' he growled. Then, 'What are you? A black belt?'

'No,' Sylvia answered. 'But I've taken Defendo. It was your Chief who said women should know something about self-defense.'

The officer shot a quick glance at his partner. The partner looked away. A man called out, 'Whatsamatter, cop, afraid of losin' yer job?' A woman yelled, 'Shame on you, Officer.' The constable's face flushed a dark red.

'I'll have to take your name,' he said gruffly.

Sylvia handed him her driver's license. He wrote down the details and gave it back to her. She put it in her purse and got into the car. The second officer leaned over the passenger side and said, 'We'll be in touch with you, Ma'am.' He was courteous, almost apologetic.

'Of course.' They smiled at each other. She started the engine and pulled away from the curb carefully. She was almost home when she remembered David's suit.

Circling the block she drove back down to Lakeshore Boulevard. A fire engine screamed behind her and she pulled over to let it pass. Every time she heard a siren she thought of the tragedy it represented. Someone's life was being irrevocably altered while the rest of the world went about its business as usual. The old woman was one of life's casualties. Sylvia wondered how badly she was hurt, whether or not she would recover. She spared no thought for the boy who had attacked her. In her mind, he had become a cypher.

When she finally arrived at the house she found Ciba waiting on the step where she had left him. After putting away her shopping, she hung David's suit in his closet and retrieved the cat cage from the basement.

When Ciba saw her emerge with the cage he stiffened and inched backward until his body was flat against the wall. Sylvia picked him up by the shoulders, talking softly to reassure him. He braced his front legs against the cage and struck out with his hind legs, raking her arm. She forced him inside.

In the car he screamed with rage and tore at the wires until his paws dripped blood. By the time they reached the clinic they were both exhausted. The partially healed gash on his neck had opened and beads of crimson spotted his white feet and front. He was still as death, but the air around him was electric. Sylvia was sweaty and blood oozed from her arm. Their entrance to the quiet waiting room was fearsome.

Sylvia set the cage on the floor and collapsed in the nearest chair. Ciba hunkered down, silent and menacing. A fat lady with a pekingese on her lap moved to the other side of the room. A huge German shepherd, anchored to a tweedy gentleman, strained at the end of his leash, sniffed at the cage, then backed away with head and tail drooping. No one spoke.

When they were finally admitted to the examining room Dr Wollmer's eyes widened and he started hissing through his teeth, a mannerism Sylvia had long suspected was inherited from his more sibilant patients. Accustomed to a well-bred clientele of mannered house pets, the vet was taken aback by the state of both Sylvia and the cat. He insisted she leave the cage on the floor while he cleaned and bandaged her arm.

'That cat, he did this, Mrs. Jenning?' Concern thickened his accent, making him harder to understand than usual.

Sylvia nodded.

His face a mask of disapproval, he asked, 'You want I should put him down?'

'Of course not.' The question came as a surprise. Wollmer had a genuine fondness for animals, placing their welfare before that of most people. 'I want you to fix his neck. Neuter him. Give him his shots. And a bath. He looks terrible.'

Wollmer shook his head. 'He is dangerous, this cat.'

Sylvia picked up the cage and set it on the table. 'The cage frightened him. He's all right now. He won't give you any trouble.'

The vet looked at her arm pointedly.

'Dr. Wollmer,' Sylvia pressed, 'I've been coming here for years. You tell me I'm one of your best clients. I want you to look after this cat. He will not be a problem.'

Wollmer finally agreed to keep him, but only if Sylvia took him out of the cage and held him while he was being examined. Before opening the cage door she said firmly, 'Ciba, these people are going to make you better. I want you to behave yourself.'

He came out of the cage quietly, allowing her to hold his legs while Wollmer swabbed his neck. When he was ready to go downstairs to the cat dorm she handed him to the young girl who looked after animals left for treatment. He didn't struggle, but he watched Sylvia, craning over the girl's shoulder, until they descended below the level of sight.

It was almost dark when Sylvia pulled back into the driveway. Having fed Millie, she fixed herself a salad and a pitcher of iced tea. Had David been home they would have eaten in the dining room; on her own, she opted for the deck. The house was part of the street and the street was part of the city; the deck was part of the backyard, remote, private, a world removed.

Setting the padded sun cot midway between vertical and horizontal she lay back and drifted pleasantly, not quite awake, yet not asleep. It had been a tiring day. When she eventually surfaced, the sun was gone and the first star was visible. The shrubbery looked dark and impenetrable.

A fluttering shape, larger than a butterfly but smaller than a bird, swooped across the pool. Sylvia grabbed a towel from the railing and waved it over her head. Bats, she'd been told, made nests in your hair. This bat arrived every night at dusk, staying just long enough to drive her indoors. On nights when the weather was good she would wait till it disappeared, then return to the deck and sit, sometimes until midnight. Tonight, although the sky was clear, she remained indoors. Restless, she tidied the kitchen, straightened the living room, turned on the television set, turned it off again when she found there was nothing worth watching.

The house was hot and airless. Sylvia was bored and restless. For once she would have enjoyed David's company, even if they didn't have much to say to each other.

At ten o'clock she switched on the news and watched a series of clips more chilling than a late-night thriller. The situation in the Middle East was worsening. Nuclear arms were proliferating. The Irish were killing each other and the cost of living was still rising. It was too overwhelming to comprehend.

The local news followed *The National* and it reduced the impersonal horror of world events to a scale that was comprehensible, thus infinitely more terrifying. A smoking-in-bed fire killed three. A downtown bank was held up, and a milk store proprietor was pistol-whipped and robbed. Another woman was followed from the subway, dragged into a vacant lot and raped at knife point. The announcer gave the impression that, the woman not having been roughed up, no harm was done. Sylvia switched off the set and went upstairs.

She turned down the bed, undressed, and wrapped herself in a bathsheet. She stood at the window for a moment, looking out over the backyard. Even on a dark night, with no moon, the pool with its cream tiles and white coping cast a pale glow over the garden.

The south wall of the bedroom was lined with windows that offered a clear view of the grounds, but the end windows on the right were shrouded with branches from the old lilac tree at the corner of the house. David had wanted to cut the tree down when they first moved in, but she had talked him out of it. In the spring, the lilacs filled the room with a light, delicate fragrance. And on hot summer mornings it was pleasant to wake to green leaves and the sound of birds singing in the branches. David felt the tree was an invitation to prowlers. Sylvia said he was being ridiculous, the slender boughs would snap under weight.

The pool looked inviting. Turning out the light, she went back downstairs.

Unlike David, she often swam after dark. He rarely used the pool. Most of his time at home was spent working on papers in his den. So much for togetherness, she thought, as she dropped her towel at the edge of the pool and slid into the deep end without a ripple.

The warm water felt like silk against her skin. The best thing about swimming at night was not having to wear a bathing suit. She swam briskly until her arms tired, then sat with her back against jet and let the water pulse between her shoulder blades. She was still in the pool when David's car pulled into the drive.

The front door was open, but the screen door was locked. She wrapped the towel around her wet body and called to him to come through the side gate. When she heard him fumbling with the latch, she knew he had been drinking.

'Jesus, Sylvia, what are you doing out here alone?' He looked at her accusingly. 'You've been swimming. By yourself.' He flipped up a corner of the towel. 'With nothing on. I swear to God, you're out of your mind. How many times do I have to tell you I don't want you taking chances like this?'

Sylvia turned away. 'David, you're worse than an old woman. It's safe here. Nothing is going to happen.'

He followed her across the lawn, walking carefully to avoid stumbling. 'You don't have the slightest idea, do you? You don't know what's going on any more. The world is a jungle and you act as though it's a goddamned tea party.'

'Oh David, you spend so much time with crime you're losing your perspective. There's still a lot of ordinary, decent people around.'

'Christ.' He stomped across the deck. 'I just left one of your ordinary, decent people. He looks like a choir boy. Married three years. Ten-month-old baby. They say he's raped fifteen women and cut one up with a knife. In the past year. And you tell me there's nothing to worry about?'

Her voice even, expressionless, Sylvia asked, 'A new client?'

'Yes, a new client.' He sounded weary.

'And he did all those things?'

David slid open the deck door and turned on the inside light. 'They say he did all those things,' he corrected.

'And you're going to defend him?'

'Yes, I'm going to defend him.'

She knew him well enough to know he did not want to discuss it, and thought how far from each other they had drifted. There were times when she felt the stocky, well-groomed man she lived with was a stranger, switched in her bed by a grown-up version of the tooth fairy who had left pennies under her pillow when she was a child while gifting her friends with dimes and quarters.

'But David, if he's guilty, why?'

He stared at her. Then, as though talking to a child, he said, 'You know as well as I do that he's not guilty until he's found guilty. He's entitled to the best defense possible.'

Long after her husband was asleep, Sylvia lay awake staring at the ceiling. She was just dozing off when she heard a low, scrabbling sound at the window.

'Those branches should be trimmed back,' she thought sleepily. 'They'll wear a hole in the screen.'

She woke up in the morning feeling tired. Her gym workout took longer than usual to bring her to par. By the time she had showered and made breakfast, she'd forgotten about the hole in the screen.

When she picked Ciba up later in the day she hardly recognized him. His body was still gaunt and out of proportion to his height, but the dingy coat glistened blue-black over an undercoat of deep, rich sable. The square head, set on a neck as broad as his body, was massive.

Sylvia gasped. 'He's beautiful.'

'He is a strange one,' Dr Wollmer said. It was not a compliment. 'Did he misbehave?'

Wollmer shook his head. 'He did nothing. No crying. No walking around. Nothing. He sits. And waits.'

As Sylvia was leaving he called after her, 'This cat does not purr. That is very unusual. If a cat does not purr, something is not right.'

Later, sitting on the deck in the sunshine, she thought of the remark. 'He does nothing. He sits. And waits.' Perhaps I'm waiting, too, she thought. But waiting for what?

The Jennings' annual pool party later that week was, as usual, a success. Sylvia served chilled gazpacho, mounds of cold lobster and iced melon balls. David served Scotch, rye, Bacardi, and Perrier on Perrier cubes. Everyone but Sylvia had a good time.

In the beginning she had enjoyed getting together with David's associates, but now she found it a drag. The eager young men had matured into pin-striped professionals with banker's gray minds. As a hedge against boredom she asked David to invite Craig Faron. When Craig begged off because of a prior commitment, she invited Anne.

Although the day was steamy hot, no one seemed interested in swimming. The company, as usual, broke up into two groups, pre-arranged by gender. Most of the wives gathered in the shade at the bottom of the garden. Most of the men lounged around David's improvised bar.

Anne was talking to the men. One hand held a drink, the other waved a finger under John Simmonds' aristocratic nose. 'The law,' she said shrilly, 'is an ass.'

The senior partner of Simmonds and Woodhouse drew back as though she had struck him. 'My good woman, the law is the foundation of society.' His neat white moustache twitched.

Anne grinned. 'Don't blame me, blame Dickens. He said it. Do you think things have improved since Oliver Twist and Little Nell?'

David reached for Anne's glass and refilled it. 'Don't listen to her, John. She doesn't mean half of what she says.'

'Then riddle me this, Mr Jenning. Why is it only the poor go to prison?'

'Not true. What about Peter Demeter?'

'And Sam Sheppard?'

'And Jean Harris?'

'Exactly,' Anne said. 'A handful of exceptions that prove the rule.'

'The truth of the matter, Anne, is that most crimes are committed by poor people.' David sounded like a kindergarten teacher.

My God, he sounds smug, Sylvia thought. Smug and patronizing.

'Seventy percent of all crime is attributable to lower income and poverty level groups,' he continued. 'Most violent crime is committed by young males between fourteen and twenty-five years of age. So if there are fewer wealthy people in prison, it's because the wealthy tend to commit fewer crimes. It's really quite simple.'

'Fuck.'

John Simmonds dropped his glass. David's face turned dull red. The ladies in the shade swiveled their heads as though attached to a single string. Sylvia, amused, felt it was time to intercede.

'Anne, how about a little help in the kitchen?'

Out of earshot, Sylvia said, 'Why do you do these things? You know how upset people get.'

Anne's dark eyes twinkled. 'They're so damn self-righteous. Do 'em good to get shook up.'

Sylvia laughed. 'You're hopeless. No wonder Ken packed it in.'

'Here, here. *I* left *him*. Remember?'

'Whatever.' Sylvia tossed her a towel. 'Here, make yourself useful.'

Anne set her glass down on the counter and wiped obediently. 'I know I'm a pain in the neck. But Jesus, Sylvia, the world's a bleeding mess. Take David, for instance.'

'I've got David,' Sylvia said humorlessly. After a moment's silence she asked, 'What about David?'

'Well he's a nice guy, right? He pays the bills. He's a good provider. He probably wouldn't lie, cheat or steal to save his soul.'

'That's bad?'

'That's good. But he earns his living, and yours, helping people who *do* lie, cheat and steal. So in a way, he's as bad as they are. Without him they couldn't go on victimizing society. It's a vicious circle.'

'Anne Campbell, are you accusing my husband of. . . . '

Anne hugged Sylvia. 'I'm not accusing him of anything. I like him. I like you. That's not what we're talking about.'

'What *are* we talking about?'

'Justice.'

'Lord. Motherhood and apple pie.'

'You don't believe in justice?'

'That's the point. I do. I believe the guilty should be punished and the innocent set free.'

'Shit, Sylvia, if that's what you think we're really up the creek. You can't believe in justice and the law. They're completely different. Maybe they started off together but somewhere along the way they went off in different directions.'

Sylvia put the last glass on the drainboard and cleared the sink. She was not willing to admit it, but she agreed with Anne.

'Take David's last case,' Anne continued.

'What about David's last case?' David asked from the doorway. Then, hand up in mock gesture of peace, 'Never mind. I'm sorry I asked. Just let me pick up some mix and I'll get out of your hair.'

Ignoring him, Sylvia asked, 'Which case, Anne?'

'The guy that got his kicks pounding the hell out of women.'

'The one you told me about, David? That hasn't come up already, has it?'

'We got it moved up.' He rummaged in the fridge and pulled out a couple of bottles of soda.

'Did he get off?'

'It wasn't a matter of getting off, Sylvia. He was acquitted.'

'But how?' Sylvia asked. 'The story in the paper said he had blood on his clothes. There was a knife. Witnesses. One woman even identified him.'

'Most of that stuff turned out to be hearsay,' Anne said dryly.

'Didn't even get into the record. I stayed for your summation, David. You were fantastic.'

Sylvia caught the undertone of sarcasm. David didn't. He looked both surprised and pleased. Whistling off-key, he trotted back to his bar. Anne stared after him, her jaw set in a hard line.

'He thought you meant it.'

'Naturally. He *was* fantastic. Why wouldn't he think I meant it?' Anne sat down at the kitchen table. Sylvia handed her a fresh drink, poured herself a Perrier and joined her with a puzzled expression on her face.

'I can't figure you out, Anne. You're dyed-in-the-wool leftwing. Against the police, the government, established order. You should stand up and cheer when someone like David rescues the under-privileged from the long arm of the law. Yet you resent him. Why?'

Anne sighed. 'It has nothing to do with leftwing, rightwing, Syl. Every time a killer is turned loose, we *all* suffer. If those who break the law are considered more valuable than those who abide by the law, we lose. A society that can't protect its citizens will fail. A system so out-of-balance that truth becomes secondary will lose sight of the meaning of truth.'

She pulled herself up. 'God, I'm sorry. I'm soap-boxing. In the middle of your party. I promise, it won't happen again.' She pulled Sylvia to her feet. 'Come on. No more sermons. Let's have fun.'

The rest of the afternoon ran smoothly. Anne made harmless small talk, and David was friendlier toward her than he had been for years. One of the wives asked Sylvia for her gazpacho recipe, and John Simmonds drank enough to forget Anne's affront earlier in the day.

Then Harold Temple stood up and proposed a toast: 'To Sylvia, the perfect wife and most even-tempered woman of my acquaintance.'

David plumped with pride. Slightly drunk, he seconded the toast: 'To Sylvia, my beloved Stepford wife.'

Everyone laughed except Anne and Sylvia. The Ira Levin sci-fi thriller about a suburb of fractious wives cloned to perfection still struck them as too close to reality to be humorous.

Much later, when their guests had left and they were alone, he called her into the living room for one of his fireside chats. His face serious, a sobering cup of coffee in hand, he said, 'I heard something last week, Sylvia, that I just can't believe.'

With conscience clear, she waited for him to proceed.

'A few weeks ago you were involved in an incident on the lakeshore. You attacked a young boy and beat him senseless. It *seems* you attacked someone,' he amended. 'Rumors get out of hand. When I find out how this one started, I intend to take action. But I think it would be wise, at this point, if you were to tell me exactly what took place. The kid's name is Germaine.'

Strange. She had tracked down the woman, phoned to make sure no bones were broken, sent flowers to the hospital, but she had not thought about the boy. She couldn't even remember what he looked like.

'Well?'

'There was an . . . an incident. A purse-snatching.'

'Someone stole your purse?'

She shook her head. 'There was an old woman. She was attacked. I helped her.'

'Good God. Why didn't you tell me?'

'You're so busy, David. Anyway you weren't around right after it happened. And then I . . . I guess I forgot.'

'You forgot!' He drew in his breath. 'You didn't actually hit him? He's got an older brother who says you tried to kill him.'

'He was getting away.'

'My God. What did you do to him?'

'Tripped him.'

He looked relieved. 'Is that all?'

'I hit him when he tried to get up.'

He sighed and closed his eyes. 'You hit him. How many times?'

'For God's sake, David, I don't know. It happened so fast. I'd forgotten about it.'

'You forgot about it? They say you put him in the hospital. That it took two men to hold you. And it just slipped your mind?' He looked at her as though she were a stranger.

Sylvia wondered if he'd thought of the incident when he likened her to a Stepford wife. It didn't matter. She felt no guilt. No remorse. 'David,' she said quietly, 'the boy was hurt. I don't know how badly. All I know is he attacked an old lady, knocked her down and stole her purse, and everyone stood around and watched. I would much rather have not been involved but no one else seemed to care.'

'Jesus, Sylvia, what if he had died? Don't you realize the trouble you'd be in?' He sat back, his body limp. 'You, of all people. You can't stand the sight of blood. Go to pieces over a dead bird. It doesn't make sense.'

It was true. She hated violence, abhorred the sight of blood shed in violence, and yet the boy's blood had not affected her. Like a teller who views bank cash as pieces of paper, only personal cash as real, the boy's nose had gushed nothing more meaningful than red dye. She could not explain it to David, although she knew he wanted an explanation. Or an apology. Or both. She could not explain it to him, because she could not explain it to herself.

He did not wish to pursue the subject. There seemed to be nothing more to say, yet he was not satisfied. He needed something, some way, to vent his feelings. He remembered Ciba.

'I saw that cat again, Sylvia.' Ominous.

'Really?' Polite interest.

'I told you weeks ago to get rid of it.' Imperious.

'I'm sorry. I thought you said you didn't want to see it around.' Courteous.

'Well I've seen it. Now will you get rid of it, or will I?' Authority pushed to its limit.

'No.' Unequivocal.

'No, what?'

'Just plain no, David. I won't get rid of it. I don't want you to get rid of it.'

He leaned forward, hands clenched on the arms of his chair. 'I don't know what's got into you, Sylvia. . . . '

'David, listen to me,' she interrupted. 'I've asked very little of our marriage.'

'For someone who didn't ask for much you certainly got your share.'

'I have never asked for anything,' Sylvia said firmly. 'I've never gone against you. But this is one thing I don't want to discuss. Ciba is never around when you're here. He is never allowed in the house. He is no trouble to anyone. He is no problem. He stays, David. Let's not talk about it again.'

David stared at her, his mouth open. He started to say something, changed his mind, sat back in silence.

There was something in Sylvia's calm, matter-of-fact voice that told him the subject was closed.

3

July/August 1984

The days of summer spun together like pale matched beads. The cat got fat. Sylvia remained slim and trim. With no outside interests, nothing to occupy her time and mind, she became increasingly preoccupied with her body. Innocent of both ego and vanity she thought of her physical self in the abstract, as she did of her car and professional-quality camera equipment. Her body was an instrument that required care if it was to function with smooth-flowing precision.

One day she drove downtown to look for clothes. The noise and confusion drove her home, empty-handed and exhausted.

Another day, when David telephoned for a set of papers he had forgotten, she delivered them to him in the cellar restaurant next to his office and they had lunch together. He ordered a small steak and carafe of wine. Sylvia had a salad and a glass of soda water.

And one day, the morning of the day Craig Faron was scheduled to come for dinner, she found the gun. It was in the night table on David's side of the bed. She opened the drawer and saw it and the sight of it made her feel faint. She closed the drawer quickly and went back downstairs. There were goose bumps on her arms and her forehead was wet with cold sweat. Tucking it away in the small room in her mind with the door that closed off things she didn't want to think about, she decided to ask David about it later.

She tidied the house before leaving to pick up the fresh fish and seafood she had ordered earlier in the week from the fish market. She remembered Craig saying shortly after they met that the only thing he missed about being inland was the daily catch sold on the docks by coastal fishermen. She had planned a menu she felt would please him — bouillabaisse, Caesar salad, fresh slices of pineapple marinated in Cointreau.

When David arrived with Faron in tow the house looked beautiful and so did Sylvia. She was wearing a light touch of make-up, her hair shone, her skin was golden against the white cotton blouse, turquoise madras skirt and silver-inlay turquoise jewelry. Accustomed to seeing her in shorts, slacks or bathing suit, David kissed her on the ear and whispered, 'You look wonderful.'

Craig held out his hand and said he had been looking forward to seeing her again.

The men went into the living room and a few minutes later Sylvia joined them with a cheese tray and raw vegetable dips.

Craig talked about his cabin and described the trip to the island on the tiny fire boat that tossed like a cork in the rough channel.

It was easy to imagine him in the wheelhouse, the windscreen drenched with spray, blue eyes bright in the lean brown face.

Craig and David were on their second drink when Sylvia mentioned the gun. David said they needed it for protection.

'You know I hate guns, David.'

'I can think of a few other things you wouldn't be too big on either,' he replied. 'How would you feel about having your head beaten in some night when you're asleep? Or being raped out there by the pool when you're out after midnight by yourself?' Turning to Craig he fumed, 'Which I've asked her a dozen times not to do, and she doesn't pay the slightest bit of attention.'

'How is a gun upstairs in the bedroom going to keep me from getting raped in the backyard?'

Craig smiled. David leapfrogged. 'You wouldn't let me get a guard dog.'

'That would be like living with a keg of dynamite. Anyway, we've *got* a dog.'

'Oh my God, Sylvia, you don't expect Millie to protect you. Thirty pounds overweight, and scared of her own shadow.'

Sylvia had suspected him of wanting the dog to get rid of Ciba. She still felt that was partly his motive, but the gun indicated a real concern.

'David, guns kill.'

'So do people,' Craig said gently.

'People do other things, as well. Guns don't. They have only one purpose. Killing.'

'For Christ's sake, Sylvia,' David exploded, 'don't you realize the kind of people I deal with? Do you think I spend my time in a fucking Sunday school?'

Craig's blue eyes narrowed. 'Has someone threatened you, David?'

'No. Not seriously, at any rate. It's just that there's so much going on. I see it every day.'

Sylvia put her hand on his arm, wanting to reassure him. 'Is that why you had the phone number unlisted?' He nodded. 'But if we're not in the phone book, and no one knows where we live, there shouldn't be a problem.'

'You tell her, Craig.' Turning to Sylvia: 'You can't hide from people who want to find you.' He dunked a mushroom in the nearest dip, ate it, said thoughtfully, 'Anyway, it's no one in particular. It could be a stranger walking along the street. He sees you. Follows you home. Watches you. Gets to know your routine. Waits for his chance. Bingo. Another statistic.'

'You're scaring her, David,' Craig remonstrated.

'It's time someone did.'

'I just don't think a gun is the answer,' Sylvia said. 'People get shot by their own guns. Just having one around invites violence.'

David was unmoved. 'I'm sorry you saw it, Syl. Try to forget it's there. If it will make you feel any better I'll keep the clip downstairs in the desk.'

'Then why. . . .' Illogical. But rather than prolong the discussion in front of Craig, Sylvia conceded. The gun would stay, clip intact.

They changed tack. Talked about people they knew and places they had been. By the time they sat down to dinner the mood was convivial.

Craig complimented her on the bouillabaisse and asked, unabashedly, for a second serving. They lingered over dinner and relaxed afterward, in the living room, with coffee and liqueurs. David and Craig debated the validity of psychiatric testimony; Sylvia, mind wandering, thought once more about the gun.

Perhaps she should have explained to David, told him how she had felt, as a teenager, when she saw the hunters come into town up north with animals draped on their cars like badges of honor.

There was one scene from the past she had never forgotten. It remained in her mind as clear, as vivid and poignant, as the day it occurred. It was a bright Sunday morning in late fall. She and her mother were on their way to church when a car pulled up on the main street and parked in front of them. There was a deer on the roof of the car. Its eyes were glazed and the head hung crooked and limp. A trickle of dried blood caked one corner of its mouth. Even in death, it was beautiful. She wanted to reach out and stroke it and make it alive again. People stopped to look. Soon there was a small crowd gathered round.

The driver of the car got out and walked to the passenger side. She expected the men on the street to start punching and hitting him. Instead they jostled against each other, laughing and joking. One of the men, dressed in a business suit, poked the deer with his finger and said, 'She's a beauty. Sure musta took some doin' to bring 'er down.'

The driver puffed up with pride. Sylvia held hard to her mother's arm. The town men were excited. It was not like hockey or baseball excitement. It was feverish. Intense. Not until much later, years later, had she realized they were sexually aroused, turned-on by the dead body, by the thought of the bullet impacting the soft flesh, the animal, staggering, writhing in its last moments of life. Nor had she forgotten that they automatically referred to the animal as 'she'.

She had looked long and hard at the hunter, feeling a deep sadness and an equally deep sense of outrage. Short and squat, his bush pants and heavy plaid shirt (bright red to save him from his own kind) made him look more ungainly than he would in street clothes. Knee-high gum boots made his gait awkward and lumbering. His hands were grimy and his jowls were covered with a stubble of beard.

She thought of the deer, alive and graceful, moving through sun-draped trees with lithe, long-legged ease. It was a sin against God that this grubby little man, uncoordinated and clumsy, had turned a beautiful creature into a rotting corpse. She wished she had the power to strike him dead. She threw up in the gutter. When she got home she threw up again, and went to bed without touching the customary Sunday dinner of roast beef and Yorkshire pudding. She had told no one of that early experience. The memory was too private to expose, too painful to dust off and lay bare.

There was a lull in the conversation, followed by David saying, 'She won't mind. She's off in a daydream.'

She looked up. They were both watching her. 'Won't mind what, David?'

'We thought we'd go into the den for awhile. Craig wants to see the Apple.'

'Of course.' She stretched. 'I think I'll have a swim.'

'Sylvia!'

'David,' Craig said, 'give her some room. She can take care of herself.' He smiled at her, his blue eyes thoughtful, seeing her not as a child to be shielded but as an equal deserving of respect.

'If I don't see you before you leave, Craig. . . .'

'Wear your bathing suit,' David interrupted.

Craig held out his hand. 'It's been a marvelous evening.'

Sylvia touched his hand briefly. 'Please come again. Whenever you feel like it. We don't see enough of you, Craig.'

She went upstairs quickly, her hand warm from the light pressure of his fingers. Craig Faron had always been scrupulously polite in her presence. Yet from the moment they met she had felt a magnetism that drew her toward him.

She swam in the raw and went to bed while the lights were still burning in the den.

Anne was seeing a new man and she had reached the stage of wanting to show him off to her friends. Three times she called with an invitation to dinner; three times David was otherwise engaged. On the fourth call she insisted Sylvia accept, with or without her illustrious spouse.

Sylvia, perfectly content to laze in her own backyard, agreed on a date, then twitted Anne about falling off the singles wagon almost as soon as she got on.

'Wait till you meet him,' Anne countered. 'You know I'm not against men, per se. It's that damned male ego stuff I can't stand. Bill isn't into that Me Tarzan, You Jane shit.'

They met in the Wilton Arms, a hotel in the downtown core off the main entertainment strip. Bill seemed nice. Tall and craggily attractive, he was obviously devoted to Anne. He was also good-humored, which was a pleasant change from Anne's ex.

The occasion called for a celebration. Sylvia hadn't had a drink since her Sunday in the pool with Anne back in May. It was now the end of July. Throwing caution to the wind she had wine with dinner, Benedictine with her coffee, and a brandy to finish off. By meal's end she felt light-headed and more than a trifle giddy.

Bill found her charming. An independent businessman with a small manufacturing plant in Mississauga, he was just beginning to export parts and equipment to the Third World. 'After years of struggle, things are finally looking up.'

Although his wife had been dead for a number of years, he still spoke of her with affection. The marriage had been traditional. When Sylvia asked if he could cope with a renegade like Anne, he grinned and said not only could he cope, in general he agreed with her.

'True,' Anne said. 'Example . . . we met over the Stouffville dump.'

Sylvia burst into laughter. She had a mental image of Anne, Calvin Klein chic, zapped across a pile of garbage by a middle-aged executive in a three-piece pin-stripe. 'What were you doing in Stouffville? And why the dump, of all places?'

'We weren't *at* the dump. It was a meeting about the dump. Chemical waste. All those poor women were having miscarriages because of the water. Remember?'

Sylvia shook her head.

Anne turned to Bill. 'Sylvia stopped the world and got off. Trying to get her out of the house is like pulling teeth. She doesn't know what's going on any more.'

'I wish I didn't,' Bill said. 'Every time I listen to the news I get another ulcer.'

'Then don't listen.'

'If everyone did that,' Bill objected, 'we'd all go down the drain.'

'We're doing that anyway.'

Anne sided with Bill. 'That's the point, Syl. We have to try. Take the economy. . . . '

'Take the government,' Bill interrupted. 'Take the whole pack of those Ottawa parasites and ship them out.'

The check for the meal arrived. Anne signed for it. Sylvia, who did not want the evening to end, suggested they move to the lounge as her guest. Pleased, they followed her into the crowded bar, pushed their way through to a freshly vacated table near the back of the room, in line with the men's washroom.

Sylvia ordered Scotch and water, and when Anne said she'd had enough to drink and wouldn't she be better off with her usual soda, she obligingly changed to a double Scotch on the rocks with soda on the side. Anne sighed and dropped the subject. If necessary they would drive Sylvia home and she could pick up her car in the morning.

They talked about women's rights, the abortion issue, the crippling effect of high interest rates on small business – which Bill described as 'the backbone of the country, God help us if it ever disappears' – and the terrible danger of nations drifting aimlessly towards global chaos.

Anne was delighted by the way her favorite man and best friend were hitting it off. When Bill leaned toward Sylvia and whispered, 'You have a secret admirer,' she tapped his wrist lightly and scolded, 'None of that, I saw you first.' It was a good-natured remark, devoid of jealousy.

Bill drew back, embarrassed, saying to Anne, 'Not me.' He turned to Sylvia with, 'There's a fellow down there who hasn't taken his eyes off you. He's been to the washroom a dozen times. Didn't you feel him touch your hair?'

'When?'

'Just now. On his way to the john.'

'I felt something brush against the chair. That's all.'

'Probably sees we're having a good time and would like to join us,' Anne said. Then, realizing the remark sounded like a put-down, she flustered, 'I didn't mean that the way it sounded, Syl. God, you're the most attractive woman in the place. But you're not exactly the pickup type. What I meant is, nobody in here seems to be having a good time but us.' She shuddered. 'Bars are dismal places. Full of lonely people. Even together, they're lonely. And it's worse for women.'

'They should take a page from Dorothy Parker,' Sylvia quipped. 'She swiped the sign from the men's room at work and put it outside her office. They literally streamed through the door.'

Bill laughed. 'I've always said women are more ingenious than men.'

'No wonder she was such a bladder mouth,' Anne said.

Bill and Sylvia groaned. 'Puns are the lowest form of humor,' Bill quoted.

'Speaking of humor, Syl, whatever happened to that mangy cat?'

'This conversation is losing me,' Bill complained. 'How can you go from humor to cats in one breath?'

'*Sylvia*'s cat,' Anne emphasized. 'The scruffiest, most ill-tempered beast I ever did see. What became of him, Syl?'

'He's still around. You wouldn't recognize him.'

'I thought David hated him.'

'He's a smart cat. He stays out of the way. Out of sight, out of mind.'

Bill nudged Sylvia's knee under the table. 'He just came out of the john,' he muttered.

Anne looked up. 'Is that him? The big blond?'

Bill nodded. Anne stared. Her face turned white. When he was out of earshot she grabbed Sylvia's arm and shook it. 'That's him. That's *him*.'

Neither Bill nor Sylvia knew what she was talking about. 'Remember when I went to court to hear David? That's the bastard he got off. Jesus, that's him. Let's get out of here.' She started stuffing things in her purse, rounding up Sylvia's change.

Sylvia threw a quick signal to the waiter when she wasn't looking. 'We can't go now,' she protested. 'We have another round coming.'

Lips compressed, Bill stared after the retreating figure.

'He was up for rape,' Anne explained.

Bill's face hardened. 'To hell with him,' he said. 'Why should we leave because of him?'

Sylvia felt excitement curling through her body. She wanted to see him. Talk to him. Know him. A prescient flash, psychic insight, told her they were linked. Fate had brought her to this table in this place at this time. Fate had done the same for him. Anne and Bill could leave if they wished. She would stay.

She heard Anne say, 'You're right. It's just that I hate being in the same room. He should be behind bars.'

'The judge didn't think so,' Sylvia said.

'Thanks to David.'

Sylvia looked at Bill. 'Tell me if he comes back.'

'I will,' he said grimly. 'And if he touches you again I'll knock his block off.'

Sylvia steered the conversation back to Bill's business, hoping to keep him engrossed. He was telling her about a new metal coating he planned to bring on the market, when he stopped short and said, 'He's coming back.'

Sylvia tensed, trying to catch his footsteps. She felt rather than heard him behind her. Feet braced on the floor she pushed back her chair, knocking him off balance.

She looked up. Smiled. Got to her feet. 'I'm terribly sorry. Are you all right?'

'No problem.' He was very tall, with broad shoulders and a trim waist. His face was smooth and clean-shaven and his eyes were a light, clear blue. Eyes paler than Craig's, lashes blond rather than dark and thick like Craig's, but attractive.

They studied each other for a moment. Then Sylvia stepped aside and he squeezed past the chair and disappeared into the washroom.

Anne was furious. 'You must be out of your mind,' she snapped. 'You did that deliberately.'

'I wanted to see what he looked like.' It sounded feeble, even to her.

'He goes around kicking women's heads in and she wants to see what he looks like. *Mama mia*, haven't you any sense at all?'

Sylvia's high had nothing to do with alcohol. 'Anne,' she said, 'you are paranoid.' She looked so calm, so unruffled, neither of them knew she was seething with emotion.

Anne gagged on her drink. Bill said it was time to go. Anne seconded him, saying it had been fun, but the party was over. Sylvia did not bother to tell her that the party was far from over; it was just about to begin.

The following week Sylvia returned to the restaurant by herself. She wore a silk dress that matched her eyes and a knot like a fist in her chest. After two hours, when he didn't show, she gave up and went home. David, who spent his rare evenings home working in the den, didn't seem to notice she'd been away.

A few days later she tried again. Again, he didn't appear. Each night she sat at the table she had shared with Anne and Bill, seated in Bill's spot with her back against the wall. On the third night, she got lucky. She was watching the door when he entered. Her heart started to pound. The palms of her hands felt hot.

He sat at the bar, drinking a beer. Dressed in grey slacks and navy blazer, he looked more like a promising young man on his way up the corporate ladder than a social misfit.

She had thought of him constantly since that first night. He had become a near-obsession, the sum of his parts inextricably bound to the whole of her being. Studying him in profile as he sat at the bar she realized she had been waiting for him for a long time, readying herself in a vacuum, not knowing why, yet going through the motions and marking time until her feelings found a focus.

She did not feel like Sylvia Jenning. She felt like an actress cast in a writer's mold. Lifescripting: a pattern of behavior shaped by a pattern of beliefs. She waited, knowing he knew she was there, knowing he knew she was waiting.

He finished his beer. Stood up. Turned in her direction. Walked toward her purposefully. She watched him, smiling. She knew she would never again see him as impersonally, as objectively, as she did at this moment.

'May I?' he asked, his hands on the back of the empty chair.

'Please.' She wondered if he remembered her.

'You were here last week.' A statement, as though he had read her mind.

'Yes,' she said simply. 'I wanted to see you again.' He smiled at her honesty.

He told her his name was Arthur Maitland and he was a freelance television producer. She said her name was Diana White and she worked in an insurance office.

He told her he was producing a slice-of-life TV commercial and she was just right for one of the parts. She said it sounded exciting, and she could certainly use the money.

He suggested they take off and discuss it. She said they could discuss it where they were. He felt it would be easier to talk in her apartment. She explained she was married, and her husband was very jealous.

It was quiet in the bar, the weekday crowd limited to lonely businessmen and a few middle-aged couples. On his third beer he suggested they go somewhere where they could dance. Sylvia hesitated. She was happy where they were. She wanted to talk to him, get to know him. He insisted. She finally agreed to accompany him in a cab to one of the packed, dimly-lit bars on Yonge Street.

He was much more relaxed in the new bar, at home with the

blaring music and frenzied crush of bodies. They danced, Sylvia trying to match her moves to his on the fringe of the small floor as he was caught up in the bodies, swaying to the music in a sinuous solo sufficient unto itself. He did not notice when Sylvia went back to their table and sat watching, admiring the tall graceful form undulating to the amplified beat.

The combo left the stage and he returned, face flushed, smiling, and asked, 'Don't you like dancing?'

'I'd rather watch you,' she answered. 'You're a wonderful dancer.'

He nodded, not at all embarrassed by the compliment. The bartender punched an intermission tape into the PA. Willie Nelson's 'Stardust.' Arthur pulled her to her feet, held her close. They moved easily together, as though they had danced in tandem many times.

'You're very good, too,' he said. They were almost the same height. His lips brushed her ear. He held her closer. She could hear his breathing, rapid and shallow. When the music ended she pulled away. She sat down. She did not want things to move too rapidly.

They did not dance together again. Instead he held her hand across the table and told her she was beautiful, he wanted her, it would be sinful to let the moment pass. He could get a hotel room. They would share an experience neither would ever forget.

She did not want to lose him, but she did not want to stay with him, either. It was too soon. She wasn't ready.

When he realized she was not going to spend the night with him, he offered to drive her home in her car so she wouldn't get picked up in a spot-check.

'Don't be silly,' Sylvia said. 'You're the one who's been drinking. Anyway, how would you get back? I'll get a cab outside.'

When she rose to leave he caught her wrists, the grip hard and painful. 'Can I see you tomorrow?' His fingers bit into her skin. She looked into his pale eyes and knew he did not intend to lose her. She was glad.

'Not tomorrow,' she said softly. 'I usually spend weekends with my husband.'

'Monday?' he pressed. She nodded, then impulsively kissed him on the cheek. He let her go. When she reached the doorway she looked back. The table was empty. He was standing on the edge of the dance floor talking to a bright young thing in a tie shirt and harem pants. She felt a quick twinge.

The weekend dragged. She walked Millie and brushed Ciba and worked on David's files, the Jenning Journal. And in between she paced restlessly from room to room, unable to concentrate on anything for more than a few minutes at a time.

Monday morning she drove to the local shopping center, Sherway Gardens, and bought a new beige pantsuit. Then, feeling it was too tailored, she picked out a rose-colored jersey dress. David would prefer the clean, classic lines of the pantsuit, but she knew instinctively that Arthur would appreciate the femininity of the soft, clinging sheath. On impulse she stopped at a wig shop and bought a carefully coiffed black wig. Before leaving the mall she dropped in to a no-appointment salon and had her hair done.

Dinner was waiting for David when he got home. After dinner, when she was ready to leave, she simply told him that she was going out and wasn't quite sure when she'd be back. He nodded, only half-listening. It was the first time she'd made a point of saying not to expect her. She was glad he hadn't asked for an explanation. If he had, she would have said nothing rather than tell a lie. Not that he was a possessive man. His concern had always been for her safety rather than her virtue. He would not suspect her of infidelity, nor had she ever given him cause to do so. Thank God for past performance. It at least gave her licence to come and go as she pleased.

She arrived at the bar a few minutes early and found Arthur waiting. They talked easily, like old friends. The atmosphere was not as feverish as it had been on Friday night, and they had time before the musicians arrived to share parts of themselves. He did not do his TV-producer number. Instead, he told her about growing up in a small town in Southern Ontario, feeling left out at school, breaking away from a mother who doted on him, getting his life together in the anonymity of Toronto.

It was hard to make friends, he said. The girls he met were cheap; women were too easy, too willing. She was the first person he had met in the city who seemed to care about him as a person. She had the uneasy feeling that he had said the same things before; the lines sounded canned, like a telephone sales pitch. It didn't matter. She had found him. He was hers. Their lives were twined in karma-like oneness.

When the band arrived and he asked her to dance she begged off, saying she'd rather 'spectate' than participate. He was flattered and danced for her benefit, smiling at her over the heads of his partners. As the evening wore on and he began to feel the effect of the beers he chain-drank, he forgot about her and danced in his own small world, oblivious to those around him. At the end of each set he returned to her, briefly solicitous, only to leave when the music started up again. It was a peacock performance, borrowed from the tribal rites of natives worked into a trance by drumbeats while their women watched.

During the last intermission he asked her again if she would stay with him. Again she said no. He looked at her coldly and she felt he was about to slip away from her, to choose instead a more willing partner. She pressed her knee against his, leaned over and took his hand. 'I've never done this before,' she explained. 'I want it to be right.'

He turned her hand over, kissed the palm. 'So do I,' he said hoarsely.

The evening was almost over and he had not mentioned seeing her again. She felt his attention wandering to a young brunette at the next table. Dressed in tight-fitting jeans and a cerise mohair sweater, the girl was flirting with him openly. She was pretty. And she was young. Much closer to Arthur's age than Sylvia was.

In an effort to regain his attention she decided to play on his ego. 'Arthur.'

'Mmmm?' Still concentrating on the mohair, only half-listening.

'What about the commercial?'

He looked at her, his face blank.

'You said you might have a part for me, remember?'

He frowned, trying to recall exactly what he had said. Finally, trapped by the image he had presented, he mumbled he would have to take some shots to see how she would look on camera. They could do it tonight. He would pick up his camera and they could go to a motel. . . .

She sighed. Back at square one. 'What about tomorrow?

Wouldn't natural light be better?' He looked uncertain. She pressed, 'I'll phone in sick. We can spend the whole day together. It will be fun.'

The thought of a day in the country, by themselves, alone with no one around, appealed to him. He grinned, like a small boy in receipt of an unexpected treat. They agreed to meet in the parking lot at Ontario Place, the entertainment centre and park on the city's waterfront, at ten o'clock.

Pleased with the arrangement, he did not object when she rose to leave. She suspected his willingness to see her go was prompted in part by the persistent brunette. She shot the girl a warning glance as she passed her table. The girl stared up at her, eyes bright and hard as buttons. When she looked back she saw them, heads together, deep in conversation.

The next morning she was up early and had completed her morning routine of workout, swim, shower, before David came down for breakfast. She surprised him with a cheese soufflé, light as a puffball with top crusted to a golden bronze. A weekday toast-and-cereal man, he was pleased by the show of attention. It takes so little, she thought, feeling almost guilty as he left the house in high spirits, step jauntier than usual.

The day was clear and sunny. It was going to be hot. Sylvia packed the picnic basket, put a bottle of Pouilly-Fuisse and two crystal wineglasses in the freezer before going upstairs to dress. She wore white linen slacks and a white shirt of handkerchief-silk, the ends knotted to reveal a band of tanned midriff. Needing a dash of color she added a brilliant silk scarf and bangle bracelet, and hoped Arthur would be pleased with the result. Before leaving the room she dabbed her wrists and the hollow of her throat with Chanel. David preferred Arpège. Arthur, she guessed, was a Chanel man.

The parking lot was almost empty and she spotted Arthur immediately. He was parked at the far end of the tarmac in a late model Chev with a tell-tale rent-a-car sticker in the back window. He got out of the car when she drove up. She thought how young he looked, how boyishly handsome in the faded blue jeans and white T-shirt. His blond hair was tousled and shower-damp at the ends.

'I was afraid you wouldn't come.' He smiled shyly. This was not the same person she had left the night before. There was none of the feverish hypertension brought on by music and strobes, the truculence whetted by alcohol. The day-person seemed far removed from the night-person.

In reply to Sylvia's question he said yes, he had remembered to bring his camera. When she mentioned having packed a lunch he looked disappointed rather than pleased. There was a seafood restaurant near Honey Harbor, a resort town two hours north of the city. It was one of his favorites; he had planned to treat *her*. There was no point in driving for miles, she argued, when they could accomplish the same thing right here in the city. When he realized she would not be dissuaded, he gave in.

They sat on the grass and talked. He took pictures of her with a camera much inferior to her own. She posed on the lawns, on the catwalks spanning the canals, and at the water's edge where the lake formed an aqua backdrop. He said she was a marvelous subject, a natural in front of a camera.

When he finished the second roll of film, Sylvia said they had done enough. It was time to eat. She spread the checkered tablecloth on the grass and set it with individual containers of salad, deviled eggs, and a mound of fried chicken while he went back to the car for the cooler of ice-packed wine and glasses. He opened the bottle awkwardly, and when she proposed a toast 'to us' he emptied his glass in response before reaching for a piece of chicken. Sylvia sipped her wine and watched him as he ate.

The fine white Burgundy was cold to the tongue but warm to the palate. It was a good bottle, at its prime, fruity and full-bodied. Arthur held out his glass and she refilled it. He drank it quickly, then continued eating with gourmand efficiency. When he finished, he lay back on the grass with his hands behind his head and said the food was wonderful, she was wonderful. No one had 'done for him' for a long time.

She pillowed his head on her knees and stroked his hair, thinking how defenseless he looked. He opened his eyes and smiled up at her.

'Arthur,' she said impulsively, 'you're beautiful.'

He reached up, locking the fingers of both hands behind her head. 'I'm supposed to say that to you,' he said softly.

'But I'm not as beautiful as you.' It was true. He smiled in acknowledgement.

'I wish this could last forever,' he whispered. His long, slim fingers twined behind her neck, strong as strands of wire.

She studied his face. Touched it tenderly. Felt the sadness she always felt in the presence of beauty, the sadness that came with knowing all things beautiful were ephemeral, could exist for a moment but not forever, knowing also that the issue was joined, the scenario cast. David would never know. None of her friends need know. The most secret part of herself belonged to her, and she could do with it as she willed.

Later they strolled through the grounds and stopped for coffee at one of the outdoor cafés. Arthur asked, again, if she would go with him, let him make love to her. She surprised him by saying yes, a quick about-face after her previous refusals. He had known, if he persisted, she would eventually submit. Because she seemed different he had not expected an answer of such quick simplicity.

He did not know that she had thought about him constantly, was ready to meet him on his terms, qualified by a minor condition. 'Not in a hotel. Friday night. At your place.'

He argued that they would be more comfortable somewhere else; if she was afraid of being seen they could drive out of town. She said hotel rooms were for one-night stands, sleazy and cheap. She did not want their relationship tainted. Finally, realizing she would not be moved, he agreed. He gave her the address, asked if she would like to meet him for a drink the next night, sulked briefly when she said she would be busy for the rest of the week and would not be able to see him again until Friday.

She arrived home minutes ahead of David. Luckily she'd done the groundwork ahead of time. The table was set, the Caesar salad was tossed and ready, the jellied cold veal was delicious. He did not ask her what she had done all day, as he sometimes did, but his good mood of the morning had persisted, making him more talkative than usual. He launched into a lengthy anecdote about one of the juniors in the firm. Her mind wandered back over the day, ahead to Friday night.

David finished his story. The resulting silence snapped her back. He smiled at her, waiting for a response. She picked up the cue and smiled back. He had told her once that she was a good listener. It was simple. All you had to do was remember that listen and silent contained the same letters of the alphabet. Early in her marriage she had learned that listening was merely a matter of keeping her mouth shut. The smile, as usual, sufficed.

After they had finished eating, David moved to the living room to watch a PBS special on Egypt and Sylvia sat outside on the deck, enjoying the warm still evening. When she went up to bed he was already there, sound asleep.

The week dragged by. Sylvia alternated between fits of indecision and calm resolve. Her doubts eased as the week progressed. By Friday she was focussed and in tune.

She told David she was meeting Anne and would probably be very, very late; not to wait up. Leaving extra food for Millie, Ciba and the outside cats she drove off without looking back.

Instead of the modern high-rise she had imagined, Arthur's building was an old brick six-plex off downtown Yonge Street. Thankfully his apartment was on the main floor; at least she would not have to climb stairs and run the risk of meeting someone in an ill-lit hallway. She pushed the buzzer beside the hand-lettered name card over his mail slot and Arthur immediately stepped into the hall and beckoned, ushering her inside and closing the door quickly.

The flat was neat but fusty. The small living room held a scarred coffee table, corduroy daybed and sprung easy chair. The windows faced a brick wall. Nothing in the room looked like the young man who lived in it.

He had a bottle of Canadian champagne on ice. They drank it, sitting side by side on the daybed. She sipped slowly, making her glass last. She had expected him to sweep her up in his arms.

Instead he talked about himself and his plans for the future. 'I will be rich. People will know me. I'm not like other men. I need a woman who is not like other women. That's what I noticed about you. You're different. You stand out. A man needs a woman he can be proud of. Who can stand beside him anywhere. We'll travel. Europe. South America.'

He finished the champagne and switched to beer. His face flushed and his voice was beginning to slur. He was getting drunk. She told herself it was her fault; she had put him off too often, made him wait too long.

She stood up, about to leave. Sobered, he came to his feet. 'Where are you going?'

'It's getting late.'

He stood in front of her, blocking the door. 'Not that late.' Then, clipped, 'Let's go to bed.'

She had been waiting for him to say it, but was not prepared for the quick rush, the flood of adrenalin. 'Where's the bathroom?' Her voice contained no hint of the emotion she felt.

He gestured toward the closed door next to the bedroom. She picked up her purse, said, 'I'll just be a minute,' and stepped into the small room with its naked bathtub, chipped basin and chenille-topped toilet.

Undressing quickly, she folded each garment neatly and placed it on the unused laundry hamper. She was standing over the basin when she heard the door creak behind her. She saw him in the mirror. Gold cross on a mat of fine golden hair. Naked. Tumescent. Blue eyes opaque as chips of glazed china. Hands reaching to take her from behind.

She turned to meet him. Stepped into the circle of his arms. Felt him move against her in a long, convulsive shudder.

It did not last as long as she had thought it would. Bells didn't ring. Trumpets didn't sound. Sylvia's moment of truth arrived silently, without fanfare. Not that it made any difference.

The waiting was over. The future was meshed with the present.

The second Anne pointed him out, Sylvia had known Arthur was special. The hunch, like most of her gut instincts, had proven valid. It did not matter that she didn't see him during the days and nights that followed. The memory of him, the feel of him, was as much a part of her as an implant.

Anne phoned mid-week. For one crazy moment Sylvia thought of telling her about the evening with Arthur. Anne was the one person she knew who would understand, perhaps even approve. But Anne had news of her own.

'Syl,' she blurted, 'he's dead.'

Sylvia's skin turned icy. 'Who?' But even as she asked, she knew.

'That man. The one David got off. Somebody finally caught up with him.'

Sylvia took a deep breath.

'They found him in his apartment with his throat slit. Didn't have a stitch on, the bastard. It couldn't happen to a nicer guy. . . .' Anne's voice rattled on.

Sylvia replaced the phone without saying goodbye. After a

while she went out and bought a paper and read the details. He was not a television producer, as she had realized from the beginning, but a truck driver. Unemployed. Fellow roomers said he had not lived in the building long but from what they had seen of him he was a quiet, pleasant young man; not the type to cause trouble. There was no mention of the rape charge or court case. The accompanying photograph showed a handsome boy-next-door, smiling into the camera. That, plus a reference to the mounting incidence of gay bashings, left the impression he was a homosexual.

There were no clues, the article stated, but the police had a number of leads and expected an arrest would be made shortly.

The arrest did not materialize. The press eventually lost interest.

Although it was not apparent at the time, Arthur Maitland's murder would come to be seen as the first in a bizarre string of killings that baffled investigators for months, from August through the following spring, casting a pall of fear over the city.

With the death of Arthur Maitland a force was unleashed; a reign of terror had begun.

Jay Smith pulled on his track suit, laced his Adidas and left his room noiselessly, careful not to disturb the rest of the family. Before leaving the house he drank a glass of orange juice and took two vitamin pills.

It was late August. The sky was clear, the sun just rising. A gentle breeze rustled the leaves of the old weed tree in the center of the backyard. He looked at it fondly. From the time he was nine he had used the tree to enter and leave his bedroom, which was set at the rear of the house directly above the kitchen. Afraid he would fall and break a leg, his parents had threatened to lop off the branch that arched between the trunk of the tree and his windowsill. They had never understood why he preferred shinnying up the tree to using the carpeted stairway, could not comprehend that one spelled adventure and the other conformity. He had stopped trying to explain. Eventually, except for one recent lapse, he had stopped using the tree.

The Smiths were indulgent parents. Jay was their only child, and they were proud of him. At sixteen he was a star athlete as well as an honors student. A handsome obedient boy, he kept to himself, never got into trouble. Jay Smith was a son any family would cherish.

Stretching in the fresh morning air, he spot-jogged to loosen up before setting off on the five-mile course he ran every morning, summer and winter.

When Jay first started jogging he had forced his body to run beyond the normal level of endurance, pushing himself until his chest felt as though it would burst and every step was back-pounding torture. Now he ran the five miles with ease, carried along by an exhilarating high that was both euphoric and addictive.

It was neat that his family lived in a small town where there was room to run through open fields and along wooded trails. Jogging in the city, through concrete canyons, would not hold the same degree of pleasure.

He loped down the hill behind the lumberyard and started along the river. It was the most scenic spot on the route, the water clear and sparkling, a curtain of willow shading the banks. It was here that he occasionally paused for a few moments of private time.

His pace slowed as he neared the small clearing in a grove of cedars. Someone had built a campfire on the bank. The patch of burned grass and ashes was circled by logs, rustic seating for a wiener roast or sing-along. Jay sat on one of the logs, legs outstretched, facing the river. He relished the feeling of solitude. He had often wondered what it would be like to be the only person in the world, to wander at will without fear of intrusion.

Jay Smith felt, had always felt, that he belonged only to himself. Even his parents were redundant. They were good people; he was fond of them in a detached way. But he would be glad when he was free of them, when he was old enough to start a life of his own.

The trail was his escape. His private world. He had staked it out three years before, when he first started his daily jogging. Only once had it been impinged upon, and then only temporarily.

That girl. He frowned, thinking of her, of the anxiety she had caused, the disruption. He had run later then, arriving home just in time to change for school. Because of her, he had moved his routine ahead to sunrise, revised and re-revised his schedule and eventually placed it in hiatus.

She was about his age, perhaps a shade older. The newspaper described her as attractive. She hadn't seemed so to him. Just a tall, thin girl with long auburn hair, damp with sweat at the ends.

The first time he saw her, he was startled. It had never occurred to him that his private time, his private space, might be trespassed upon. He slowed down to let her pass; stared after her until he lost sight of her in the trees ahead.

The next morning he left the house at the same time, hoping she would not appear; telling himself she would probably never take the same route again. When he heard the rhythmic footsteps approaching from the rear he felt his muscles tighten. He forced himself not to look. She passed, taking the best of the day with her.

The next day he started later and caught up to her almost at the end of the trail. He arrived in class after the bell, sweaty and panting.

The following morning he set out earlier. He was on the side road a few yards from home when he looked back and saw her crossing the field near the old Sampson house.

For a week he didn't run at all. It was then he discovered he was addicted, that jogging was a fix he was not prepared to do without. So he continued to run, but the pleasure was gone. He ran with the weight of the girl on his mind. Even on the rare days when she didn't appear, she was there. He listened for her footsteps. Checked ahead and behind. Lost the sheer joy of running free.

He had considered asking her to run somewhere else but discarded the idea. There was something about the loose stride, the set of her shoulders, that told him she would be difficult to dissuade. He would wait. Patience, he knew, could perform miracles.

He was right. The girl ran the trail for a few weeks. Then one day her body was discovered on the riverbank.

Now Jay stretched, breathed deeply; it felt good to be alive. Overhead a redwinged blackbird perched in one of the cedars chattered noisily, breaking the early morning silence. Jay smiled in empathy. Running, his body skimming the earth, verging on flight, he felt like a bird, felt he would lift from the ground and soar overhead with the graceful ease of a gull.

Caught up in his daydream he did not hear the light sound of footsteps. Not until he heard the whisper of his name did he turn, look up, go numb with fear.

A tall figure stood poised above him, fence post clutched club-fashion, ready to strike.

They stared at each other wordlessly. A breeze rustled the leaves in the birch trees across the trail. Water rippled over the stones in the creek bed. The bird preened, flapping its wings. Sounds, unnoticed a moment before, magnified.

Jay's eyes widened, darkened in terror. For one stark moment he sat frozen; saw the glint of a nail, shiny and untarnished, protruding from the rough splintered wood; saw a heavy black curtain shot with scarlet blot out the sky.

The blow landed on the crown of his head, shattering his skull. His body lay propped against the log, limp as a rag doll. The bird, alarmed, flew away.

The assailant bent over him briefly before moving through the cedars to the riverbank, downstream to the neglected Sampson pasture, along the back lane to the abandoned homestead.

The car was parked in the toolshed. It was an old Ford, battered and mud-splattered. It looked like a cast-off, left behind when the Sampsons moved out, but it was not. The pitiful body contained an engine smooth and powerful, tinkered into superb running condition by a moonlighting master mechanic. The vehicle had cost three hundred dollars. Performance-wise, it could outclass many of the newer models on the road.

The driver paused behind the forsythia bushes at the end of the lane to make sure no one was coming. Once in transit on the concession road, the Ford blended into the local traffic.

It was a short drive back to the city. The car was parked at a meter in the suburbs, doors unlocked and key in ignition to encourage theft. The driver boarded a streetcar to the municipal parking garage located downtown.

After the cramped interior of the vintage Ford, the top-of-the-line import felt richly luxurious. It wheeled easily on the spiral ramps, stopped briefly at the attendant's cage, moved smoothly on to the street. In seconds, car and driver were swallowed up in the flow of city traffic.

The Smiths were devastated by their son's death. Mildred,

who had been one of the community's leading volunteer workers, retreated behind drawn shades. Jason, Jay's father, withdrew behind a wall of silence. They avoided old friends; soon, old friends avoided them. The loss of Jay's life brought an end to theirs.

The piece of timber used to stave in Jay's skull was buried in the wound. The first officers on the scene thought it was glued in place by dried blood. When it was finally worked free they discovered the nail. The heavy spike had pierced the skull and penetrated the brain. The post was old. The nail was new. The police were stymied.

There were no fingerprints on the crude weapon and the nail was a common variety that could be purchased anywhere. Aside from the post, the only extraneous item was a shipping tag tied to Jay's shoelace. There was a number on the tag. The number was 3.

4

September 1984

The National Ballet was performing at the O'Keefe Centre. Sylvia had tickets for *Swan Lake*, her favorite, and she had been looking forward to the evening for weeks. The night before the performance, David spent one of his increasingly rare evenings at home.

They were relaxing in the living room after dinner, David with the day's paper and Sylvia with a paperback copy of Jack Abbott's *In the Belly of the Beast*, the book that, with Norman Mailer's help, gained Abbott temporary release from a near-lifetime behind bars. When she glanced up and saw David watching her over the top of the newspaper, Sylvia set her book aside. He was wearing his 'I have something to tell you' look. She knew from the faint smile and restrained excitement in his eyes that whatever it was, it was important.

'I've been asked to do an interview.' Low-key. Offhand.

'That's not unusual.' It was true. David Jenning was becoming one of the city's most visible, audible spokesmen on matters pertaining to law. When he didn't elaborate she obliged him by asking, 'What kind of interview?'

His chest expanded. 'On *Nightline*.' A pause for effect. 'The Ted Koppel show on ABC.'

'David, that's marvelous.' She was thrilled for him. Doing local interviews was one thing; appearing on a major U.S. TV news program was another.

He stopped pretending indifference and grinned boyishly. 'You approve?'

'Of course I approve. It's terrific. But how . . . why. . . . ?'

'They're doing a show on the legal definition of insanity in different countries. There'll be someone from England. Germany. Lee Bailey for the States.'

'And David Jenning for Canada. David, I'm so proud. When is it?'

He swallowed hard. 'Tomorrow night.'

'Oh no. What about the ballet? You promised. . . . ' She caught herself. A night at the ballet was a mere bagatelle compared to this once-in-a-lifetime opportunity. 'They don't give you much notice, do they?'

'I knew about it a couple of weeks ago,' he said lamely. 'I didn't want to tell you about it until it was absolutely sure. You know what happens. If a big story breaks at the last minute, they jump on it. With a live show you have to be ready when they are.'

She hid her disappointment. The program would catapult David into an international élite of legal superstars. He had every right to feel proud.

He cleared his throat. 'About the ballet. . . . '

'David, it's not important. We can go next year. I can go by myself, for that matter.'

'That wouldn't be the same, Syl. I asked Craig to take you, and he said he would.'

'Oh no. David, you shouldn't have done that. It's like conning your best friend into a date with the village wallflower.'

David roared with laughter.

'It's not funny.' She was annoyed at him for placing her in an embarrassing situation. She was also disturbed by the thought of an evening alone with Craig Faron. There was a bond between them, a deep-running current, that neither had acknowledged. She did not want to run the risk of either being swept away.

'It *is* funny, Syl. A wallflower? You? My God, I've seen the way men look at you. If I didn't know you so well I'd be out of my mind with jealousy.'

It was Sylvia's turn to laugh, a sound as cool as ice tinkling in a glass.

'Look,' David said, 'I knew you wanted to go. I knew you were geared for a night out. Dinner. Dancing. A real evening. And I knew you wouldn't go at all or you'd ask Anne and that wouldn't be the same thing. Also . . . ' the clincher, 'Craig is the only man I'd trust with you. He's as straight-laced as you are, Syl. Most of the men I know would be all over you in a flash. I didn't want to subject you to that.'

His best friend. His best wife. If it were anyone but David, she would suspect a set-up. A test. But David wouldn't do such a thing. Not that he wasn't capable of it. He would go to any lengths for a client. But she knew that where she was concerned, he was childishly naive. He accepted her as she seemed to be. It was a peculiar blind spot for a man who prided himself on his ability to read human nature. At one time she had considered his trust in her a touching tribute, a token of the depth of his emotional commitment. More recently she had come to think of it as the complacent ownership of a possession that, appraised when acquired and value thus set, is forevermore taken for granted.

'Poor Craig. He probably detests ballet.' She hated the thought of forcing him to sit through an evening he would probably find boring. The thought of sitting beside him, watching the male dancers in their tights, cleavage and baskets clearly defined, made her uncomfortably warm.

'Sylvia,' David said in his patient voice, 'Craig loves ballet. And *Swan Lake* happens to be his favorite. He was like a kid when I asked him.'

Comparing Craig Faron to a kid was like comparing a panther to a housecat. She was about to say she wouldn't go, Craig could have both tickets and take someone else, when David forestalled her by suggesting a drink to celebrate. He poured himself a Scotch and handed her a glass of wine. She held it up in a toast and said, 'To you, David. And to *Nightline*. May you out-Bailey Bailey.'

He kissed her on the cheek and sat down again, pleased that everything was settled. 'Incidentally,' he said, 'I told Craig to dress. I thought you might want to wear that spaghetti thing. Or the Chinesey silk.'

'Honestly, David. You can be a real pain.'

He grinned as though she'd handed him a compliment.

They were quiet for a moment.

Then, trying not to sound overly interested, she asked, 'Why hasn't he ever married?'

'Who?'

'You know who. Craig. He rarely talks about himself. Not about his private life. Never about women. Has he ever been engaged?'

David leaned over and picked up his paper. 'He's a dyed-in-the-wool bachelor. The prize catch that got away.' He started reading where he had left off earlier.

'David.' Sylvia was exasperated. 'Why hasn't he married? Doesn't he like women?'

David lowered the paper and looked at her coldly. 'What are you suggesting?' His lips were pressed into a thin line.

'Good God, nothing.' She was nonplussed by his reaction, the edge of hostility.

He studied her face, decided the question was innocent of suggestion. 'He *was* engaged.' He said it slowly, as though infringing on Faron's privacy.

'When?'

'A long time ago. Before I met him. I don't know much about it. He mentioned it once, but it's not something he talks about.'

'What happened?'

'Sylvia, I really don't know.'

'Does he still care for her?' Sylvia realized he didn't want to continue the discussion, but she had to know. 'Why didn't they get married?' She couldn't imagine any woman who was engaged to Faron letting him go. And if he was still carrying a torch it seemed unlikely that he would have been the one to call it off. 'Does he ever see her? Is she here in Toronto?'

'She's dead,' David said tersely.

'Dead?' The word registered slowly. 'Dead? How? When?'

'Syl, I honestly don't know.' He was becoming more and more impatient with her. 'All I *do* know is that he was very much in love. They were going to be married. Just before the wedding, something happened. It was sudden. It was violent. It was tragic. He still thinks about it. And I would advise you to never, ever mention it. I did. Once. And he scared the hell out of me. He went into shock or something. Whatever it was, it was goddamn terrifying. I don't think he knew who he was, who I was, anything. He just went into this . . . this thing . . . a bloody psychotic trance or something. He was like a different person.'

'You think he's psychotic, yet you want me to spend an evening with him?' She was ragging him, teasing to see what he'd say. She could not imagine being frightened of Craig Faron.

'Jesus Christ, the man's as normal as I am. I knew I shouldn't have told you. In all the years I've known him that was the only time it happened. And it was my fault. I started digging up something he'd buried, and it got to him. He didn't actually do anything. He was just out for a couple of minutes.' He went back to his paper.

Closing her out. David would not, she knew, speak of the

matter again. Sylvia picked up her book, looked at the type, tried to see past the fleeting images of Faron to the printed page. Faron — smiling and relaxed the night he came to dinner. Faron — frowning in concentration as he cross-referenced David's files. Faron — staring off into space, expression somber, eyes dark and troubled. She had recognized his moments of sadness, had known there were dark depths beneath the calm, controlled exterior. But she had never felt, never could feel, that he was a man to be feared.

As part of his plans for the evening, David had made dinner reservations at Winston's. Sylvia wore the spaghetti-strap dress he had suggested and felt, looking at herself in the mirror, like a schoolgirl on her first date. David came into the bedroom while she was applying her make-up and told her she looked gorgeous, not to hurry home, he'd probably be late anyway.

She heard Craig's car drive up. Later when she went downstairs she found both men having a drink at the bar. David was in his shirt-sleeves, tie loosened, collar undone. Craig was wearing a tuxedo and ruffled shirt. He looked as comfortable in black-tie as he did in faded jeans and sneakers. David in a tux looked like a waiter. Craig looked like a man accustomed to corporate boardrooms and private Lear jets.

Animated, both hands gesturing, David was talking about the upcoming interview; Craig, leaning against the bar with one foot on the brass rail, provided an attentive audience.

David stopped talking when he noticed her, and Craig, following David's glance, turned and smiled. She caught her breath. The stern face was radiant, the dark blue eyes sparkling. He had never looked as handsome as he did at that moment with the late afternoon sun touching the sharp, high cheekbones with bronze, the heavy black hair with a shimmering blue sheen.

'Are you ready?' His lips would not say what his eyes were saying. She could not have coped if they had.

She nodded, handing him her wrap, braced for his touch as he placed it over her shoulders.

David beamed at them both, telling them they made a handsome couple, saying he wanted them to have a good time.

Sylvia kissed him and wished him luck on the interview. Walking them to the door he stood there, waving.

Returning his wave as they backed out the driveway she

noticed how old and tired he looked. Pricked by guilt she rolled down the car window and called, 'Are you sure you don't want me to stay? I can go to the studio with you, if you like.'

'Don't be silly.' He straightened up, putting on his public face. 'You'd just be in the way. I have to make a few notes. Do a couple of things. There's no point in you sitting around for nothing.'

Craig started the engine. 'I think he wants to be alone, Sylvia. Tonight means a lot to him. He wants to do it right.'

He turned and smiled at her and she felt, again, the animal magnetism, the sheer energy that vibrated around him like fine, thin feelers. His hands rested on the wheel of the Mercedes lightly, the long graceful fingers manipulating the car with an economy of movement.

She remembered that David had told her Craig didn't own a car. When she mentioned it, he said David was right; he preferred to take cabs or rent, as he had done tonight.

'We could have used my car. You shouldn't have gone to this expense,' she protested.

'I wanted this night to be special,' he said simply. He looked straight ahead, watching the traffic. His face in profile told her nothing.

Sylvia hadn't been to Winston's for a couple of years. The popular dining spot was as pleasant as she remembered it. The food was excellent and so was the service. Craig was attentive, albeit carefully formal. They talked easily and the time went by quickly.

When Craig finally looked at his watch and said it was time to go or they'd miss the curtain, she told him he must be joking, they couldn't have spent that long over dinner. When she discovered they had, she was amazed. The time had gone by much too quickly. Isolated in their private pool of candlelight, she had been conscious of nothing but the vibrant, handsome man sitting across from her. Reluctantly, she rose to leave, wishing that more of the evening stretched ahead.

They arrived at the O'Keefe Centre just before the lights dimmed. Their seats were upstairs on the aisle, chosen in deference to David who hated scrunching along the narrow rows, a blessing that allowed them to take their places without fuss as the lights went down.

Sylvia had always enjoyed *Swan Lake*, but never had it held more magic than it did that evening with Craig. Never was there a prince more charming, an Odette more lovely, a villain more sinister. Never had Tchaikovsky sounded more romantic, more melancholy, more majestically ominous.

When the lights went up after the first act she sat, mesmerized, until Craig placed his hand on her arm and shook her gently back to reality.

Turning to him she saw that he, too, was caught up in the enchantment of Tchaikovsky's make-believe world. The sharp planes of his face were softened, the hooded eyes were candid and serene. They smiled at each other, each unwilling to turn away, each conscious of his hand on her bare arm.

It was Sylvia who moved first, jostled by a stout lady who was trying to squeeze past into the aisle. They both stood to make way. The spell broken, Craig asked politely if she'd like a drink.

'Only if you would.'

He looked at the stream of people inching down the staircase and shook his head. 'It's a short intermission. Maybe next time.'

After the second act they left their seats, not for a drink but to stretch their legs. Sylvia was conscious of people looking at them, at Craig particularly. Craig did not notice. He seemed oblivious to everyone and everything but her. As he told her about the original version of the work, she felt a tap on her shoulder and turned to discover Anne and Bill at her elbow. She was not glad to see them, did not welcome the intrusion. Anne tugged at her arm, edging her away from Craig and Bill who were making polite conversation about the performance. Out of earshot, Anne looked at Sylvia with knowing, narrowed eyes and said, 'I didn't know you had a thing for this gorgeous, sexy hunk. Where in hell is David?'

Sylvia explained about the interview. Anne whispered, 'It's fate. You two are perfect together. If you don't get this guy into bed you need your head read. Forget David for once. You probably haven't had a good fuck since your honeymoon.'

'That's not the way it is,' Sylvia snapped.

'Oh no? Yours truly knows high voltage when she sees it. You're both throwing off sparks.'

The lights flickered and the audience began filing back into the auditorium. Relieved, Sylvia made her escape but she continued to hear Anne's voice through most of the third act. Not until the death scene, blue half-light shadowing the stage, the ballerina crumpled with arms undulating like fragile wings, did illusion again become reality. They remained in their seats until the final curtain call, rising only when the house lights came on and the crowd had thinned.

Sylvia waited under the canopy while Craig retrieved the car. When she was settled, he asked quietly, 'What would you like to do? Go for a drink? Dancing?'

She did not want to be with other people. She did want to be with Craig. She wanted to know more about him, wanted to see where he lived, wanted to know about his aborted engagement and the girl he had loved.

As though he had read her mind he said casually, 'Why don't we go to my place for coffee? It's just a few blocks.'

His voice was impersonal, free of suggestion or hidden meaning. She knew he was trying to tell her that he was inviting her as a friend and he would not impinge on that friendship. She accepted readily. There was nowhere for the evening to go, yet neither wanted it to end.

The building was a glass-and-steel phallus that dominated the surrounding business area. Riding up in the high-speed elevator, conscious of the lean body beside her, Sylvia felt her pulse quicken, her heart palpitate. Outwardly she was calm. Inwardly she was in turmoil. A tinder box. One spark and she knew she would be swept beyond fear of consequence. It was a relief to step out of the confined space of the lift into the hallway, from the hallway into the spacious apartment.

Craig took her wrap, suggested she make herself comfortable in the living room, was pleased when she insisted on joining him in the kitchen. As he ground the coffee, set the coffee-maker, he talked about the early days of the National, how it had evolved into a world-class company, how the corps now rivaled that of the legendary Sadler's Wells, once famed for its immaculate precision and consummate grace.

While they waited for the coffee to drip he showed her his view of the city, the flash of neon below, the lake beyond, silvered by moonlight.

She felt his warmth, smelled the faint musk of his cologne, thrust David between them as a shield by suggesting that they turn on the television set to see if they could catch the end of the program.

Craig handed her the remote control and left her to find the channel while he poured the coffee. The show was almost over. Koppel was winding up his summary. The credits rolled. She pressed the off button as Craig emerged from the kitchen with coffee and liqueur. He did not join her on the couch, choosing instead a leather slingback on the opposite side of the coffee table.

The bottle on the tray was Benedictine. She knew it was there because it was her favorite. He knows everything, she thought, everything about me there is to know. But I know nothing about him. She felt a moment of panic. And then she looked up into his eyes, saw the gentle warmth, the total acceptance of her as she was, knew there was nothing to fear from this strange, compelling man. She knew, too, that in this moment of limbo there was nothing she couldn't ask, nothing he wouldn't answer.

Accepting the small snifter of Benedictine, she inhaled the sweet piney fragrance, saying softly, like someone in a dream, 'What was she like?'

He looked down at his hands, fingers laced, knuckles white. The vein along his temple rose in a thin blue ridge. A muscle contracted in his cheek. Stricken by his grief, she leaned toward him, reached across the table to touch his clasped hands. He jerked away, as though the brief contact inflicted unbearable pain.

'You should talk about it,' she said softly, aching to help.

Slowly he raised his head and the face before her was the face of a stranger. Her breath caught in her throat. It was not grief with which he lived, but rage, rage so primitive that his features were twisted into a mask of hatred.

Sylvia sat motionless, unafraid. She gauged the measure of his discipline, understood the effort of will that kept him poised on the precipice, immobile until the fury passed, the pressure eased.

Slowly his pupils, distended until only a thin rim of blue remained, retracted. The death's head transposed, became familiar. She handed him his cup of coffee, waited for him to speak.

He drank the coffee, pressed his fingertips against the still swollen temples. When he finally spoke she had to lean forward to catch the soft, muffled words. 'I've never. . . . ' He paused, searching. 'It's not something I like to talk about, think about. I've never discussed it. . . .'

'Then don't,' Sylvia said. 'I know you must have loved her a great deal. I thought perhaps if you shared it, brought it out in the open, you would be able to put it behind you. Start again. But if it's too painful, if you loved her so much. . . .'

He came to his feet, began pacing the floor with long, rhythmic strides. 'Loved her? Yes. In a way. Not like. . . .' He caught himself. 'She was young. We both were. Young. And vulnerable.' He stopped pacing. Stood with his back to her looking out over the balcony.

'Avril. Pretty little Avril. Seventeen years old. We didn't know how young we were. Old enough to want each other. Old enough to get married. She was so delicate. So frail. I wanted to protect her from the world.' He laughed harshly. 'She made me feel invincible. Her slayer of dragons.' He turned back to Sylvia. 'She trusted me. I failed her. Because of me, she's dead.'

Sylvia held him then, cradling his head on her shoulder until she felt the stiffness drain, leaving him limp and relaxed. He was exhausted, but the story was not complete. She did not want to know more. But neither did she want to let the moment slip by, the rendering fall short. 'What happened?'

He pulled free, turned away as if to shut her out.

'Let's make some more coffee,' she suggested. She carried the tray to the kitchen, willing him to follow. She wanted him to finish his story, lay low the ghost, and the brightly lit, antiseptic kitchen offered safe ground for the telling.

'What happened to Avril?' Deliberately blunt.

He poured the coffee, hand steady. 'She was raped and thrown in a gully. They said she lived for two, maybe three days.' His voice was as steady as his hand. 'She was found on the day we were to be married. The body was still warm. If it had been a few hours earlier. . . .'

She took his hand in both of hers. He did not pull away.

'She wanted to pick something up for the wedding. Some kind of surprise. For me, probably. She wanted to borrow the car. I said no, I'd drive her when I got off work. It was a heap of junk. I was afraid she'd get in an accident. Hurt herself. So she decided to walk. And that was the last we saw of her till they found her. If I had let her have the damn car. . . .'

She held his face between her palms. 'Craig, it's over. You

can't pretend it didn't happen. Accept it. And let it go.'

He took her hands, brushed a palm with his lips. 'It was because of Avril I met David.'

The remark came as a surprise. Avril had died years earlier.

'After she died I thought I'd go crazy. I had to get away. I hitchhiked to Vancouver. Got a job on a tramp steamer. Skipped ship in Sydney. I did a lot of things in between. Built a business. Made money. Got rich. But she was always there, in my mind. After I came back I started thinking about the law, how it works. I'd never seen a trial. So I went, and I saw David.'

She had never understood why a man financially independent would spend his time tracking undesirables through the sin bins and clip joints in the maw of the city. 'You work with David because of Avril?'

'In a way.'

'But you're working *for* criminals. Helping them get away with whatever it is they've done.'

'No. That's not true. If I think a person is innocent, yes. But I do very little aside from special reports now, Sylvia. And you know about that. I think it's just as important to know where these really dangerous types are after they get out as before they go in.'

And now she understood. 'The man who killed Avril. . . .'

'Yes. The man who killed Avril was a repeater. He served his time. They let him out. Two weeks later he got Avril.'

'But they caught him.'

'Yes. And he's out again. But this time it's different. I know where he is. And he knows I know. I can't prevent him from pulling the same thing again. But I drop around just often enough to make him think twice.'

'When you see him . . . does it bother you?'

'Yes. I think if I'd still been in Canada when they caught him I'd have killed him. Now he's old. No money. No family. Killing him would just put him out of his misery. It would have been worth it back then. Not any more.'

They had talked enough. Sylvia asked him to call a cab, offered no objection when he rode down in the elevator and waited with her in the lobby.

Holding her hand, he traced her cheek lightly with his fingertips. 'Thank you for tonight, Sylvia. You've been more of a friend than you know.'

When the cab arrived he held the door open for her, watched as the car swung out and along Yonge Street. He felt empty and alone and lonely. Avril belonged to the past. And Sylvia belonged to David.

Sylvia did not get up to see David off to work in the morning; and it was late afternoon before she managed to get through to him by phone. Henny Henderson, his secretary, told Sylvia the lines had been busy because people had been calling to congratulate him. Henny said he'd been terrific, by far the best of the lot. Compared to David, Lee Bailey just didn't rate. Sylvia smiled. She had long suspected Miss Henderson of having a thing for David. Not that it would do her much good, poor soul.

When Sylvia finally spoke to David, he said modestly that everything had gone very well. He had picked up two new clients because of the program, and a British journalist had called from overseas requesting a copy of his remarks.

He did not ask her about her evening with Craig and she did not tell him, then or later, about Avril.

5

Mid-September 1984

Roly Burns had lived out of a suitcase for more years than he cared to remember. His job as field sales manager of a cosmetics firm took in a broad territory. He was never home during the week, often away on weekends as well. His wife and children had long since adjusted to his schedule. They looked upon him more as a distant relative than head of the household. He didn't mind. He had married in a moment of youthful exuberance. When the novelty wore off, so did his enthusiasm.

Usually Roly enjoyed working Toronto, but this trip his sales were off and he felt down. It was a dull fall day, the sky gloomy and overcast. The weather did not add to his mood. Skipping his last appointment, he headed for the Marpole Hotel. He left his sample case in the car and stopped in the lobby just long enough to register. In his room he changed into slacks and a velour V-neck, splashed cold water on his face and hurried back downstairs.

The Marpole was Roly's favorite stopping place. Most of his time was spent in small towns where he had to be mindful of his p's and q's. A straight-laced lot, those small town merchants. Cut you off soon as look at you. In the city you were lost in the crowd, free to do whatever you liked. And what five-foot-three Roly liked most was tall, leggy women with a penchant for action.

The Marpole was one spot where Roly always got lucky. After picking up a package of cigarettes in the lobby, he took the escalator to the lower level and the long bar that offered an underwater view of the hotel swimming pool. Seating himself at a porthole table he watched the swimmers while he sipped his double rye on the rocks. The brightly colored bodies with pale, flipper-like limbs looked like exotic sea creatures.

The pool reminded Roly of the aquarium he had as a child. His parents bought it for him one Christmas, and it remained in his room for years. It wasn't until the fish started dying, their golden bodies floating on the surface, that the tank was drained and given away. The day the aquarium was removed, he took his pint-sized fishing gear down the street and threw it in a trash can waiting on the kerb to be emptied.

The last swimmer left the pool and Roly turned his attention to the dim interior of the bar. It was early. The evening crowd had not yet arrived. A few of the tables were occupied by office workers having a drink before starting home. A couple sat in a corner holding hands. There was only one other single in the room, an attractive dark-haired woman with oversized designer eyeglasses.

He caught her eye and, with the confidence of more wins than losses, gave her a broad smile. When the waiter came by to check his drink he ordered another rye for himself, whatever she was drinking for her.

When it arrived she said something to the waiter in a low voice. He nodded toward Roly and she glanced in his direction, raising her glass in acknowledgement.

When the waiter went back to the bar Roly walked over to the woman's table and asked if he could join her.

'Please. I'd like company.' Her voice was deep, slightly husky. She looked even better close up than from a distance.

Roly computed the possibilities. Too much class for a streetwalker. Not enough class for a call girl. Either a businesswoman in transit or a bored housewife looking for some action. Not that it mattered. He'd been known to pay if need be, although he much preferred a more personal relationship.

'Do you come here often?'

She shook her head. 'Just on special occasions.'

He wondered what sort of special occasion would bring her to a bar on her own. 'Your birthday?' he ventured.

'Dear me, no.' She laughed, amused by the question. He waited for an explanation. Instead she motioned toward the porthole and said, 'It's relaxing, isn't it? There's something hypnotic about water.'

Slipping into his boy-meets-girl patter, he quipped, 'As long as you don't have to drink it.'

They bantered back and forth easily, content with conversation rather than communication, and after the first few rounds he asked her to join him for dinner.

She ordered more to drink.

The waiter brought a small dish of peanuts and he ate those

instead. By eleven o'clock, Roly Burns had consumed more liquor in one sitting than he usually put away in a month. When they got up to leave he was glassy-eyed and his legs felt like rubber.

His companion, who was not nearly as drunk as he was, gathered up his change and put it in his pocket. He was dimly aware of her hand sliding along his leg, separated from direct contact only by the thin lining of his trouser pocket. He was much too drunk to respond. When she stopped groping and slipped her arm around his waist to steady him, he sagged against her limply.

The woman half pulled, half pushed him out of the bar and onto the escalator. In the lobby she manoeuverd him into the nearest easy chair and informed the men at the desk that someone would have to help him to his room.

She waited while they searched his pockets for the key he had picked up earlier. Unable to find it, they checked his wallet for identification. They finally located his room number in the registry and picked the duplicate key from the board. The night manager and his young assistant wrestled Roly to his feet and held him erect while they waited for an elevator.

The woman watched while the assistant steered Roly into the elevator and tried to hold him up with one hand while he punched the floor with the other.

When the manager returned to the desk, shaking his head in disgust, she left through the main entrance, caught up in a party of husbands and wives hurrying to get home before their baby-sitters ran into overtime.

On the tenth floor the young man half-carried Roly along the hall. By the time they reached the room he was puffing, out-of-breath, fed up. It was his first week on the job. If this was it, they could have it. He had better things to do with his life than wet nurse middle-aged inebriates. Opening the door, he dragged Roly to the bed and dumped him on top of it. Then with one last look over his shoulder he stepped out into the hall, closed the door, and left the hotel.

Roly Burns woke before dawn with a raging thirst. He was still fully dressed, his clothes wrinkled and damp with perspiration. The room was dark except for a thin wedge of light from the bathroom.

He lay still, his head pounding, and tried to remember what

had happened the night before. There was a woman who kept ordering drinks, calling for a new round every time he suggested they have something to eat. There was a tall young man who got him into the elevator and upstairs. And there was some kind of commotion about a missing key.

Roly cursed under his breath. He seldom drank to excess. He knew only too well how dangerous alcohol could be, how a momentary blackout could become a lifelong regret.

He swung his feet to the floor and sat on the edge of the bed with his head in his hands. More than anything in the world, he wanted a drink of water. If only the bathroom weren't so far away. Palms pressed against his temples, eyes fixed on the carpet, he sat pole-axed. The room was hot. Stuffy. He had a heavy day lined up. One of his appointments was with his biggest account. If he lost it, he'd be up shit creek. He must have had a mental seizure, gone right off his rocker to let himself get in this condition.

He was so disoriented that when he first heard the voice he thought it was an imagined echo inside his head. 'Burns,' it said. And again, 'Burns.' And then again, louder, more insistent, 'Roly Burns.' He raised his eyes, saw the wedge of light widen, the tall figure silhouetted against it, an apparition. He knew it was not real, knew too much alcohol could bring on gallon distemper, the d.t.'s. He closed his eyes. Told himself he was hallucinating; when he opened his eyes the phantom would be gone. He looked, and it was there. Moving forward. A silent glide on cat feet.

Roly fell back across the bed, tried to scrabble his body out of reach. His arms and legs were heavy, weighted, as though he had taken one too many sleeping pills. He felt a terrible, suffocating fear, a sense of time spinning beyond his grasp.

He rolled over and reached for the opposite side of the bed in an attempt to pull himself across and out of reach. His fingers clutched the edge as other, stronger fingers closed around his throat. His body heaved as he gasped for air. His eyeballs, curtained by a fine red film, felt as though they were bursting from their sockets. White sound exploded in his eardrums.

It was over in moments. Roly did not feel the quick, sure hands stripping him to the skin or the shorts being wrapped round his neck and tightly knotted. He was unaware of being dragged off the bed and left sprawled on the rug he had walked across just a few short hours before.

The killer placed the key to the room on the night table and eased the door open slowly. There was no one in the hall. In a few hours the chambermaids would be on duty, but now the floor was deathly still. The guests were asleep, the early morning shift had not yet arrived. There was no one to notice the unregistered guest emerge from the stairwell on the lower level and slip through the side entrance to the deserted pre-dawn city street.

The maid discovered Roly Burns' body shortly before noon. It was lying in full view of the doorway, nude, with shorts knotted around the neck and a tag bearing the number 4 wound round the toe. The girl did not enter the room. First she screamed, then she fled to the floor below where she told the housekeeper what she had found. The housekeeper notified the manager, and the manager notified the police.

Aside from the corpse, there were no signs of violence in the room. No clues were found, nothing seemed to be missing. Roly's belongings and billfold were intact, his samples were in the trunk of his car and his car was in the garage.

Mrs. Burns said her husband had no enemies and his superiors described him as a hard-working, God-fearing man who would be difficult to replace. The following week they assigned his territory to a bright young comer they had been grooming to replace Roly at the first opportunity.

The Burns family, well-compensated for their loss by a trio of insurance policies fortified with double indemnity clauses, settled back into the routine of their lives.

When Mrs. Burns married Roly's best friend, the neighbors said it was wonderful how she had taken hold. After all, they said, life must go on.

Sylvia's life, having idled in neutral through spring and summer, moved smoothly into high gear. Whether it was the brief encounter with Arthur Maitland or the presence of Craig Faron, the quiet days at poolside were over. She still swam daily, weather permitting; worked out in the gym; enjoyed the occasional skinny dip at midnight. But the rest of her time was spent sorting David's files and cataloguing the information that would eventually make up the computer data base.

David had decided to do the job right. His appearance on *Nightline* had established him as Canada's most widely known criminal lawyer. He was considered the country's leading authority on M'Naghten, the still enforced nineteenth century insanity ruling based on the attempted assassination of Sir Robert Peel by lunatic Daniel M'Naghten. He was also in receipt of a growing number of blue chip clients who retained him more as a deterrent to would-be litigants than through immediate need. The Apple, he decided, lacked both the versatility and capacity to fulfil the requirements of the future. He bequeathed it to Sylvia as a replacement for the TRS and invested in a multi-user, multi-function Prime, a versatile system with the added advantage of compatibility with a wide range of mainframes. It would enable him to access the data base of law enforcement agencies both at home and abroad. It would also keep records, handle accounts and process contracts and agreements for the firm. Craig and Sylvia had been assigned the task of setting up the master file for the Journal program. The master would then be turned over to an analyst who would finalize it for the programmer. The hardware was in place, the software was weeks away.

Craig and Sylvia spent hours together but they were careful, always, to keep their relationship on an impersonal plane. They did not talk about themselves, did not mention the evening at the ballet. It was only when David was present that they allowed themselves the luxury of being friends.

It was during one such evening, when they had worked late and David insisted Craig stay for dinner, that she again glimpsed the man behind the persona. While in Vancouver he had attended a meeting of victims of crime. He was impressed; felt more should be done to assist such groups.

David disagreed, saying it was a mistake to feed on tragedy. Far better to try to forget.

'That's exactly what these people have been told,' Craig said. 'Go home and grieve. Then bury your dead, and forget.'

'The only sensible thing to do,' David said. 'Talking about it won't bring them back.'

Sylvia, with a lifelong affinity for the hunted rather than the hunter, with Avril fresh in her mind, said, 'I've often wondered,

David. What would you do if someone did me in?'

'You're making my point, Syl. What would you want me to do? Spend the rest of my life brooding about it? Would you want that?'

'I suppose not. I guess what I'm really asking is whether you'd defend whoever was responsible.'

Both Craig and Sylvia waited for his answer.

David shifted uncomfortably. 'That's a hypothetical question. It wouldn't be allowed.'

'But *could* you? Would you be capable of defending such a person?'

'Probably not.'

Craig was intrigued. 'How would you feel about it?'

'I'd be angry. Torn up. I'd want to see him behind bars.'

'Would you want revenge?'

'Oh, no.'

'Would you want him hanged?'

'What good would that do? It wouldn't bring Sylvia back. You know I've never believed in the death penalty. Violence breeds violence.'

'My Lord and Protector,' Sylvia said.

Craig bore in. 'It wouldn't bother you that Sylvia was dead and in a few years her killer would be walking around free? You wouldn't want to get your hands around his throat and strangle him?'

'And put myself in the same category? A common killer? Of course not. And do you think it would be worth it . . . worth spending the rest of one's life in prison?'

'No one spends his life in prison. Not in Canada.'

'Sylvia's right, David. If it were me, I'd risk the few years. And you can forget that business about being a murderer because you kill a killer. There is a big difference between murder and retribution.'

'Retribution is the right of the state, not the individual.'

'But if the state reneges, then what? Do we let ourselves be led like lambs to the slaughter?'

Sylvia knew that not even Craig could shake David's deep commitment. He had worked on one of the briefs submitted to the government during the debate on abolishing capital punishment. Phrases, sentences from that brief remained in her mind.

'The death penalty is not a deterrent. If the individual does not have the right to take a human life neither does the state. One innocent man hanged is too high a price to pay.' He quoted from the Bible, ignoring the ringing resonance of 'eye for eye, tooth for tooth, hand for hand, foot for foot,' choosing instead the cryptic commandment, 'Thou shalt not kill.' Society must think in terms of rehabilitation, not punishment. And he cited the case of Jim Henry, rehabilitated, paroled, now a useful and productive member of society. Sylvia had not approved of the brief, had wondered whether it contributed to the decision of the House. More cynical than David, she doubted whether the arguments on either side had affected the outcome. She had felt, still felt, that the issue was decided before the motion was made.

Now, with the practicality born of having to balance a household budget, she said, 'The cost of life imprisonment, even if it isn't life per se, is astronomical. We can't afford it. Sooner or later something will have to be done.'

David was shocked. 'You're suggesting we should hang people because it's too expensive to keep them alive?'

Craig sided with Sylvia. 'Have you ever thought about it, David? Between forty and forty-five thousand a year to keep just one person locked up. Families live on less than that. A hell of a lot less. And in the special handling units that goes up to sixty thousand a year. And we can't afford to keep people on welfare. It's insane.'

'Politicians spend more than that on junkets,' David said stubbornly. 'You can't put a price on human life.'

Sylvia's eyes narrowed. 'That's what it always comes down to, isn't it? But have you noticed it's always the killer's life you can't put a price on? The victim's life isn't worth two cents.'

'Two wrongs don't make a right,' David said smugly. 'You can't bring the victim back. What does it solve to add another life to the list?'

Sylvia leaned forward. 'If you truly believe you can't put a price on a human life, the question begs the answer. If a life can't be measured in monetary terms, it leaves only one standard of currency. Another life.'

Craig smiled. David glowered. 'That's barbaric.'

'*Murder* is barbaric. And so is bleeding the taxpayer to feed a pack of killers who will get out, and do it again, and the whole thing goes on forever, ad infinitum.'

'The real bottom line is that capital punishment is not a deterrent.'

'It is for the Mafia,' Craig pointed out. 'And what about the multiple killers? Manson. The Hillside Strangler. Bundy.'

'All American.'

'The border doesn't make them any different. People are people.'

'Some people are off-balance. They would kill anyway.'

'Exactly. So how do we stop them?'

David sat back, arms folded across his shirt front, and addressed them both. 'What you have to understand is that murder is an irrational act. These people don't sit around the kitchen table discussing what will happen if they're caught. They don't plan these things ahead of time.'

'Sometimes they do,' Craig contradicted. 'Bonin, the Freeway Killer, did exactly that. He sat at his kitchen table after killing a kid and said, "I still feel horny, let's go get another one," and by God, that's exactly what they did.'

'That has nothing to do with the death penalty. And again, you're using an American as an example.'

'Then what about Betesh. Right here in Toronto? They sat around the table with that poor little kid tied up in the corner and discussed what they should do. And they decided it was safer to kill him than to let him go.'

Sylvia gasped. 'I didn't know that. That's terrible.'

'The bottom line,' David reiterated, 'is that capital punishment is not a deterrent. You can't put a dollar sign on a human life. And another thing. Juries are made up of ordinary men and women. They would rather acquit than bring down a verdict of guilty if they knew that verdict meant the rope. So you'd end up with more killers running around loose than you have now.' He signaled an end to the discussion by asking, 'What's for dinner, Sylvia?'

'Chicken.' He pulled a wry face. 'Marengo,' she added.

He brightened. 'How much time have we got?'

'*You* have half an hour,' she said pointedly.

From the kitchen she heard the sound of drinks being poured, the low murmur of conversation. They were talking about the nuclear arms race. She turned on the radio, listened to music while she washed spinach for the salad and stashed it in a paper bag to crisp, then sautéed pieces of chicken and placed them in the Corning casserole. It took only a few minutes to make the sauce, blending flour and wine, garlic and tomatoes. A mouth-watering aroma filled the kitchen and wafted into the living room.

'You're making me hungry,' David called out.

'It won't be long,' she assured him. She added fresh mushrooms, parsley and a pinch of thyme and stirred till thick and velvety smooth.

Millie sniffed the air from her mat in the corner, then rose laboriously and ambled across the floor to Sylvia. She looked up, brown eyes soft and pleading. Sylvia speared a piece of chicken from the casserole and covered the remainder with the sauce. She put the casserole in the oven, then sliced Millie's chicken into bits, feeding them to her one at a time.

Glancing through the window she saw Ciba, waiting patiently under the hedge in the front yard. She fed him quickly, put down extra dishes for the other strays, and checked the oven.

'Five minutes,' she called to David.

Both men moved to the dining room and she began her juggling act. Lobster tails in a pot of boiling water. Fresh shrimp sautéed quickly in butter. Fried bread. Fried eggs. Arrange the platter with chicken and sauce in the center, lobster, shrimp and eggs on diagonals of fried bread around the outside. It was an entree that would do credit to a fine French restaurant. David kissed her, Craig said she was a genius.

They did not return to the subject of capital punishment but Sylvia questioned Craig about the Vancouver meeting and David listened politely. He asked for the salad and said again that rehabilitation was the answer, there should be more money, more programs set up.

Sylvia passed the salad bowl and said nothing.

Craig said there *were* programs, it was up to the inmates to take advantage of them.

'License plates and shoemaking,' David said scornfully.

'And typing and computers,' Craig added.

'Computers?' David looked pleased.

'Not really,' Sylvia said.

'Really. They spent a hundred and twenty thousand dollars to put fifteen computers into maximum-security Collins Bay.'

'Money well spent. Now that makes sense.'

'Yes,' Sylvia said evenly. 'This is the computer age. They say computer crime will be the crime of the future. There's nothing like getting in on the ground floor.'

Good food always reduced David's appetite for argument. He ignored the remark, helped himself instead to another lobster tail and more shrimp. 'Sylvia,' he said pleasantly, 'how someone who eats so little can cook so well, I'll never understand.'

They finished dinner amicably and Craig insisted on clearing the table. Following his lead, David scraped and rinsed the plates and Sylvia stacked them in the dishwasher.

Craig left early, saying he had to pack for a short trip. Another of his unexplained absences. David walked him to the door.

The house, so full of life and energy a moment before, seemed drained and empty.

Arthur Maitland's death occurred in August. The bodies of Jay Smith and Roly Burns were both discovered in the first half of September.

The next body was mutilated. Nat Berger, the victim — described as happily married, the father of three young daughters, a pillar of the community — had been severely beaten by what the papers termed a blunt instrument. His nose was broken, one temple was staved in, and his Adam's apple was crushed. There was a piece of pipe jammed up his rectum and both nipples had been sliced off with a razor blade.

The officer in charge called it the most sickening crime he had encountered in all his years on the force. He had said the same thing eighteen months earlier with the discovery of a small boy, raped and strangled, in the east end of the city.

None of the men had known each other. Examination of their private lives ruled out the obvious explanation of homosexuality. That they were connected, there was no doubt. Each body bore a numbered tag. This vital piece of information was not revealed to the public, nor was the sinister jump in sequence from tag number to tag number. Body number 2 was never found.

Number 6 was forthcoming. Once, like real people, he had a real name. Now he was known simply as Bottle Bob. The appellation was apt. Bottle Bob always had a bottle in his pocket. When he was flush, it was full. When he was down on his luck, it was empty. Either way it served as a weapon against the violence of the streets.

Casual acquaintances considered Bob and his bottle a joke. Those who had seen him use it knew otherwise. In spite of his bleary eyes and unsteady limbs, Bob could move with lightning speed when the occasion warranted. Old timers still talked about the night he warded off an attack by three young punks with the jagged end of a Bright's special, smashed against the kerb in one swift movement, lethal as it slashed out at his attackers. Taken off-guard by the unexpected resistance, the youths backed off, abandoning Bob in search of easier prey. Among those who knew of the incident, Bob's reputation was made.

With his double layer of soiled pants, and old jacket over frayed sweater over limp shirt over dirty T-shirt, it was hard to think of him as anything but what he was at this moment; impossible to imagine him as a baby held in loving arms, a toddler learning to walk, a schoolboy confidently preparing for the future.

Once upon a time he had been married. He had a family, a good job, a paid-for home and two cars. He never talked about those days, not even to the compassionate men and women at the Salvation Army hostel, Harbour Light.

For years, Bob had thought of Harbour Light as home. It was here he ate when he was hungry. It was here that he occasionally attended Sunday morning service, the familiar hymns touching off vague feelings from the past.

The days were not too difficult. Some he enjoyed. Sitting on a park bench in summer, feeling the warmth of the sun and the weight of a full bottle in his pocket, he was content. But the nights were always bad. There was danger on the streets. Finding a place to sleep was a constant struggle. Finding a place that was safe was next to impossible.

Still, he was luckier than most. For the month of September he had bedded down in an empty garage in a ramshackle row of wooden units behind one of the old apartment buildings just a block away from Harbour Light. He had been disturbed only once, when an old drunk staggered in through the door backing on the lane. The man was too inebriated to be a threat, but Bob did not intend to share. He knew that once people started moving in on your territory it was only a matter of time until you were routed.

The garage was his. He had seen the tenant loading boxes into the trunk of the car, filling the back seat with clothes on hangers. It was obvious the man was moving. Just to make sure, he had waited a few days. Then, late one night, he had moved in as silently as a shadow and had remained ever since. The roof leaked when it rained and the floor was bare oil-soaked earth, but just being surrounded by four walls gave him an almost forgotten sense of security.

Most of the street people slept in the open, even during the bitter days of January and February. They huddled on the heated ramps at City Hall, under the expressway, in open stairwells. They would have given their eyeteeth for a setup like Bob's. He knew this, and covered his trail carefully each night. Aside from the old drunk who was too out of it to remember, he was sure no one knew where he holed up.

But he was wrong. Someone did know.

The week after Bob moved into the garage he was followed to the entrance of the lane by a tall, dark-clothed figure. He knew there was someone behind him. A quick glance told him it was not one of the street people. He waited in the shadows near the mouth of the lane and heard the footsteps continue along the sidewalk, recede, fade to silence. He was inside, asleep, when the door at the front of the unit was eased open. He did not know that someone entered as he slept, listened to his breathing, left him to dream undisturbed.

Nor did he know that the following week the superintendent of the apartment building received a call asking if he had any vacancies. The super said it was a shame the caller hadn't contacted him sooner, he had just rented his last flat. The caller said it was too bad, the problem wasn't so much finding accommodation in the downtown area, you could always find a room, but it was a hassle trying to come up with a place to keep a car. The superintendent brightened and said the new tenant was a young girl who had just moved to the city and didn't have a car, so her unit was available. He'd be willing to let it go for a price. The price turned out to be a monthly stipend of fifty dollars. Three days later, a hundred dollar bill arrived by mail. The super congratulated himself on a sweet deal and put the money in his pocket.

When the garage remained empty he decided the caller must have come up with a more convenient arrangement. Fine by him. The space was paid for. Empty or used, it was no concern of his.

Bottle Bob had resigned himself to the inevitable when the No Vacancy sign went up in front of the building. He continued to use the garage but he arrived later, left earlier, and slept fitfully. When a couple of weeks passed and it became obvious the new tenant didn't have a car, he relaxed into his old routine. Perhaps he'd be able to stay through the coming winter, after all.

He and his friends seldom discussed it, but winter was a threat that hung heavier in their minds with each passing day. Sleeping in the open meant you never knew, when you closed your eyes at night, if you would open them in the morning.

But the freeze-up was still weeks away. He did not think of it on this pleasant autumn morning as he shuffled along College Street on his way to the Scott Mission. Some days he ate nothing until the Sally soup line at night. Today he was hungry. The Mission started serving at ten. He'd stoke up and maybe run into somebody with a bottle to share. If not, he'd head back to Jarvis Street and spend the afternoon on a park bench soaking up the sun.

He ignored the passersby. They all looked the same. It had bothered him, once, when women and men, too, sidled away as though his touch would contaminate them. He no longer cared what they did.

There was a lineup at the Mission. He recognized some of the faces, but there was no one there that he had hung out with. Not that it mattered. Street people for the most part were loners, but they belonged to the same fraternity. There was an ebb and flow of the subculture that brought strangers together in brief encounters, free of bonding and unwanted ties. When three of the men, noticing the bulge in Bob's pocket, asked if he'd like to share their stash, he didn't hesitate. He knew he would be expected to share in return. He didn't tell them he was dry. He had often been counted in on the strength of what he was assumed to be holding. Sometimes, when the first bottle was finished and his expected contribution was not forthcoming, there was trouble. But he was always careful to point out that *they* had invited *him*;

it was not his fault if they jumped to conclusions. If they wanted another drink he'd go see what he could come up with. Usually, aside from a few muttered obscenities and some drunken shoving and pushing, he managed to get away without too much trouble.

The men led the way to an old rooming house in a lane off Spadina. One of the trio went upstairs to get the bottle and the other two headed for the backyard. Bob followed.

The yard, full of trash and weeds, was shielded by a tall wooden fence that ran along the back and sides. They sat on the sagging porch and talked about how things had changed on the street: you never knew what was going to happen anymore. . . . Did anyone know what had happened to Old Bessie, the bag woman?

They drank straight from the bottle, not bothering to wipe it before passing it on. When they reached the last few swigs Bob stood up and said he had to leave. It was always easier to get away while there was something left in the bottle. He expected an objection, but no one seemed to notice. As he turned to go, one of the men said he was going up to get the other bottle. Bob could have kicked himself for being so hasty. Unable to think of a reason to stay he scuffed out of the yard, grumbling under his breath.

After walking back toward Jarvis Street, stopping to look in shop windows, he paused to rest at the foot of the fountain in Eaton Centre. A chubby little girl in shorts was tossing pennies into the pool and he watched her, rheumy eyes fixed and unwavering. He liked children. He had a particular fondness for little girls.

When the child was finally led away by her mother he continued his trek, stopping again to speak to the hamster woman who lived in a vacant lot next to the Friendship Centre, across the street from Harbour Light. She was bundling her brood into a lopsided Loblaws' buggy, a task she repeated endlessly throughout the day. As she loaded the tiny bundles of fur in one end of the buggy they scurried out the other. Bob thought she might as well try to carry water in a sieve.

When she saw him leaning on the fence watching her, she walked over and said, 'I am a non-person. I do not exist. I have no number. If you have no number from the government you are nothing. That is how they get rid of you. Do you have a number?'

She didn't expect an answer. Whenever anyone stopped within hearing distance she told them about the government plot to get rid of unwanted people. He listened sadly, wishing someone would come and take her away where she'd be safe. It wasn't right for a young woman to be living in an excavation in a vacant lot in the middle of the city.

She said the same things over and over. After a while he got tired of listening and walked away. He crossed over to the park and lay down in the grass. With eyes closed, he listened to the city sounds of traffic and children playing and a dog barking in the distance. The sun was warm. He fell asleep.

When he awakened the shadows were lengthening and the air was beginning to cool. He stood up and stretched. It should be just about the right time for the soup line.

He crossed over to the building and met Jack and Scotty on their way in. They sat together at one of the long wooden tables and ate directly from their trays. The food was hot and wholesome. When they finished they carried the trays to the back of the room and filed out to the street. Scotty was sharing a room with a friend and asked if they'd like to come over for awhile and play cards. Bob and Jack were pleased. It was better than hanging around the street.

Seated on the lumpy couch in Scotty's room, Bob thought back over the day. It had been a good day, much better than most. Full of food, with friends, with a private sleeping spot assured, the world seemed less bleak than usual. He was still in good spirits when he finally left his companions and made his way to the garage he now thought of as home.

He made sure there was no one around before opening the door and slipping inside. He felt with his foot for the heavy boulder he used as a doorstop and shoved it tight against the door. It wouldn't stop someone from getting in, but it would alert him if anyone tried. Door secured, he moved to his sleeping corner and curled up in his bed of newspapers and old rags.

It was quiet. So quiet he could hear himself breathing. He listened to the regular rise and fall, the rhinal inhalation and exhalation, and wondered why he had never noticed it before.

It was a few minutes before he realized it was out of sync.

He held his breath to make sure. The sound, like an automated bellow, continued.

He lay still, back against the wall, eyes searching frantically, coming to rest on a shadow darker than the rest crouched near the door.

His street smarts told him this was no itinerant drunk looking for a place to sleep. This was the body snatcher he had always known would come some day and carry him away, the bogeyman he had hidden from as a child, shivering in bed with the covers pulled over his head. But then his parents had been in the next room, ready to come if called. Now there was no one. Bob and the cloven hoof, alone together at last.

He forced himself to remain motionless, to breathe deep from the diaphragm until the panic eased and his mind cleared. He had faced danger before. Years of surviving in the underbelly of the city had made him streetwise, capable of defending himself.

He slid his arm across his body and felt relief when his fingers closed on the neck of his bottle. The heavy dark blackness was an advantage. This was his place and he knew it well; knew every piece of litter on the floor, how many steps from wall-to-wall and corner-to-corner.

Prepared for sudden attack, he was not prepared for the flash of light. Like an animal caught in headlights on a country road, he was blinded by the beam. And then the light flicked off and a voice called: 'Robert Willard.'

Bob recoiled. *Robert Willard*. No one had called him by name for years. It had an unfamiliar ring, as though it belonged to someone else, someone he had known in another lifetime. The sound of it, the sound of the voice speaking it, filled him with bone-chilling dread.

He fingered the bottle, worked it free. He needed a hard surface, something to turn it from harmless flask to jagged weapon. The only hard surface was the stone against the door on the opposite wall.

He tensed his muscles, readied his body for the roll to his feet and lightning dash across the intervening space. As he started to roll, the shape moved forward and around. An arm closed across his windpipe, crushing his larynx, pulling him to his knees. He struck backward with the bottle, tugged at the arm around his throat. The bottle did not connect. The arm tightened. Forced his head up and back. A thin line of fire scorched the exposed flesh.

Something warm and sticky spread across his chest. The bottle slipped from his hand, shattered, too late, against the stone. Time stopped. Moved backward. He watched as the little girl tossed coins in the fountain. He drank wine from the bottle in the back yard off Spadina. He spooned up the lumpy chocolate pudding he and Scotty had for dinner.

He convulsed, and bled, and then lay still. It took only a few moments to finish the job with the broken bottle and wind the tag round a button on the scruffy overcoat.

Bottle Bob's body was discovered by the superintendent, who responded to a complaint about a strange odor emanating from the premises. A week later he resigned, saying he had urgent business back in Nova Scotia. He remained convinced that the tragedy never would have occurred if the person who rented the garage had not allowed it to stand vacant.

Jack and Scotty were questioned and released.

The men at Harbour Light said Bottle Bob had been a good old boy.

His family, not knowing where he was, never knew he was gone.

6

October 1984

There was nothing on that crisp autumn evening to indicate that the celebration of John Simmonds' birthday would have a profound effect on the course of future events.

The party was well underway by the time David and Sylvia arrived at the imposing stone house in the Kingsway. John was in his cups. Myra was in a dither. The guests seemed to be having a good time. So did the guest of honor, who was standing in the middle of the living room surrounded by a group largely made up of lawyers' wives.

'The trouble with the women's movement is that you have one group of women telling another group of women how to live their lives.' The women nodded agreement, not bothering to point out that men had been doing exactly that for centuries.

David joined the group to wish John a happy birthday while Sylvia headed for the bar where she asked the Rent-a-Host bartender for a glass of Perrier. Standing alone, she checked the room for familiar faces. A few of the guests she knew personally, some she had seen at social functions in the past, and a few she recognized from press photos and appearances on TV.

Bob White, David's senior law clerk, was talking to an animated redhead in plaid taffeta and old-fashioned hoop earrings. Harold Temple and a clutch of lawyers were paying homage to Justice Pemberton, who looked unfamiliar without his black robe. A woman in red chiffon was getting drunk and two middle-aged men were agreeing that the new boxing regulations would emasculate the sport and turn it into a pastime for sissies.

Among those she had seen on TV were a man called Parker who had something to do with the Parole Board, Patrick Flaherty, the new Crown Attorney, and Alfred Bretz, the man in charge of the male murder investigation. David, who disliked Bretz intensely, said he was a sonofabitch who would stop at nothing to get a conviction, and that included fabricating evidence and threatening witnesses. Sylvia felt he looked more like a scholar than a detective, his stoop-shouldered frame topped by an ascetic face and mild gray eyes magnified by thick glasses.

There was no one Sylvia wanted to talk to. Unlike David, she found large parties a bore. She wasn't good at small talk and didn't relate easily to strangers. It wasn't that she felt ill at ease or uncomfortable. She simply couldn't be bothered.

She moved from one group to another, content to remain on the fringe, listening to snatches of conversation.

'Parole is from the French 'la parole' which means word, the idea being that early release was contingent upon the prisoner giving his word that he would abide by the conditions of that release. Know what I mean?'

'I make no apology for the plea-bargain process. It has saved the taxpayers of this country hundreds of thousands of dollars. It is vital to the administration of justice.'

'Voiceprints do create a problem. Too subjective. Too dependent on the examiner. On the other hand, there's the wristprint. I solved a case on a wristprint. A little girl who was strangled. The only clue was a wristprint on her neck. I kept on the lab till they figured out how to lift it. Got a conviction. Only thing with a wristprint, it changes with age. Not like fingerprints. They stay the same.'

Sylvia moved toward a couch occupied by two young girls deep in conversation, wending her way through the press of bodies and a cacophony of sound.

'He's getting it on with his secretary.'

'So what's wrong with foreign investment if it keeps people working?'

'He asked her if she was bilingual and she said no, she was cunnilingual, and he said he could just speak English himself.'

Finally she reached the couch and sat down at the far end from the girls. They were talking about a young teacher who had been murdered in her apartment the week before.

'So she let him in, and the next thing she knew he was beating on her with a hammer.'

'Why would she open the door to a stranger like that? That's just asking for trouble.'

'But it wouldn't occur to you. I'd have let him in, too. And doll, I'm super careful.'

'Well he wouldn't get past me. I don't open my door for nobody.'

'Shit. The creepy little freak said he was from the Bell. He was wearing a Bell uniform. And he even left a message on her answering machine telling her he was coming because there was trouble with the phone.'

'How do you know all this if the girl's dead?'

'Because he pulled the same thing a week later, the prick. Only the next one got away.'

Sylvia knew about the case the girls were discussing. She had just set up a preliminary file on the bogus repairman. He was in custody at the moment but would probably be released on his own recognizance pending trial. Wearily she leaned back against the couch and closed out the voices. She was drifting into alpha, the relaxed state between waking and sleeping, when she felt a hand on her shoulder, heard David saying, 'I've been looking for you. What are you doing over here by yourself?'

He pulled her to her feet just as Patrick Flaherty walked up, hand outstretched. 'Mr Jenning, I caught you on *Nightline*. You were excellent.'

Flushed with pleasure, David introduced Sylvia. Flaherty acknowledged the introduction, then turned back to David. 'I got the impression from something you said that you're not completely in favor of psychiatric testimony.'

David said psychiatric assessment was essential. It was the courtroom presence of opposing teams of psychiatrists that he opposed. 'They cancel each other out, confuse the jury. The entire body of testimony is often disregarded because it's impossible for the layman to make sense of it. It seems to me. . . .'

He was interrupted by John Simmonds, swaying on his feet. 'David, my boy. What's this I hear about a computer?' He made it sound slightly disreputable.

David explained that the firm had acquired a number of new clients and he felt the time had come to upgrade the office procedure.

'I understand the software can be a real problem,' Flaherty said.

'Nothing is a problem for David,' John interjected. Sylvia guessed he was suffering from early pangs of jealousy. David had always admired John's firm, considering it one of the finest in the city, but in the last couple of years his reputation had grown while John's lost luster.

'We're working on it now,' David said to Flaherty. 'It won't take long once we have the main menu finalized.'

'The main menu? It sounds as though you're running a restaurant.'

David smiled, then outlined the different programs the computer would contain. The list ranged from accounting and standard contracts to case law. 'Main menu' was an umbrella term for the listing of these various programs. He would have access to the full menu, while staff members would be limited to programs relating to their specific function. He used Bob White as an example. Instead of spending hours poring over law books for past precedent, he would merely have to punch up the information he needed on a screen. Each department would have its own terminal, and any number would be able to access the central unit at the same time.

'Including *Mrs*. Jenning.' John looked at Sylvia accusingly, as though she had no business meddling in David's affairs. She was startled. David didn't try to hide his hobby, but he didn't make a point of talking about it, either. She wondered who had told him about the extra terminal. Then she remembered having seen him earlier with Bob White. Bob knew about the additional program. He also knew that Craig and Sylvia were working on it.

'That's right,' David replied, explaining that the original intention was to set up a smaller computer at home to house the information he had put together on crime and criminals. Some day, he said bashfully, after he retired, he hoped to write a book.

Sylvia noticed that Bretz, standing with his back to David, appeared to be listening to their conversation. He tilted his head in their direction, then turned and said, 'I didn't realize you were personally interested in crime, Mr. Jenning. Perhaps there is something in your records that we've missed in ours. Something that might help with this current investigation.'

'I doubt it,' David said politely. He smiled at Bretz and Bretz smiled back. Baring their fangs, Sylvia thought.

She turned away from the men and caught sight of Myra talking to a plumpish woman with short gray hair. The woman had her back to Sylvia but something in her stance, in the way she held her head, struck a chord. She riffled through her memory, made a connection with her mother, made a further connection with the lifelong friend who had gone to school with her mother, spent a week visiting when Sylvia was a child. Selma May Roberts. For years Selma and her mother had corresponded faithfully, exchanging secrets and sharing the details of their lives. The last letter had arrived when Sylvia was at home during the Lucy Menard trial. It contained a photograph of Selma, surrounded by a group of handsome young men. She had written on the back: 'What do you think of my boys? Love, Selma May.' Sylvia had never forgotten the faces in the photograph.

The woman could have been Selma May Roberts. But Sylvia knew that was impossible. Selma May Roberts was dead.

She interrupted David in the middle of a sentence. 'Please take me home, David,' she said. 'I think I'm going to be sick.'

The first weekend in October brought with it the best of autumn. Clear, cloudless skies. Scarlet maples. The perfect formation of Canada geese heading south.

Faron invited David and Sylvia to spend the weekend at the island. David was too busy. Sylvia declined. Craig went off on his own and Sylvia drove into the country to see the colors.

As she drove she thought about the purse snatcher and how strange it had felt to sit in the witness box and recount the events of that day. The old woman was still in the hospital. Sylvia was the principal witness.

The boy's lawyer was pushy and aggressive. She answered his questions briefly and wasn't surprised when, in view of his youth and lack of a previous criminal record, the accused was given a suspended sentence. His family applauded. Brother Lou cheered.

He had stared at her on the stand and she had stared back, unmoved by the hatred that flared in his eyes.

She was angered by the verdict, but glad it was over.

Buddy Thompson paused in the doorway leading from the sub-level of the apartment building into the underground garage. He was wearing a tight-fitting suit and carrying a beige trench coat over his arm.

In the dim light he could just make out the gleaming grille of his new Cadillac parked against the opposite wall. All his life he had wanted to own a Caddie. Three months ago he bit the bullet, emptying his bank account and borrowing the difference to purchase a Fleetwood limousine. He carried the specs in his pocket and rhymed them off to anyone who would listen.

'A one-forty-four wheelbase. HT 4100 power system. V8-6-4 fuel injection.' He didn't understand the technical jargon, but he memorized it anyway.

It was three o'clock in the morning. He had intended to drop Wanda off and get home early. When she insisted he come up for a goodnight drink, said he could park in her stall and not on the street (which he hated because of the fucking poor drivers), he decided, why not? I'll tell Chrissie I had a business appointment. Who's to know?

Wanda. He straightened his tie and grinned. She hadn't expected things to get out of hand. For that matter, neither had he. But she shouldn't have led him on. It wasn't as though he'd hit her or gone out of control. He hadn't been into anything heavy for a long time.

He started across the floor, footsteps echoing in the stale air. The tightly packed cars, cement-pillared stalls and shadow-filled alcoves were unnerving. The memory of Wanda's soft body was replaced by a vague unease. He crossed the floor quickly, on tiptoes, half expecting something to leap at him from the shadows. When he reached the Cadillac he heaved a sigh of relief, then frowned as he realized the driver's side was hemmed in by a battered Dodge.

'Damn,' he muttered. 'They build these places for kiddy cars.' He got in the passenger side, locked the door, and wriggled across the front seat. His mouth was dry and he was trembling. He felt hemmed in, claustrophobic.

He started the engine. Relaxed as the car roared into life. With doors locked, windows closed, motor humming, he was safe. It was like being in a suit of armor, sealed in steel. The limo's bulk was almost too much for the narrow aisles. He drove slowly, negotiated each turn at a snail's pace lest he nick the finish. It seemed as though eyes were watching him, boring into his back. When he reached the ramp and the automatic door slid back allowing access to the street, it was like a release from solitary.

The tree-lined street was as quiet as a country lane. He drove to the end of the block and swung onto the city's main street. At least here there were a few signs of life: a cyclist pedaling along the sidewalk; a young couple huddled in a doorway with their arms around each other; a police cruiser inching along the curb behind a street-cleaning machine. He had intended to head straight north but changed his mind when he saw the cop car. Force of habit. He looped the block and turned south instead, toward the freeway that curved north from the lakefront and afforded an uninterrupted run through scenic ravines to the new development where he and Chrissie had bought their first home.

On a clear road, unhindered by traffic, the car was a joy to drive. He turned on the radio and let his mind drift. So much had happened so fast. From a shitty start his life was now a green-light. He finally had his front uptight. Wanda didn't matter. A one-night stand. It wasn't the first time he'd copped pussy since he met Chrissie. It wouldn't be the last. As long as she didn't know. He'd die if she ever left him. She was the best damn thing that had happened to him in his whole fucking life, the Caddie included.

The sky was clear and bright, stars glinting like diamonds on velvet. Deep ravines edged both sides of the road. The lights of the city shone to the left. Trees and tangled shrubbery fell away to the right. The car floated effortlessly through space.

Chrissie. She'd be asleep when he got home. He would get into bed quietly, be inside her by the time she woke up. She said she hated it when he did it that way. He didn't believe her. Besides, it was a real trip for him.

Thinking about her naked under the covers excited him. He was starting to get a hard on. God, if Wanda only knew. Absorbed, he was barely aware of the cobweb touch against the back of his neck. Absent-mindedly he brushed along his collar. A moment later he felt it again. Brushed again. Probably a loose hair. He made a mental note to check his hairline. Time to look into one of those hair-loss clinics if he was losing more than he was growing. Skinheads were for the birds.

The music segued into 'Laura' and he hummed the melody, sotto voce. Halfway through the chorus he felt it again. A touch. Definite. Insistent. Persistent.

He stopped humming. Glanced in the rearview mirror. No oncoming headlights. No backseat passenger in silhouette.

Nothing but the faint outline of the rear window and the blackness beyond.

He ran his index finger along the inside edge of his collar. It stopped midway. Made contact. Felt an obstruction cold to the touch. Hard. Slender. Thin-edged. Sharp metal with the feel of blue steel.

The wheel jerked in his hand. The car lurched to one side. He pulled it back on track, tried to swallow. His throat was so tight he could hardly breathe. There was a great rushing sound rolling in waves that beat against his eardrums, rising and falling like the wings of hundreds of birds in flight. It filled his body. Drummed in his brain.

With a superhuman effort he began the exercise he used to control his claustrophobia. 'Relax the frontalis muscle. Lower your blood pressure. Slow down your heartbeat.' The panic began to subside and with it the terrible roaring sound; the sound, he now realized, of his own blood and heart-beat.

As his body returned to normal he dared another glance in the mirror, saw another reflection of empty space. He told himself he was imagining things. He had dozed off, slipped into another of his nightmares. Better to pull over and catch forty winks than risk a pile-up. He braked lightly and edged toward the gravel shoulder.

There was a rustle of movement from the back seat. A gentle plosion, warm against his nape. A voice. Soft. Almost a whisper. 'Keep driving.' Expressionless. Terse.

His scalp prickled. His heart palpitated, then slowed. It seemed to stop beating. The frontalis, crucial barometer of relaxation, contracted. His forehead creased with worry lines.

He tried not to look in the mirror. This time, he knew, it would not show vacant. He tried not to look, but his eyes were drawn as though by invisible threads. And it was there. As he had known it would be there. A head and shoulders. Hulking. Visible only in outline. Lacking dimension. Flat. A shape cut from cardboard.

'Who . . . who are you?' His voice was falsetto, like the time he had been hatpinned in the balls by a streetwise chick who did him in at the last minute.

There was a soft click, the sudden glare of a flashlight. The beam, cone-shaped, came up from below, turning the face into a death's head of light and shadow.

The features were indistinguishable. He could not tell whether or not he knew the person. He looked into the hollowed sockets. Tried, in the split second of light, to read the eyes and determine intent. They were blank. Not glazed or spaced-out. Not fired by bloodlust or rage. Simply implacable, made all the more terrifying by lack of emotion.

His mind flashed back to another car in another lifetime. A time when he was young, really young, and what he wanted he took. What he had wanted at that point in his life was the female vocalist of a combo playing the neighborhood hangout.

It had been surprisingly easy. The first night he watched the girl get in her car and followed her home. When she came out the second night he was in the car, crouched in the back seat. He waited until they were on the lonely stretch of road he had earmarked the night before. When he rose from the floorboards and pressed the knife against her throat she looked up and their eyes met. The terror he saw sparked a surge of raw excitement. She was the first woman he had taken by force. The experience was one of the most intensely satisfying of his life.

He had known then that the girl was terrified. Only now did he comprehend the depth of that terror.

'There's a road to the right. Take it.'

He knew the cutoff. Two overgrown ruts that angled from the freeway into riverbank scrub. It would rip the bottom out of the car, ruin the finish. He decided to take a chance, to overshoot the cutoff and aim for the bright lights ahead. He would be safer on the freeway than down in the bush.

'Turn here. Now.' The razor-thin blade pressed against his throat. The flashlight rekindled the face in the mirror. The eyes held his. The blade rested on his Adam's apple. He swung onto the dirt road and inched over the ruts.

'Pull over. In those trees.'

Robotized, he eased the car through the bush into a small clearing, braked to a stop and turned off the key. He released the seat belt. Groped for the door handle. Tensed for flight the moment the blade eased.

The blade did not ease. It sliced deep in a single sweep, severing the jugular. His throat gushed crimson, drenching the dashboard, forming puddles and pools on the white broadloom and turning the immaculate upholstery into a crazy quilt of scarlet. The front seat looked like a slaughterhouse. The back seat was unmarred.

An hour later a jogger boarded a subway car at the end of the line. The ticket collector, grumpy and graveyard-shift-envious of nine-to-fivers who could be home in their beds, frowned disapproval. 'Nut city,' he grumbled. 'Home of the loonies.'

There was a train waiting. The jogger got on board, glad the car was empty. There would be time for a brief nap. And at the other end, a hot breakfast and a fresh pot of steaming coffee.

Chrissie Thompson knew when she saw the policemen at the door that something had happened to Buddy. She did not expect that something to be his demise. She paled, swayed on her feet, was grateful for the arm that encircled her shoulders and led her to the new sofa, as yet unpaid for, in the attractive living room.

Her mind refused to accept Buddy's death until the day of his funeral, at which time the finality of her loss became real. She had loved Buddy in an immature, naive way. Improbable though it seemed by current standards, she had come to him as a virgin. Buddy had prized her virginity, had boasted of it to his friends. 'Like finding a needle in a haystack,' he would brag. He did not know she didn't enjoy his lovemaking. He did know that she depended on him as a child depends on his father. It was this unquestioning faith that had drawn him to her, just as it was her image of him that was helping to re-shape his life.

Chrissie had left her parents as a child bride. She returned to them less than a year later as a grieving widow. She did not remarry. Buddy, she felt, could never be replaced.

7

December/January 1985

In November the killer went into hiatus. No bodies with numbered tags were found. Bretz and his men, grateful for the lull, worked frantically to clear up the backlog of leads and telephone tips.

Veterans on the force said the murders had stopped because the killer was in custody, picked up for theft or some other misdemeanor.

A psychologist said the killer had expended his inner rage and was not likely to strike again.

A psychiatrist said the killings were cyclical and would recur during the same time-frame the following year.

Ever since the night downtown with Anne and Bill, Sylvia had planned to have the couple over for dinner. It wasn't until just before Christmas that they finally got together.

David had resisted the evening because Anne got on his nerves, but he took an instant liking to Bill. By the time they had reached the brandy-and-coffee stage in front of the fireplace, he was having such a good time that he was even civil to Anne.

It started to snow, and thick, heavy white flakes drifted past the window. David added more wood to the fire. The room was warm and cozy. Sylvia remembered that Ciba was still out, and excused herself to make another pot of coffee. She entered the garage through the kitchen and opened the side door. He was there waiting, his heavy coat layered with snow. He disappeared into the box she had carpeted for him. It was behind the pool fittings and David didn't know it was there. The corner would provide a safe hideaway until the diving board and pool ladder were removed in the spring.

When she returned to the living room the conversation had shifted from the riots in Britain, which Bill felt were economic in nature rather than racial, to the proud tradition of the British police. David was talking about the difference in public attitudes toward the constabulary. 'We call them fuzz. Pig. In England they're bobbies. A term of affection.'

Anne interrupted. 'It may be better than pig, but what does it mean?'

David explained that the name went back to Sir Robert Peel who reorganized England's police system in the nineteenth century. The idea was to put men on the street that the public could relate to, men who would prevent trouble. That's why they were unarmed. Sort of an early breed of social worker.

'I wonder,' Bill mused, 'if an approach like that might have prevented the situation we're in now. These terrible killings.'

We had to get around to it sooner or later, Sylvia thought.

'It didn't stop the Yorkshire Ripper,' Anne said.

'That's different,' David said quickly. 'He was killing women.'

There was a stunned silence, broken by a red-faced Anne. 'Why is killing women *different*?'

Embarrassed by his slip-of-the-tongue, David stammered, 'Ah . . . well . . . you know . . . it happens all the time. I mean . . . well, you know what I mean. Men don't kill women for *nothing*. There's always a reason.'

Bill looked uncomfortable. Anne was speechless.

Sylvia, like Anne, seethed with anger. Unlike Anne, she kept it hidden. 'You mean,' she said coolly, 'we carry the seeds of our own destruction between our legs.'

'For God's sake,' David exploded, 'do you have to be so damn crude?'

'Crude. Oh my God.' Anne buried her head in her hands.

'Come on,' Sylvia said lightly. 'David's right. I shouldn't have said that.'

Anne looked at her as though she were demented. Bill bridged the awkward silence by asking, 'What do you think is behind these killings, David?'

'It's just another male strike,' Anne said sarcastically. 'Nothing to get excited about.'

Bill frowned at Anne. 'It's not something to joke about,' he said reprovingly. 'Please, Lord, don't let them have their first quarrel in our house,' Sylvia thought. Aloud she said, 'Bill's right. It's grim. If I were a man I'd be afraid to step out of the house.' No one noticed the thread of irony in her voice.

Responding to Bill's question, David said, 'I don't think we're dealing with a mass murderer like Olson or Bundy. There's not enough similarity. It doesn't compute. I think we have people jumping on the bandwagon. They see this as an opportunity to settle old grudges. It's happened before in cases like this.'

Bill shook his head. 'I don't know. They've set up a special task force under Bretz. They wouldn't have done that unless they felt there was a connection. They probably know who's responsible and they're just waiting to trip him up.'

David snorted. Although he spoke well of the police in public, Sylvia knew he considered them a dismal lot.

'Take that first one: Maitland.' Sylvia's stomach tightened into a hard, hot knot. Anne shot her a quick glance. Innocently, Bill continued, 'He was the one we saw the night we had dinner, Sylvia. The one you bumped into.'

David looked at her curiously. 'You didn't mention that, Syl.' Bill ignored the aside. 'The way I see it,' he went on, 'Maitland's death ties in. Why else would he be naked? I figure he was a homosexual and one of his lovers caught up with him.'

'That doesn't make sense,' Anne objected. 'He was a big, good-looking, masculine guy.'

David and Bill smiled at each other knowingly. Sylvia bit her tongue and said nothing.

'Besides,' Anne said, 'why would he be running around raping women if he was queer?'

'Men don't rape women because they like them,' David said. 'They do it because they hate them.'

'And they call women ball-breakers,' Anne sighed. 'Anyway, it didn't sound like a sex murder to me. He wasn't cut up or anything.'

'No, but he was naked. And there was no sign of forced entry. Which means the killer was already in the apartment, and it was someone he knew.'

Anne, who was getting high, quipped, 'Only their hairdressers know for sure.'

'The travelling salesman,' Bill said. 'That had to be a sex killing.'

'The one with the pipe up his ass,' Anne giggled.

David glared at her. 'It's not something to joke about,' he said coldly.

'Mr. Jenning, if rape is inevitable, relax and enjoy it. Men have been telling women that for years.'

David looked at her with disgust. Heedless, Bill said, 'I hope you're right, David. If they're grudge killings at least there's a motive for each one. Which means the rest of us can stop worrying.'

'Whether it's one or a dozen, there's always a motive somewhere,' David replied.

'Because you cunt find it, it don't mean it ain't there,' Anne slurred.

'Anne,' Sylvia remonstrated.

'I think it's time to leave,' Bill said.

It was after midnight. Bill helped Anne into her boots and coat and stood in the doorway with his arm around her, saying how much he had enjoyed the evening. He and David shook hands soberly, and said they would have to get together and do it again.

David's multiple-killer theory was not shared by the public. The man-in-the-street was convinced the deaths were connected and a mass murderer was at large. Each killing sparked fresh protest. Pressure mounted against the police. The public was angry and impatient.

The police, in turn, were baffled. They knew the murders were connected because each one was neatly numbered. But aside from the tell-tale shipping tags, there was nothing. No witnesses. No fingerprints. And most frustrating of all, neither a motive nor a clearly defined MO.

In multiple homicides which involve the indiscriminate killing of strangers by a stranger, the method of killing becomes a signature. There was no single method operative in the Toronto deaths. Slashed. Strangled. Bludgeoned. Mutilated. Unmutilated. The common denominator of a set MO was missing.

In murders of passion, where the victim is known to the killer, motive is primary. Although it may not weigh heavily in the courtroom, it is an early road sign for investigators. This, too, appeared to be lacking.

Some officers felt the killer was an insider who, knowing what his colleagues looked for, satisfied his lust for killing by striking at random, thus running the least possible risk of discovery. They told each other, with covert pride, that he had to be one of their own. A novice would have left a footprint, fingernail scrapings, any clue, however minor.

There was talk of conspiracy and a secret society like the Manson family, organized to disrupt the social structure by spreading terror and mistrust. Still others were convinced the killings were gangland executions, a comforting thought that meant law-abiding citizens had no cause for fear.

There was a masculine outcry demanding protection. The Chief of Police suggested avoiding dark streets, elevators and underground parking garages. Men, accustomed to telling the same thing to their wives, were outraged. While the men paid to protect them demanded bigger guns, bulletproof vests, two-man patrols, taxpayers were told to look after themselves.

Women, inured from puberty to the threat of attack, watched quietly as their men came to know the full meaning of fear. They also noted that as the murders of men mounted, murders of women decreased. There were still wife beatings and the occasional rape, even the odd murder, but these were the normal crimes of a normal society. Even the most titilating were no longer front-page news.

There was an eerie force at work and all men felt vulnerable. Some turned to tranquillizers, unable to cope with a world seemingly gone mad. Tire chains came out of the trunk and into the front seat. Sales of penknives soared. Macho males who had never worn jewelery took to heavy, square-cut rings. A few packed guns and hunting knives. When their wives told them it was against the law to carry a weapon, they refused to believe it. 'A man is entitled to defend himself,' they argued. 'But only within limits,' their wives told them, fully aware that 'self defense' is a rigidly defined term that states the degree of resistance must be commensurate with the degree of force employed in an attack.

The men told them they must be mad to believe such poppycock. Survival was a basic instinct, they said. How could there possibly be a law that denied the right to that survival?

At first their wives were astonished by their husbands' naivete. Later they came to realize there was much their husbands didn't know because they had never felt the need of such knowledge.

Men who had never known the meaning of fear were developing a victim mentality. And with the murder of Keith Hallworth, that fear flared into hysteria.

Keith Hallworth was a prominent businessman who lived in an exclusive lakefront condominium with his attractive wife and two teen-aged sons. He was dynamic, handsome, brilliant. His death was bannerline news.

During a routine check at four a.m. the security guard found Hallworth sprawled on the floor of the underground garage, half under his vintage Rolls Royce. His trousers were tossed over the hood of the Rolls and his undershorts were stuffed in his mouth. The tire iron that had crushed his skull lay next to his outstretched hand.

The body was not mutilated, but there was something painfully obscene about the lean white buttocks, fully exposed below the flipped-back shirt tail and expensive tweed jacket.

The security guard took a deep breath and closed his eyes. He counted to three and looked again. The body was still there. Putting out his hand, he steadied himself against the side of the car. Then he started to shake; the flashlight dropped from his hand. As he leaned over to pick it up the body twitched and he heard a low, racked gurgle. Galvanized, he tugged at the shorts, pulling them free and releasing a clot of blood that slid over his shoe. He knelt down and felt for a pulse. The body was still warm. He thought there was a faint flicker in the wrist.

With a start, he realized that the attack had just taken place. Perhaps he had even interrupted it. He hunched over the body, listening. There was no sound except the thump of his own heart. He huddled, braced for a blow from behind. After a moment he thought he heard the door into the building ease open.

He waited for a few more minutes, painfully aware that time was vital if Hallworth were to be saved. When he knew he could wait no longer he picked up the tire iron, holding it like a club in case the intruder reappeared. Before leaving the body he dropped the iron bar and covered the naked lower half with the trousers that were lying on the hood of the car. The naked posterior was more disturbing to him than the smashed and bloody head.

Keith Hallworth was still alive when he was placed in the ambulance, but at the hospital he was pronounced dead on arrival.

Mr. Hallworth's days as one of the city's prime movers-and-shakers were over. His widow was sedated, and a relative was asked to contact his sons, who were away at school. Residents of the plush condominium, roused from sleep as the police conducted a door-to-door precautionary search, were horrified. Bretz and his squad were jubilant.

Although the body had been removed before the photographers and plainclothesmen arrived, the scene was an investigator's dream. The tire iron contained a perfect set of fingerprints. There was a palm print on the Rolls, and a pair of bloody footprints that showed an unusual tread. They did not need the numbered tag, which would be recovered from the hospital later with the victim's personal effects, to know that this killing was one of the series.

'Find the shoes, you've got the killer,' Forensics said.

'With the blood on them, once we've matched it up, he's nailed,' one of the officers seconded.

It was after dawn when the forensic team finished. The evidence was bagged and tagged, and the Rolls was towed away.

The story was headlined in the afternoon papers, accompanied by a statement from the Chief saying that, thanks to the opportune arrival of the security guard, who interrupted the perpetrator in the commission of the act, the police now had solid evidence to work with. It was only a matter of time, he assured the public, before the perpetrator was apprehended.

Discussing the case with Sylvia and Craig, David said it would have been much more opportune for Mr. Hallworth if the guard had arrived a few minutes earlier. Sylvia agreed. Craig said he had almost sublet one of the apartments in the building, and was glad now he hadn't. David said he didn't know how anyone could get through the security in the building; the time he and Sylvia attended one of the Hallworths' many cocktail parties they practically had to show identification. 'Where there's a will, there's a way,' Craig said.

In the days that followed, the guard assumed the role of celebrity. His picture appeared in all three dailies and he was interviewed on radio and local and national television. The first interviews were sparing of detail and matter-of-fact, but gradually the accounts improved. The day he described the assailant and how he had found him standing over the body with tire iron raised to strike another blow, the guard was nominated for a special citizen's award.

The police, miffed that he hadn't mentioned the attacker

earlier, but elated at finally having an eyewitness, brought him in to work on a composite drawing. The picture that emerged was round-faced and glowering, with lank hair, shaggy brows and a cruel, down-turned mouth. The face was filled with such brooding evil that those who saw it said they would recognize it on sight. Hundreds of copies were run off and distributed to everyone from rookie policemen to senior officials to shop owners.

Copies were also sent to newspapers and television stations from coast-to-coast in Canada and throughout the U.S. Within the first three days of the picture's release, the man was sighted in New York, Halifax, Victoria, Los Angeles and Copper Cliff.

Every policeman on the force was required to follow leads and check alibis. Vacations were cancelled and officers on regular shifts were asked to work overtime.

None of the leads panned out. The fingerprints were not on file. They and the palm print were useless without a suspect for comparison. With only the bloodied footprint remaining, officers started a systematic canvass of shoe manufacturers and repair shops. They discovered the tread was so common it would be impossible to come up with a 'make' unless they could provide more information.

Homicide detectives, too often bedeviled by a suspect minus evidence, now had ample evidence but no hint of a suspect.

The police were convinced that if they could track down the shoes that wore Keith Hallworth's blood they would have their killer. The man who found the shoes was not a policeman, but a veteran newspaperman.

Joe Parsons was a senior police reporter and dedicated crime buff. Nothing appealed more to Parse than a good, gutsy murder. He had been known to climb out of a panting lady's bed and rush to the scene of a slaying at the first chirp of his beeper. His friends accused him of following in the footsteps of a famous predecessor who had once worked on the same paper and was known for his lifelong preoccupation with death.

They were wrong. There was nothing Hemingwayesque about Joe's feelings.

He did not see death as something fine and ennobling.

He detested war and was sickened by the sight of blood.

He found murder fascinating, not because it involved death but because it revealed the darkest, most primitive side of life.

Joe was not interested in the corpse. He was forever snared by the mind of the corpse-maker.

Parsons knew about every murder recorded in Canada for the past one hundred years. He rhymed off dates and places, depositions and sentencings, the way some men talked sports. His cluttered three-room apartment contained book shelves, files and scrapbooks filled with information about murders, both past and present.

Joe knew almost every police officer in the city, and the majority of lawyers and judges as well. He spent so much time in police stations that many lawmen thought of him as one of their own, talking as freely in his presence as they did to each other.

Joe did not know about the numbered shipping tags, but he did know about the footprint. He also knew it was the most tangible lead to the killer. He felt if he could get permission to run it in a lead story, there might be someone out there who could identify it. It was a slim hope, but with nothing else to go on it was worth a try. As it turned out, the authorities agreed with him. He was given a glossy and told to go ahead.

The day after the paper appeared, a west end shoe repairman phoned and said he had a shoe that matched the photo. It had come in for a heel lift, freshly polished but with rusty brown stains in the tread. The shoe, still stained, was ready to be picked up.

Feverish with excitement, Parsons told him not to release it until he got there. He arrived at the shop to find the owner trying to placate an irate woman who was threatening to have the law on him if he didn't find her husband's shoe this very minute.

Joe introduced himself and asked the repairman if he could examine the shoe. The woman, furious, tried to snatch it from his hand. Joe stepped back, out of reach, and turned the shoe over. The moment he looked at the sole he knew he was holding the shoe that had made the footprint in the garage.

'Madam,' he said sternly, 'this shoe will have to be handed over to the police.'

The reaction was swift and unequivocal. 'That is the property of my husband. You give it to me this minute or I'll turn *you* over to the police, and lay a complaint besides. I have come here for years and this is the last time you will see me here you . . . you bozo. I think you have both gone crazy out of your heads. . . .'

She paused for breath and Joe said, 'This shoe may be evidence in a murder. It must be turned in to the police.'

She stood stock-still, like a windup toy with spring unsprung. Then the blank expression brightened. 'A murder, you say? You mean poor Mr. Hallworth hit in the head and dead and a man that did no harm to no one and every Christmas sent a card with ten dollars to buy us a treat and him dyin' alone in the dark, a Christian shame it is. . . . '

'You knew Keith Hallworth?'

'Sure, and wasn't it my poor husband what drove the killer off with the very weapon he used to beat the poor man senseless, and it was himself that covered up the poor man's shame, him lyin' there naked to the world, killed dead by a pervert still running loose. . . . '

'It was your husband who found him?' Joe sagged against the counter, limp with disappointment.

She reached over and took the shoe, turning it in her hands lovingly.

'It was a night of terror, it was, and my poor darlin' fighting for his life against a murdering rascal what will stop at nothing to fill his bloodlust to the brim and this here is the shoe he was wearin' whilst standing over that poor man's bleeding body battling with the powers of darkness. . . . '

'Your husband handled the weapon?' Joe asked dully.

'That he did and sure if it weren't the only thing standing between him and certain destruction. . . . '

Wordlessly, Joe turned and left the shop.

He called Homicide about the shoe and suggested they check the palm and fingerprints found at the scene against those of the security guard. The detective he spoke with said that would already have been done; it was routine. Joe suggested they do it again, just to make sure.

When he checked back later they told him the prints matched. Embarrassed, they said that somehow in the confusion of that night, the many people who had come and gone — ambulance men, uniformed policemen, plainclothesmen, lab men, reporters, residents of the building — they had not checked out the guard. They said of course they always checked prints against those of everyone at the scene — it was elementary procedure — but mistakes and omissions could occur.

Joe hung up the phone in disgust. 'They bungled it,' he told himself bitterly. 'They were so close. He was just a few minutes ahead of them and that's where their minds were. They had so much to work with, it was all they could think about. They were so fucking close. God damn.'

He took the rest of the day off and got drunk.

The police issued a statement saying they expected an early break in the case, but it was up to the public to co-operate.

The security guard quit his job and lived on unemployment insurance until the benefits ran out, at which time he applied for worker's compensation on the grounds that he was too tense and nervous to continue working.

The male population avoided back streets and some took to the buddy system.

The Christmas season was bleak for the families of the victims. For David and Sylvia it was a quiet time; they had Christmas dinner at home and saw Craig only once over the holidays.

There was a general sense of relief when the old year rang out and the new rang in.

Sylvia hated January. A confirmed sun worshipper, the only thing she enjoyed about winter was the annual vacation down south. She was working on a list of things to do before leaving the day David called and asked her to pack an overnight bag and send it to the office by cab. He had to make a rush trip to St. Catharines but would only be gone overnight.

The cab arrived in a swirl of fine powdered snow. The sky at noon was charcoal grey and gusts of wind whipped branches from the trees and funneled along the street, causing the few pedestrians to walk backwards and doubled over. Sylvia was glad to be home, but she felt uneasy about being alone.

She thought of asking Anne to spend the night, but dismissed the idea as childish. Then, as the day faded and the house moaned and groaned with frost-creaks, she changed her mind and dialed Anne's number. No answer.

The street lamps came on, sparkling like diamonds in the still, frosty air. It seemed to Sylvia that eyes, sly and cunning, followed her from room to room.

The phone rang. She picked it up. There was nothing but the

sound of breathing. She said, 'Yes, who's there?' and the line went dead. Instead of Anne, as she had hoped, another wrong number.

It was quiet in the house, so quiet the click of the furnace starting up was like a rifle shot. She heard sounds she had never heard before. She was imagining things, she knew, but the feeling of unease persisted.

When she finally went to bed, after the late show and wrap-up news capsule, she retrieved the gun and placed it under her pillow. She had steeled herself to touch it, blanking her mind to past prejudice. It felt cold in her hand. Lethal. But it also seemed dissociated, like the viscous red fluid that dripped from the boy who stole the purse. She drew comfort from the lump under the pillow, slept better because it was there.

The following morning when she went out to feed the birds she discovered the footprints in the snow. When she told David about the prints he appeared unconcerned but when he thought she wasn't looking he tested the bolts on the doors. Later, when she went upstairs to help him unpack, she discovered him checking the clip in the gun.

When he suggested they eat out, she was quick to agree. Over dinner he asked, 'Do you remember Jim Henry?'

Her mind flashed to a pimple-faced adolescent who had matured in prison to an attractive, self-possessed young man. 'Wasn't he the boy who killed that young girl in Ottawa and stuffed her body in a plastic garbage bag? He chopped her up.'

'He's the one they said killed her. He was just a kid when they sentenced him. Some of the evidence was suppressed.'

'You handled the appeal.'

'That's right. A lot of people felt he was innocent. There was a committee set up that worked for his release.'

'I remember when it happened. There were marks on his body. Blood on his clothes. He was the last known person to see her alive.'

'Circumstantial,' David said impatiently.

'As I recall, you put in a lot of time for a very small fee.'

'The kid needed all the help he could get.'

'He was released, wasn't he?'

'Yes. Five years ago. We set him up with a new identity. Got him a job. He got married. Everybody liked him.'

Sylvia unconsciously fell into the past tense established by David. 'Did they know who he was? The people he worked with?'

'No,' David said peevishly. 'That was part of the cover.'

'Did the girl he married know?'

'No. I told you. We gave him a new identity. A brand new life.'

'So he was living in St. Catharines under an assumed name. And he's in trouble again. And you had to rush off to get him out of it.'

'Jesus Christ, Sylvia, you can be a pain in the ass. The kid serves years for a crime he didn't commit and you're still ready to think the worst.'

Sylvia could have kicked herself for upsetting him. When he sensed a difference of opinion, he clammed up. She had concluded early in their marriage that his stonewalling at home was a reaction against his professional life, where all his efforts were channeled into refuting opposing points of view. 'I'm sorry, David. What happened?'

Feathers smoothed, he said, 'He's missing. His parents called and said he left for work three weeks ago and hasn't been seen since.'

'Why did they wait so long?'

'They didn't. They reported him missing. I guess they kept expecting he'd turn up.'

'Maybe he had a fight with his wife.'

'No. We checked with her. She said they've never even had a disagreement.'

'Everyone fights sometime, David.'

'Syl, if you knew Mary. . . . She's one of the sweetest girls I've ever met. So are the kids. A boy and a girl. Both babies.'

'Probably it was all too much for him. Working. Taking care of a family. Maybe he was having trouble on the job.'

'He was one of their best workers. Hadn't missed a day since he started. They had moved him up to shop foreman.'

'He's bound to turn up, David. People don't just fall off the face of the earth.'

She knew David well enough to know he was deeply worried, too worried to settle for false comfort. 'It must be difficult to give someone a new identity,' she said finally.

'In some ways,' he agreed. 'There's always the chance they'll run into someone they know. It's hard on the parents, too. Mrs.

Henry told me one day that the most difficult thing to remember was not to call him Jim anymore. It's the little things. . . . '

'How *do* you pick a new name for someone?'

'Verrrry carefully.'

She rewarded his attempt at humor with a faint smile. 'Does the person choose it? I can think of a lot of things I'd rather be called than plain old Sylvia.'

'I like Sylvia,' David said automatically. He buttered a piece of roll and chewed it the prescribed thirty-two times.

'What name did he pick?' she asked.

'We picked it. We felt it would be safer. He might have dredged something up from his subconscious that was a dead giveaway.'

She tried again. 'So what did he end up with?' He hesitated. 'Oh, David, come on. If you can't trust me, who can you trust?'

He stared at her, undecided. Then he leaned across the table and whispered, 'Kevin McGregor.'

'Aka Kevin McGregor.' The name seemed to amuse her. 'A fine Scottish lad. Quite a switch from plain old Jim Henry. Did you pick it out of thin air?'

David looked down at his plate without answering and she knew the conversation was over. He was irritated by her lack of concern. They drove home without speaking and when she asked him if he'd like a cup of coffee he said he was tired and would rather go straight to bed.

Shortly after the Jennings' talk Kevin McGregor turned up. Two boys hiking along the canal found his frozen trunk in a plastic garbage bag. It wasn't until the second bag was found some days later that the body was identified. The second bag contained the arms, legs and head. There was a tag on the bag inscribed with a number 9. The hands and feet were never found. The genitals were never found, either.

When David heard of the discovery he was devastated. 'Some lousy bastard knew he was making it and couldn't take it,' he raged. 'The lousy bastard should be strung up.'

The outburst was so out of character it left Sylvia dumbfounded. David was deeply opposed to capital punishment, abhorred what he called judicial violence. Nor did he, as a rule, become emotionally involved with his clients. He had obviously felt a personal commitment to the case and cause of Jim Henry.

'Do they have any idea who did it?' Sylvia asked.

He gritted. 'They think it was a local, the fools. They've got some poor little bugger locked up because he dated Mary a couple of times before she got married.' He banged his fist on the table. 'They're going to fart around until the guy is miles away. By now he's probably out on the coast or down in the States laughing his goddamned head off.'

'Do the police know who he really was?'

'No. As far as they're concerned he was Kevin McGregor. No one knew but the members of the committee.'

'Then you can't blame them for looking close to home. Maybe if you told them?'

'Jesus, Sylvia, do you know what that would do to Mary and the kids? That's the last thing I'd do.'

It seemed to Sylvia that the truth would have to come out eventually. Everyone connected with Kevin McGregor was being questioned. His parents had sold their home in Ottawa and had moved to St. Catharines to be near him. They, too, were living under an assumed name. They, too, were being questioned. It seemed highly unlikely to Sylvia that they would be able to explain their relationship to the young family without raising more questions than they answered. Much to her surprise, with David's coaching they came up with a story no one challenged. Unable to claim their son in life, they would gladly have claimed him in death. They refrained from doing so for the sake of Mary and the children.

Kevin was quickly dubbed 'the mystery man' by the peninsula press. Reporters, accustomed to fleshing out their stories with intimate details dating back to early childhood, were intrigued by Kevin's lack of a past. They harassed his friends and co-workers, and drove Mary into seclusion. Amid rumor and speculation, Kevin was described as everything from the son of a prominent family who preferred to make his own way in the world to an undercover agent in league with the RCMP. The few people who knew Kevin's identity were determined to keep his secret, even if it meant the killer would go free.

The truth might never have surfaced if it hadn't been for Joe Parsons and his incredible memory.

8

January 1985

Joe Parsons dragged himself out of bed and stumbled into the kitchen of his small flat. He had a hangover and his hands shook as he poured a glass of tomato juice and plugged in the kettle for coffee. It was Sunday morning, and he was thankful he didn't have an assignment on tap.

After drinking his juice at the kitchen sink, he added the glass to the week-long build-up of dirty dishes. He took the coffee into the living room along with the morning paper which was delivered, Saturdays and Sundays only, by a skinny kid with a speech impediment.

No longer headline news, the story was on one of the inside pages. It was accompanied by a photograph of Kevin, neatly dressed in shirt and tie, smiling at the camera.

Joe glanced at the picture, read the brief item, then looked at the photo more intently. There was something familiar about it, but he couldn't quite pin it down. The name Kevin McGregor meant nothing. He shrugged and turned the page. Small-town killings seldom interested him. Most were one-shot affairs aimed at settling a grudge or eliminating a rival. Crude cut-and-slash, sloppy in execution and begging solution.

He was on his second cup of coffee, dashed with rum, when it registered. Pulling the newspaper out of the garbage, he looked at it again. 'Holy Mary, Mother of God,' he breathed. He found the Jim Henry folder in his filing cabinet and spread the contents on the kitchen table. Sure enough. An article written before his release featured before-and-after photos of Henry. The first showed a scared kid, flanked by detectives. The second was taken in the prison yard. He looked tanned and healthy, and was wearing the same half smile as in the Kevin McGregor shot.

'Well I'll be a sonofabitch,' Joe muttered. His chest tightened with excitement and his hands began to shake. The murder was a month old, yet no one had made the connection. He had a fingertip on the biggest story of his career. If he could just keep it to himself, keep it away from the competition until he had it pinned down, had the details, maybe even that one vital piece of information that would lead to a successful denouement of the case.

The Henrys' telephone number was written on the inside of the file folder. Joe dialed it, his hands now sure and steady. He wasn't surprised when the person who answered the call said he had the wrong number. Over a decade had passed. The Henrys would be in retirement, perhaps even dead.

He called Information in St. Catharines and asked for Kevin McGregor's number. It was unlisted. Nor was there a listing for anyone called Henry.

Joe cursed himself for having ignored the killing when it was first reported. All he needed was one slim lead, a lead that may well have been contained in the local coverage.

Too canny to contact one of his St. Catharines colleagues, he decided to call the news director of one of the local radio stations. Joe felt the average newscaster, unlike newspaper bloodhounds, merely sat in the station and read whatever came over the wire service. A safer bet than tipping his hand to a hotshot looking for a byline and pickup by the metro dailies.

Joe's contact wasn't on duty. He sweet-talked a home number out of the switchboard operator and got through. The newsman said yes, he knew about the case, he had followed it carefully, he had gone to school with Mary McGregor so you might say there was a personal connection. In answer to Joe's next question he said of course he knew her parents. Their name was Hollander and they lived on a small farm just outside the city. He gave Joe the Hollander telephone number and told him where the farm was located and the best way to get there. Joe thanked him and hung up, his heart pounding with the excitement of the chase.

Within half an hour he was on the Queen Elizabeth Highway headed for the Hollanders. Traffic was light. It took less than an hour to reach St. Kits. Taking the bypass, he turned off into open country, swung onto the concession road and saw the house immediately. It was set back in a flat, treeless field. He had expected to find reporters swarming the area, but there was no one in sight.

The house looked deserted. The curtains were drawn and the

only sign of life was a battle-scarred German shepherd that circled the car, hair stiff along its spine. He kicked at the dog as he got out of the car and it backed away, snarling viciously. Joe tried to pretend it wasn't there.

As he crossed the old-fashioned porch he caught sight of movement behind one of the curtains. The house reminded him of the Olson farmhouse in Maine, painted and re-painted by Andrew Wyeth. He knocked. And waited. Knocked harder. Nothing happened. He sensed the dog, slinking. Knowing it wouldn't attack while he was facing it he half-turned, watching, continuing to pound on the door.

When no one answered he went around to the back, picking up a piece of firewood on the way to use as a club. Wary, the dog backed away.

The backyard was littered with old pieces of farm machinery. The door was glass-paned and uncurtained. He climbed onto the stoop and banged on the door until the glass rattled, determined to stay all night if necessary. He could see directly into the kitchen. There was a pot cooking on the stove. He knew someone would eventually have to appear and remove it. He waited, thumping on the door at regular intervals.

Finally a small, gray-haired woman appeared in the archway at the back of the kitchen. She stood there, undecided, then came toward the door and opened it a crack. Joe wedged his foot into the opening. 'Mrs. Hollander?'

She tried to close the door, to balance his weight with hers. 'I'd like to talk to you about Kevin.'

'Please go away.' She threw her weight against the door. Joe's foot was an effective stop.

'I'm a friend of his,' he lied. 'I grew up with him.'

She relaxed just long enough for Joe to push against the door and shove her aside. 'I have a message for Mary,' he continued. 'Something he wanted her to know.'

Joe's sharp eyes caught the slight movement of Mrs. Hollander's head toward the open arch. There was a faint stirring, a whisper of motion in the other room. He stood very still, hands clenched, not breathing. He had found more than he bargained for. He knew, as surely as he knew his own name, that Mary McGregor was in the house and that if he did it right she would come to him.

Mrs. Hollander looked at him suspiciously. 'What's your name?'

'Joe Parsons.'

'Kevin never talked about you.'

'Perhaps not. But we kept in touch. He phoned me just a few days before the . . . uh . . . the accident.'

She hesitated, unsure. Then, 'If you have a message I'll see Mary gets it.'

He shook his head. 'No. I'm sorry. It's personal. I'll have to tell her myself.'

She stood in front of him, shaking her head. He decided to play a long shot, turned away as though about to leave. As he stepped off the stoop a different voice, younger, wearier, called, 'Wait. Please. Don't go.'

He turned, and there she was. A slim, pale, childlike figure in a sleeveless white blouse and wraparound denim skirt. Her long brown hair was wispy and lifeless, her light blue eyes watery and red-rimmed.

'I'm Mary McGregor.' She looked broken and helpless. Joe read her quickly. A little tender loving care and she would open up, let it all hang out. He put his arms around her and held her close.

'He loved you, Mary. He said you were the best thing that ever happened to him.'

Her body started to shake. He half carried her to one of the straight-backed wooden chairs and eased her down. Then, as though it were his house and she the visitor, he got her a glass of water. He sat across from her, covering her hand with his.

'Kevin was one of the finest men I ever knew,' he said, feeling his way.

She stared at him. Said nothing. He had expected her to cry. When she didn't he decided she was cried out, there were no tears left. Nothing but the film of moisture that gave her eyes a strange underwater look.

He tried again. 'Kevin spoke of you often, Mary. You and the children.'

She looked up, her eyes blank. 'He never talked about you.' An echo of her mother.

'But he didn't talk much about the past, did he?'

'Sometimes he did.'

Joe stared at her incredulously. The little sonofabitch told her and she married him anyway, he thought. He knew about women who were turned on by killers, the jailhouse groupies who sent letters, money, proposals to strangers on death row. They were sick. But how sick would a woman have to be to marry a sexual psychopath? Mary McGregor didn't fit the mold. She couldn't have believed he was guilty; she must have thought he was framed. He felt a grudging respect. Whatever she had thought about Kevin, she had managed to keep his secret. To make a life for them both.

'Did he tell you about growing up? Going to school?' Joe probed carefully, his voice soft and sympathetic.

'Yes,' she answered. 'He wasn't very happy.' She pulled a wad of Kleenex out of her pocket and blew her nose. 'You went to school with him?'

Joe nodded.

'In Vancouver?'

Joe's stomach tightened. She didn't know about Jim Henry after all. Whatever he had told her, it hadn't been the truth. He computed the odds. He could win her confidence by playing accessory to the lie. Or he could go for broke and run the risk of losing her before he had what he needed. He decided to play it safe. Ignoring her question he asked, 'Mary, do you have any idea who did this?'

She shook her head.

'Do the police have a suspect?'

Mrs. Hollander came over to Mary and put her hand on the girl's shoulder. 'If you have something to tell Mary you had better say it and leave.'

'Do you think it was someone he knew here or someone he knew before?' Joe persisted.

'Everybody liked him,' Mary said softly.

'He was a good person,' Mrs. Hollander said flatly. 'We don't want to talk about it. I want you to go now.'

'You want whoever did this punished, don't you?' The question was aimed at both of them. Mary nodded. Mrs. Hollander tugged at her arm. 'It's time to lie down, dear.' And to Joe, accusingly, 'She needs her rest. You have to go.'

Joe took a deep breath and played his trump. 'Your husband wasn't from Vancouver. He grew up in Ottawa.'

'No. He lived in Vancouver until he came here.'

'You didn't know Kevin at all,' Mrs. Hollander said. Angry. Accusing. Her lined face livid with rage. 'I want you should leave now and never come back.'

As though she hadn't heard, didn't comprehend what her mother was saying, Mary rambled on in a monotone. 'His parents were killed when he was a little boy. He lived with the Wilsons. They took care of him. They loved him like a son. They came here to be near him.' She leaned against her mother, eyes closed and body trembling. 'I can't believe he's gone,' she whispered. 'I can't believe we'll never see him again.'

Joe kept his voice steady. 'The Wilsons? Where do they live?'

'They've had enough grief. They've taken this as hard as Mary. If you don't go now I am going to call the police.' Mrs. Hollander was very, very angry.

Joe knew he had nothing to lose. 'Mrs. Hollander, I have something here I want you to look at.' He took the Jim Henry clipping out of his wallet and unfolded it on the kitchen table. 'Read this.'

Mrs. Hollander glanced at the twin photographs. 'That's Kevin.'

'No,' Joe said. 'That's Jim Henry.'

Mrs. Hollander leaned over Mary, her face a puzzled frown as she read the clipping. Curious, Mary read along with her.

Mrs. Hollander finished the item and stared at Parsons, her face a mask of bewilderment. 'Who is this person?' she asked, shoving the clipping back across the table. 'Why are you showing us this?'

'Don't you know?' Joe asked. 'Can't you tell? Kevin was Jim Henry. Jim Henry was Kevin. They're the same person.'

Both women stared at him wordlessly. He rushed on, words flowing in a torrent. 'When he was still in public school he killed a little girl and cut her up with a saw and butcher knife. In the basement of his own house. He stuffed the pieces in a garbage bag and hid the bag on the banks of the Rideau. They didn't find her until spring. Parts of her were never found at all.'

'You're lying,' Mary screamed. 'Kevin never hurt nobody in his life.'

'Everyone has a double,' Mrs. Hollander said. 'Anyway,' triumphant, 'it says here this Jim Henry is in jail. So why are you telling such a crazy story, making such trouble, driving Mary out of her mind when she's had so much already that is more than she can bear?'

'Jim Henry was released from prison five years ago. He was given a new name. A new place to live. A new life.'

'It's not true,' Mary sobbed.

'It's true.'

'He wouldn't have done nothing like that. I don't believe it.'

'Maybe you don't, but there's somebody out there that does.' Joe folded the clipping and put it back in his billfold. 'Don't you see? It's a copy. Jim was killed because of what he did to that little girl. It could have been a relative. Maybe a young brother who waited till he was grown to get even.'

They were both looking at him as though he were mad. He gave up trying to convince them. 'I'd like to talk to the Wilsons.'

'You've talked enough for a month of Sundays. And said nothing but a pack of lies that you should be ashamed of telling on the dead.' Mrs. Hollander wrapped a protective arm around Mary.

'Tell me where to find the Wilsons and I'll go.'

The sad, small woman did her best to look menacing. 'My husband will be home soon,' she threatened. 'It will be too bad for you if he finds you here. And Mary in such a state that you're responsible for.'

As if on cue, a car door slammed outside and the dog barked excitedly. Mrs. Hollander blanched and Joe braced himself for her husband's wrath. The front door opened and a woman's voice called, 'Mary, we're back.'

They came into the kitchen, the woman carrying a baby and the slightly stooped white-haired man holding a small boy by the hand. Mrs. Hollander held out her arms for the baby. Joe stood, still as a statue, staring at the couple. He hadn't seen them since the trial, wouldn't have recognized them on the street. But now, in context, he knew.

They had aged more than their years. His hair, once thick and dark, was sparse and white. Hers was streaked with gray and heavy lines creased the face Joe remembered as being fresh and rather pretty. Joe took a step forward. Casually, as though greeting old friends, he said, 'Mr and Mrs. Henry . . . it's good to see you again.'

The man staggered back as though Joe had struck him. Mrs.

Henry screamed. Mary fainted.

Joe knew he had his finger in the brass ring. All he had to do was hold on.

Mrs. Henry couldn't stop talking. Years of pent-up misery were pouring out in a flood of words, memories, reminiscences. Joe caught it all on tape. All he had to do was sit back and listen.

'He was such a good boy. A handsome boy. All the girls liked him. Everybody liked him. He was never in any kind of trouble; always building things, making things. He wanted to be an architect when he grew up and he talked about all the things we'd do together, the places we'd go. . . . '

In the first few minutes of confusion at the Hollanders' Joe had managed to get the Henrys out of the house and away from Mary and her mother. He wanted to talk to them alone. They refused to tell him where they lived. When they realized he intended to follow them they agreed, reluctantly, to accompany him to a motel. He got a room at the Parklane and there, in unfamiliar surroundings and on neutral ground, Helen Henry was letting it all out.

'He knew the girl. She lived right next door. A pretty little thing but old for her age, if you know what I mean. And used to looking after herself because her mother worked and she was the only child so she was always visiting the neighbors. . . . '

Joe's ears pricked up. 'No brothers or sisters?' No brothers or sisters, she confirmed, nor, for that matter, uncles or nephews. 'The only visitors we noticed were men. Her mother was separated and she had a lot of boyfriends; they kept coming and going, and it was one of *them*, not my Jim. But the police questioned them and let them go and said they could account for their time when it happened so they put the blame on Jimmie. They had to come up with someone so they picked on a child who couldn't defend himself. . . . '

'What about the girl's father? Could he have wanted to get back at Jim?'

'He was down on the east coast. He loved the girl but the mother wouldn't let him have her. He came for the trial and we tried to talk to him, tell him how sorry we were and explain to him that Jimmie would never have harmed her; he loved her like a sister. But he cursed at us and said some day, if it took him the rest of his life, he'd put my baby where he couldn't harm anyone any more. . . . ' She started to cry, the scene etched in her mind as though it had just happened.

Joe tensed. 'Do you think he. . . . ?'

'No. We heard he died not long after the trial. We know it's true because we were afraid he would come back and do something, so we kept track of him through a friend who lived in Halifax. He sent us the clipping so it wasn't him. We were so relieved when we heard he was gone. . . . '

Becoming impatient with her rambling, Joe said, 'I knew Jimmie, Mrs. Henry. He got a raw deal when he was sent up. And another raw deal here. For his sake, we have to find out who's responsible. You want that, don't you?'

She looked at her husband. 'I don't know,' she said, her voice uncertain. 'He was such a sweet boy and if it all comes out now people will start saying those terrible things about him all over again. And it won't bring him back. So maybe it's better to try and forget and give Mary and the children a chance. . . . '

'It has come out,' Joe said bluntly. 'Mary knows. Her family knows. The newspapers are bound to find out. Do you think it was someone he met in prison?'

'No. They liked him. He was a model prisoner.' She sounds like a goddamned broken record, Joe thought. 'Did you know he found God? He was a born-again Christian. The other inmates came to him for help. We saw him every week and took him things and he always shared with everyone. When he was released they held a party for him and it was one of the happiest days of his life. . . . '

'A lot of things go on in a prison, Mrs. Henry.' He didn't want to offend her, but he had to know. 'Was there one friend? A special friend?'

She nodded. 'There was a guard who was like a big brother to him. He took care of him and for a long time he was the only person Jim saw, while he was being kept away from the other prisoners, that is. . . . '

'Was there one prisoner that was . . . you know . . . closer to him?'

Mr. Henry broke in harshly. 'If you're asking if my son was . . . ah . . . ,' he shot a quick glance at his wife, '. . . one of those, the answer is *no*. He was a good, God-fearing lad. Would he have married Mary?' Even in anger he was old and defeated.

Joe knew it would be useless to point out that men in the pen did what they had to do to survive. Naivete and blind faith had been the Henrys' shield for so long that it had become integral to their lives. He called room service and ordered food for three. He would let Mrs. Henry talk, without interruption, for as long as she wanted to. Perhaps, somewhere on the hours of tape, there would be a hint, a clue, something worth following. One consolation was that he now had their license number. Getting their address would be no big problem. If he needed them again he would know where to find them.

Joe did not connect Henry's death with the Toronto killings. Unaware of the numbered tags, he had no reason to tie the St. Catharines slaying to the wave of metro murders. He did not know who killed Jim but he knew why he was killed. Revenge, pure and sweet. Administered by someone from the past, someone who had known the little girl in Ottawa and waited over a decade to do unto him as he had done unto her.

And Joe knew also that if he could come up with the answer, he'd have two scoops in one. The McGregor masquerade. The Henry killer. He'd be able to write his own ticket. Other papers would know him. Want him. He'd have a regular column. Be syndicated. Life would be a bowl of cherries. And best of all, he'd be able to pick and choose his stories, work full-time on the cases he liked best.

Dimly aware of Mrs. Henry's voice feeding the tape recorder, he stretched full length in the uncomfortable chair, feet propped on the bed, arms behind his head. It was going to be a long night.

David cancelled the trip south because he wanted to be on hand in case anything broke in the Henry case. When Sylvia asked if he planned to defend Jim's killer with the same dedication he had applied to Jim's appeal, he stormed out of the house without answering. The next day he told her he would be spending a couple of days in Ottawa and she knew, without being told, that it had something to do with Henry and the Ottawa group that had worked for his release. She was sorry then that she hadn't taken David's advice and gone south without him.

She no longer felt comfortable at home alone. She was fine during the day, but she was nervous and uneasy in the house after dark. She thought of checking into a hotel but that would leave no one to look after Millie and Ciba. Finally she phoned Anne and coerced her into staying until David got back. 'It's only for one night,' she said. 'You can get along without Bill that long, I'm sure.'

It was dark when Anne arrived and she hadn't eaten. When Sylvia suggested going out for dinner she said it was a splendid idea. Just the two of them — like old times.

They drove along the Queensway to Latina and ordered a liter of house wine from the waiter who seated them. 'The last time I saw you drinking was the night we saw what's-his-name,' Anne remarked.

Sylvia tensed. She reminded herself that Anne didn't know about her relationship with Arthur. 'I still drink occasionally,' she said coolly. 'How's Bill?'

Launched on her favorite subject, Anne talked abut Bill through antipasto, cannelloni, baskets of warm garlic bread and another liter of wine. By the time they were ready to leave they were both slightly high, pleased with themselves and the world. Sylvia now knew as much about Bill as she did about David.

Their good spirits lasted until they pulled into the Jennings' driveway. The street was deserted. The dark outline of the house was somber and threatening. They sat in the car for a moment, not speaking.

'It isn't just me,' Sylvia thought to herself. 'Anne feels it too.' She shuddered.

As they crossed the porch, Sylvia noticed fresh footprints on the front walk. Not wanting to alarm Anne, she said nothing. Safely indoors, she switched on all the downstairs lights and talked to Anne, non-stop, at the top of her voice.

'You're nervous.'

'Yes,' Sylvia admitted.

'It's the house,' Anne said, looking over her shoulder. 'It feels as though there's someone here. Waiting to pounce.'

'It's not the house, it's this damned winter. It drags on and on.'

Anne slid one of the cutting knives out of the butcher block. 'Let's check to make sure.'

They roused Millie from her spot behind the sofa, coaxing her into following them as they went from one room to another. Anne, who was leading the way, knife in hand, paused at the foot of the stairs. 'I think I hear something,' she whispered.

They listened. A faint scraping sound came from above. Sylvia pressed the light switch and the upstairs hall light came on. They started up slowly, conscious of the shadows at the end of the hallway.

'There's a gun in the bedroom,' Sylvia whispered in Anne's ear.

'Good,' Anne whispered back. 'Stay behind me. If there's anybody there, run for it. I'll keep him busy with this.' She brandished the knife, sword-fashion.

They inched their way upstairs; were relieved when they reached the bedroom without incident. With the light on and door closed behind them, they began to feel foolish, like two kids playing ghosts. Anne threw the knife on the bed. 'We're turning into neurotic old maids,' she grinned.

The scraping sound came again, much louder. Anne made a grab for the knife. They both turned toward the window, hearts pounding.

'It's those damn branches,' Sylvia whispered, trying to keep her voice from shaking.

'Where's the gun?'

Sylvia opened the drawer. The gun was gone. 'It's not here.' She was beginning to tremble uncontrollably.

Anne reached for the phone and dialed the emergency number. She reported a prowler and gave the address in a crisp, businesslike voice. With help on the way, Anne regained her confidence. She checked the window, noticed that the spindly branches of the lilac tree were moving slightly, but they weren't rubbing against the wall. She looked more carefully. There was a small cloud of steam near the bottom corner. And, barely discernible, a tear in the screen between the panes.

The patrol car pulled up moments later. The flashing lights patterned the snow with blood-red splotches. Anne took Sylvia by the hand and led her back downstairs.

The officers were young, handsome and polite. They checked the grounds, and then at Anne's request searched the house. They found no sign of attempted entry, no indication of a foreign presence.

Sylvia apologized for bothering them and they said it was no bother, better safe than sorry. Hoping they would stay awhile, Sylvia offered them a cup of coffee. They declined, saying it was a busy night but they would make a point of cruising by during their rounds, they were sure there was no cause for alarm. They left, taking with them the eerie sense of foreboding both women had felt prior to their arrival.

'We should have told them about the gun,' Anne said ruefully. Although it was the reason she had called, they had forgotten to mention it.

Sylvia said it was just as well. David knew she didn't like having it around. He had probably put it somewhere else.

'Better tell him, just in case,' Anne suggested.

'In case of what?'

'In case someone ends up dead, shot with your pistol,' Anne joked. Then, her voice serious, she asked, 'Where is David? Does he often leave you alone like this?'

'Hardly ever,' Sylvia replied. She explained about Jim Henry and the release committee and Kevin McGregor and how David was determined to find out who was responsible.

Anne was fascinated. An avid reader of mystery stories, this one sounded good enough to out-Agatha Miss Christie. 'Do they have any clues?' she asked.

'That could be why David's in Ottawa. Although frankly I doubt it.'

'The way I see it,' Anne reasoned, 'the first thing they have to pin down is which one was murdered. Was it Kevin McGregor, or was it Jim Henry?'

'Does it matter? Either way, he's just as dead.'

'True. But they won't find the killer till they find the motive. And they won't find the motive till they know whether it was Jim or Kevin who got stuffed in that bag.'

'In that case, they're bound to come up with something. They're looking for Kevin's killer in St. Catherines. And David and the committee are concentrating on Jim Henry.'

Sylvia lit a firelog and they sat in comfortable silence, watching the tiny flame flicker into life.

Anne was the first to speak. 'Do you think he killed that little girl, Syl?'

'Yes.'

'I always thought so, too. But then, when David got so involved . . . well . . . I sort of thought you both felt he was innocent.' She looked at Sylvia, a wisp of suspicion forming in her mind. 'David did think he was innocent, didn't he?'

Sylvia looked into the fire, thinking. Finally she said, 'I don't know. I don't know what David thinks anymore. At first I thought he felt sorry for the boy. He was so young. And he did serve some time. And there did seem to be room for doubt. But I've never seen him this personally involved. Perhaps it's some sort of ego thing. He wanted Henry out. He got him out. Maybe it was a power trip. And now someone has come along and ruined it all.'

'Was there anyone else that could have done it? Killed her?'

'I don't think so.'

'Wasn't there something in the appeal, something David came up with about some strange man who was seen going into the house that day?'

'Anne, don't be naive. David found someone who had seen a stranger in the neighborhood that day and he made a big thing of it.' She paused, then said softly, 'Hacking someone to pieces is bloody business. No one could walk away from a crime like that in broad daylight.'

'David is very bright, Syl. He wouldn't think Henry was innocent without good reason.'

'David is a criminal lawyer. He spends his life convincing people like you and me that people like Jim Henry are as pure as the driven snow. Sometimes I think he even convinces himself.'

'I've always thought if I ever got into real trouble, I'd want to have David on my side.'

Sylvia's smile was as cold as the frost on the windows. 'So would I, Annie. Believe me, so would I.' She stood up and stretched. 'Ready for bed?'

Anne yawned. 'Should we put the fire out?'

'It'll be all right.'

On their way upstairs, Anne said, 'Do you know that last year Toronto had twice as many murders as Buffalo? We set a record.'

'At least most of them were men,' Sylvia said evenly. 'That's quite a switch, isn't it?'

Sylvia got Anne settled in the guest room and climbed into bed on David's side. Drowsy, she thought of the patrol car making its rounds and Anne in the next room.

Feeling warm and protected, she fell into a deep, untroubled sleep.

Joe Parsons sat in a bar on Yonge Street with a friend from the paper and two policemen who were off duty. The officers were talking about the rash of unsolved murders in the city and how, even if they caught the perpetrators, it wouldn't make much difference; they'd be back on the street so fast it was hardly worth picking them up.

'There's this punk in Florida,' one said. 'He snatches a fifteen-year-old kid off the street, drags her into his car, and stabs her seventy-five times. The kid is a cheerleader on her way home from school and this guy just stuffs her in the car and cuts her up like hamburger. Then he throws her out on the side of the road and she bleeds to death.'

'And?'

'And the little bastard gets off. His lawyer pleads insanity, saying what he needs is help; it's not going to do any good to lock him up. Everybody knows he's guilty as hell; people saw him do it! He doesn't deny it, and the goddamn jury goes along with the defense, thinking he'll go into an institution for treatment and be out of circulation for years. When he gets there they find he's sane and doesn't need any treatment, so they let him go. Now he's out, free as a bird, and there's nothin' can be done about it.'

'So much for the jury system.'

'Yeah . . . well . . . they're on everybody's hate list, but they just didn't know. They think he had to be crazy to do it in the first place. Then his lawyer convinces them he's crazy — legally that is — and when push comes to shove, the state psychiatrists say he's sane. The guy that shoots the Pope gets life for wounding; *this* abortion gets nothing for assault, rape and murder.'

'He wouldn't be walking around free if it were my daughter.'

'And then what? You'd get the book thrown at you. What it comes down to is, the punks with nothing to lose have it made. Let you and me step out of line and we're in bad trouble.'

'Can't have the public taking the law into their own hands,' one of the officers pointed out.

'Yeah, that's what you tell the good guys. The bad guys do

whatever the hell they like, and the rest of us are supposed to sit around like a bunch of clay pigeons.'

Joe listened to the conversation half-heartedly. He'd heard it all before. With a lot of friends on the force, he knew they did the best they could. On his good days he felt maybe the system wasn't perfect, but it was better than a hell of a lot of others. On his bad days he knew the whole thing was a stinking mess and would eventually collapse in chaos.

He was tired. He had spent a lot of time, and his own money, running down Jim Henry leads in and out of town: St Catharines, Ottawa, Kingston. The interview with Mrs. Henry had given him nothing but a headache. Hours of tape, played and re-played, and it was strictly zilch. The same with the guard in Kingston. He'd liked Jim, said the other prisoners liked him, too. None of the inmates had it in for him. It had to be someone on the outside, something dumb like maybe a card game or a fight at work. The guard, like Mrs. Henry, had been no help at all.

Joe had even tracked down the mother of the little girl who was murdered. She had re-married, and it took him a long time to find her. She didn't want to talk about her daughter. Her current husband ran a small trucking business and they lived quietly in a new development outside of Ottawa. They had two teen-aged children and it was apparent to Joe that she lived completely in the present. He didn't blame her. Kept alive, the memory of that terrible day would have driven her mad.

Her husband, a gruff lumbering man, knew of the tragedy but refused to discuss it. He had insisted that his wife get rid of everything she had owned prior to their marriage. She did not even have a photograph of her firstborn. The strategy had worked so well that, talking to her, Joe felt he was getting a third-hand report from someone who had read about the murder and knew of it only from written accounts.

It was obvious, within the first few minutes, that neither had any knowledge of Jim's death. Nor had the child's father. The woman corroborated the fact that he was dead, that even his own family had not been sorry to see him go, that he had many enemies but no friends, that all his life he had talked big and done absolutely nothing.

The boyfriend who at one time had been a minor suspect was also dead, killed in a rock-cut car crash near Parry Sound shortly after the trial. His friends said he crashed the car deliberately.

The little girl's mother had coped by wiping the past from her mind. The boyfriend, who had truly loved the little girl, coped through oblivion. He, too, was a dead end.

Before leaving Ottawa, Joe visited the house where the murder had taken place. At first the woman who answered the door didn't want to let him in. She knew the house had been the scene of a tragedy, but she knew none of the details. She had moved in recently, and made it plain that she was not one to have anything to do with her neighbors. It wasn't until Joe told her he was a writer, working on a series of articles about neighborhood homes, that she agreed to let him in. He showed her his press card and said if she didn't mind he would like to start with the basement. She switched on the light at the head of the cellar stairs and told him to help himself, she had things to do.

He descended the stairs and stood in the damp, unfinished basement and tried to imagine the horror it had contained. The old enameled laundry tub was still under the window. The glass in the window was streaked and dirty, and a cobweb was spun from the latch to the pipe above. No light came through the smeared pane.

Dark rust spots mottled the tub where the enamel was chipped. The spots looked like old, dried blood. Joe thought this was how it must have looked when the killer washed the pieces of the little girl before putting them in the bag, washing himself clean before leaving.

There was an old wooden folding table beside the modern washer and dryer and Joe wondered if it was the same table on which she had been dissected. He removed the oilcloth cover and ran his hand over the wood surface, worn butter-smooth by years of use. The wood was scrubbed almost skeleton white. He replaced the oilcloth and looked at the drain in the center of the floor. The gray concrete was rough and pebbled.

'He stood here,' Joe thought. 'Perhaps right where I'm standing now. He had taken his clothes off, because he knew there would be a lot of blood. He hosed it down this drain and then he hosed himself and when he left here, except for a few small splatters he had missed, there was nothing left to see. Nothing but a boy in tennis shoes carrying a green garbage bag.'

Closing his eyes as the room vibrated around him with chill, evil energy, he could almost feel the knife slicing through flesh, hear the saw grating on muscle and bone.

The scene played against his eyelids like a horror film. A thin, intense boy, his body wet with sweat, pimpled face frowning in concentration, working methodically as though he were dismantling a life-size doll assembled from a hobby kit. There was no need to hurry. The house was empty. It would be empty all day. The boy knew he could take his time; there would be no one to interrupt.

Joe shuddered and opened his eyes. The basement was drab and ugly. The single light bulb hanging from the center of the ceiling cast shadows in the corners. The place was spooky. Joe was glad to go back upstairs, into the bright sunny kitchen.

The woman offered him a cup of coffee and he accepted. They sat in the kitchen beside a large window that looked out at the house the Henrys had owned. There was a wide mutual drive and adjoining garages. Each house had a side entrance into the driveway.

He went out the side door, directly into the garage for his bicycle. If anyone noticed him they didn't think anything of it, Joe thought. They were in and out of each other's houses all the time.

'Would you like to see upstairs?' the woman asked.

'I think I've seen enough,' Joe answered. He asked, 'The table downstairs. Was it here when you moved in?'

'Yes. I was going to get rid of it, but it's handy when I do my laundry. No one ever sees it down there, anyway.'

'Have you made any changes in the house?'

'Just paint and wallpaper. We haven't been here very long.'

Joe wondered how many people had lived in the house since the little girl's mother moved out. And how the first occupants had felt. 'Do you like it?' he asked.

She shrugged indifferently. 'It's all right. The rooms are nice and big. But sometimes there's a feeling in it. . . . ' She paused. 'Sometimes, when it's raining or the sun isn't shining . . . it gets kind of depressing, if you know what I mean.'

Joe did know what she meant. Even now, with friends, surrounded by noise and activity, he could feel the dark brooding malevolence of that cement vault. And it, too, had yielded nothing. He still felt the best clue in a murder case was the motive, and he was convinced that the motive for Jim Henry's murder was the little girl. There just didn't seem to be a connecting link.

A fight broke out at one of the tables and the bouncer moved over to break it up. The commotion snapped Joe's attention back to the present and he waved his glass for a refill. One of the policemen said jokingly, 'She sure must be a hot number.'

'Who?' Joe asked.

'Whoever you were thinking about. You were off in dreamland.'

'I was thinking about that Kevin McGregor case down in St. Kits,' Joe confessed. 'Is there anything new on it?'

'Not that we've heard. Homicide might know something. But they don't get that much into other jurisdictions.'

'I suppose not, Joe said wearily. As an afterthought he asked, 'What about the TO cases? Anything new there?'

'Another body,' the second cop said nonchalantly. 'A young supermarket clerk. Gruesome.'

'Gruesome how?'

'Found him in his apartment, one of those Parkdale bachelorettes, with his tongue sticking out and a pencil stuck in each eye. The guy who found him fainted.'

Joe felt as though he'd been struck by instant malaria. He was hot. Cold. Sweat broke out on his forehead. 'Was there a cross on the body?'

The policeman stared at him. 'How'd you know that?'

'Did he have make-up on? Lipstick? Eye shadow?'

Both officers were staring at him suspiciously. The details hadn't been made public. These were things no one outside the department was supposed to know.

Joe read the answer in their faces. The weariness was gone. Excitement curled through his insides like a supercharged rush. It was more than coincidence. The pieces were beginning to fit together.

'What've you got, Joe?' The other newspaperman was suspicious, too.

'Nothing, nothing at all.' He'd have to get away by himself and think about it. Check and double-check. Look for other match-ups in his files.

'If you know anything, Joe, you'd better report it. We'll see it gets to the guys working on the case.'

Joe pushed his chair back. 'Fellows, I swear, I don't know a thing. I've been out of town. Out of touch.'

'Withholding information, Joe,' his reporter friend said meaningfully.

Joe shook his head. 'Not me. You guys know me better than that.'

The three men stared after him, wondering. He knew more about crime than all three of them put together. What the police pursued as a profession, he followed as a hobby. What they did for pay, he did for pleasure. There was no comparison between the depth of his commitment and theirs. They knew this and felt a momentary twinge of guilt.

But what the hell. They were off duty, out of uniform, on their own time. They ordered another round and settled into the evening.

9

February 1985

The apartment was a mess. Every flat surface was obliterated by the litter of living. Stacks of newspapers and old magazines covered the floor, overflowing ashtrays, sticky glasses, half-filled coffee cups held squatter's rights on tables and counters. Joe's first priority was to clear a spot in which to work.

He bundled up newspapers and lugged them to the incinerator, piled dishes into his plastic laundry basket — thank God it was solid and would catch the drips — and stashed it on top of the sink. And then he was ready. He pulled out his scrapbooks, poured himself a drink, and began leafing through page after page of clippings in search of the Clown Murder.

It had been one of southern Ontario's most grotesque homicides. He remembered the grossness of it, but not the year nor even in which of the peninsula's many small farming communities it had taken place. He searched until well after midnight and then, head splitting with a headache of near migraine proportion, admitted defeat. The information was there in his filing cabinets. But the scrapbooks served as a cross-index. Without the year and location of the crime which the clippings provided he didn't know where to look in the hundreds of folders he had on file.

Realizing he was hungry he made himself a fat sandwich and ate it in his favorite easy chair, feet on the coffee table, mind racing. Jim Henry's murder was a carbon copy of the one he, Henry, had committed years before. Now there was the Clown Murder, which appeared to be a second copycat killing. Was it possible, could it be that the Toronto deaths followed the same pattern?

Joe had started a new scrapbook for the Toronto snuffs. They were together in one book, not because he had felt they were connected but simply because they had occurred within the same short time frame and in or near the city. He found the scrapbook, re-read the clippings. the first was dated August. It was now February. Seven months of bizarre slayings, all men, each crime seemingly perfect, each crime seemingly devoid of motive. But suppose the motive lay, not with the killer, but with the victim? It was a possibility. But until each murder was checked against the victims and their past, the possibility was merely a theory.

The first step was to cross-check the Clown Murder for similarities, and he knew of only one other person who might have the information at his fingertips. David Jenning. That cold fish lawyer.

Joe had interviewed David a number of times and once they had even compared notes on their murder memorabilia. Joe considered David highly capable but thoroughly ruthless, a man who would walk roughshod over anyone who stood in his client's way. He did not know Sylvia but he had seen her with David and felt they made an odd couple: she tall, blond, aloof, and with an almost mannequin-like stillness; he short, dark, heavyset and phlegmatic.

Joe reached for the phone. It was well past the witching hour, no time to phone an enemy much less someone from whom one wanted help, but he was much too hyper to sit and do nothing.

He checked the number in his little brown book and dialed. It rang three times. He would have let it ring all night if necessary. On the fourth ring it was picked up and a guarded female voice said, 'Hello?'

'Mrs. Jenning?'

There was a long pause. Finally the voice answered in the affirmative.

'Is your husband at home?'

He heard a click and the line went dead. He sat for a moment staring at the phone, then dialed again. This time she answered immediately. 'If you don't stop calling me, I will notify the police.'

Before she had time to hang up he blurted, 'Mrs. Jenning, it's Joe Parsons. I know your husband. It's important that I speak with him.'

The tone was friendlier. Not warm, but less tense. 'I'm sorry. I thought it was. . . . ' A pause. Then, stilted, 'My husband is asleep. You can call him in the morning. Do you have his business number?'

'It's *extremely* important.'

'Perhaps if you tell me what it's about.'

It was obvious she did not intend to call her husband unless there was a dire emergency. But perhaps she could get the information for him. All he needed was the year and the place. So he told her about Jim Henry and the interviews he had conducted and how everything had led to a dead end. She did not seem particularly interested, although she did seem surprised that he knew Kevin McGregor was really Jim Henry.

Then he told her about the Clown case, and how the two together seemed to be too much of a coincidence. She remained non-committal. When he had finished she asked why he was calling her husband instead of the police.

He explained that he needed more information on the original murder; he didn't want to fly off half-cocked.

'My husband didn't handle the case,' she reminded him.

'But he does have a tremendous amount of material. Do you have access to his files?'

Instead of a direct answer she said, 'I don't share his interest, if that's what you mean.'

'But does he keep his files at home? Could you just check the date for me?'

'I'm sorry. I wouldn't begin to know where to look.'

'Could I come over and do it?'

'Certainly not. You will have to discuss it with Mr. Jenning.'

There was a hint of steel in her voice. Accustomed to wearing down opposition through sheer persistence, Joe acknowledged defeat. He thanked her and hung up. Frustrated, he spent the rest of the night catnapping in front of the television set, impatient for morning and the chance to begin his search in earnest.

The ringing of the phone as she entered the house had startled Sylvia. For the past few weeks there had been strange calls. Sporadic. Irregular. Always late at night. When she answered, a polite voice would ask for David. Told he was asleep, the caller would hang up. When she mentioned the calls to David he told her to let the phone ring. Simple for him. *He* could ignore a ringing telephone.

She hung up her coat and went directly to the study. She didn't know whether David was awake, but she did know he was at home. His car was in the driveway and the upstairs lights were out. Awake or asleep, she had no intention of disturbing him.

She closed the study door and opened the drawer containing the Clown Murder file. The folder was complete with photos, clippings, and information on the trial and disposition.

The crime had occurred in Myron, a small farming community composed of a general store, gas station, theater and poolroom. There were a few small homes clustered behind the main street, occupied for the most part by older couples and retired singles long since widowed. There were few young people in the town. As they came of age they moved to larger, more active centers that offered better jobs and more exciting forms of recreation. The few in evidence, either visitors to aging parents or stopovers on their way to somewhere else, hung out at the pool hall where there was a greasy-spoon cafe, pinball machines, a jukebox and two pool tables.

Like those who lived there, Myron was a town waiting to die.

Elsie Abodeen lived in a small frame house at the south end of town. She was a quarter of a mile from her nearest neighbor. The house was set back from the road, the plain frame lines softened by a small flower garden and a knee-high picket fence.

Elsie and her husband had moved to Myron when they sold their small farm ten years before. They had enough land for a vegetable garden out back and some chickens. When Mr Abodeen died, Elsie decided to remain in the house. As she told her friends, there was nothing like having your own place, on top of which she could live there for practically nothing.

Mrs. Abodeen was a small, wiry woman in her late seventies. Active all her life, she kept her small home spotless, rode a bicycle to town to do her shopping, and attended church and Myron's weekly card games regularly. The only thing she could no longer handle by herself was the outside work. When she needed someone to dig the garden or make repairs to the house and outbuildings she did what everyone else in Myron did — she posted a handwritten notice in the poolroom.

Elsie did not know that the ad she posted for a handyman that fateful spring day was a death warrant. The young man who appeared at her door did not look like an instrument of death and destruction. He was road-worn and unkempt, but his candid eyes reflected the innocence of the very young. He was wearing blue jeans stiff with dirt, a denim jacket, and a bedroll on his shoulder. His name was Willie, and he was hitch-hiking to Toronto where he intended to get a job and go back to school at nights.

Elsie Abodeen was not one to judge a person by his appearance. When her friends talked about the younger generation's long hair and shiftless mode of dress she told them the Lord had room for everyone. 'Judge not that ye shall not be judged.' All these young people needed was someone who cared. If women were at home raising their children instead of taking jobs away from men who had families to support, young folks wouldn't be in the fix they were in. Her friends told her she was much too tolerant and should be more careful.

She opened the door and invited Willie in.

He stayed with her for two weeks, sleeping on the old couch in the summer kitchen and working far beyond the sum of his meager wages.

He dug the garden, repaired the roof where it leaked, and offered to freshen up the peeling exterior if she would buy the paint. He was a pleasant, undemanding companion and she enjoyed having him around. He did not shave off his beard or cut his hair, nor did she ask him to, although she did point out that he would find it easier to get along if he looked more like other people. Willie, who looked exactly like most of the people he knew, paid no attention.

Evenings when he didn't go to town or withdraw to his room, which she considered off-limits because she felt everyone was entitled to some privacy, they sat in her small kitchen and talked. He told her about his stepfather who beat him, and his mother who never seemed to take his side. She told him about Mr Abodeen and their life on the farm and occasionally she read to him from the Bible, hoping to get him interested in God's word. He listened politely, often with a faraway look in his eye that convinced her he was a very spiritual young man.

The only thing that seemed to bother Willie was staring. He told her wherever he went people stared at him, and it drove him crazy. Sometimes, lying in bed, he felt eyes staring at him in the dark, great yellow animal eyes that he was afraid would devour him so that some morning there would be nothing left in his bed but a pile of empty clothes. Once, standing at the sink getting a drink of water, he whirled round and accused her of watching every move he made. She was so astonished that she apologized, even though she was reading the weekly paper at the time and was hardly aware he was in the room.

What turned out to be their last day together was a bright spring Saturday. He helped her take the flats of seedlings outside for planting, but she could see he was restless and edgy. Around noon she sent him off to buy the paint they had talked about. His nervousness had made her nervous too, and she was glad to be by herself.

Although the hardware store was within easy walking distance, as was everything else in Myron, he didn't get back until early evening. He hadn't bought the paint because he didn't like the brand they carried. She had given him a twenty dollar bill and two tens. When she asked for the money he said he would go into London on Monday and check out the bigger stores like Sears and Canadian Tire, so he might as well keep it till then.

The day in town had done him good. He seemed a little tired but there was no trace of his earlier nervousness.

She fixed him something to eat and he played with the food, muddling it on his plate the way a small child might. She watched him idly, her mind on the garden she had just planted. A couple of times he looked up from his plate and met her eyes, but he said nothing. When he got up and went into his room she cleared the table and put the dishes in the sink, leaving them to wash in the morning before she left for church.

She got ready for bed. Then, remembering she hadn't latched the screen door, she pulled on her housecoat and re-entered the kitchen. Willie was there, sitting at the table staring dreamily into space.

He looked so friendless and alone that she wanted to take him in her arms, to hold and comfort him, but she knew he did not like being touched. So she sat across from him and smiled and tried to convey, through her presence, that she was his friend and she cared. His eyes were wide open, fixed through her on the opposite wall. He did not seem to know she was there.

She reached over and touched him lightly, so lightly she barely made contact.

He snatched his hand away as though she had seared it with a hot poker. His eyes, uncomprehending, filled with terror. Slowly, in a dream, he stood up. The chair clattered to the floor. He moved around the table. Deliberate. Mechanical. His thin body was an implacable, moving force. Elsie Abodeen sat transfixed, unable to move or scream.

She felt his hands around her throat, each skinny finger a strand of steel. She struck out at him then, hands flailing the air like the wings of a dying bird. The last thing she saw was Willie's face, as remote and unfeeling as a bust of bisque. He let go and she fell to the floor, face blue and body still twitching. Willie looked down at her. Elsie looked up at Willie, her eyes sightless and unwavering. Willie looked around the room, slowly, as though he, Elsie and the room were fragments of a dream.

At the end of the kitchen counter, underneath the phone, there was an old coffee mug filled with the pencils Elsie used for phone messages and her weekly crossword. They were little more than stubs, their points worn down to the wood. He chose two of the stubs and walked back to Elsie's body. Carefully, like a six-year-old planting miniature fence posts in a model setting, he forced the stubs into the staring eyes. He felt an immense relief when he knew she could no longer see him.

He had been fond of Elsie. She was a nice old woman and she had been good to him. He felt sad that her friends would find her with her hair mussed and without the make-up she always wore when company was coming. He went into her bedroom and found her purse. It contained a small make-up case. He brought the case back into the kitchen and applied the lipstick and eye shadow to the cooling flesh. Then, on impulse, he took a paring knife from the drawer and traced a cross on her chest. He did it lightly, so as not to hurt her.

By the time Elsie's body was discovered, Willie was settled in a rooming house in Toronto. The case was solved quickly. Folks in Myron knew that the young man Elsie had hired was on his way to Toronto. Willie did not attempt to hide his whereabouts, unaware that he had anything to hide. When he was picked up in a drug bust in an after-hours club he was quickly identified as the Clown Killer.

He did not attempt to defend himself. When he was shown photographs of Elsie's body and told he had killed her, he refused to believe it. He knew vaguely that something not quite right had happened in Myron. But he also knew that never, in his entire life, had he physically harmed another human being.

The court-appointed lawyer made much of his non-violent past, adding the further insurance of pointing out that he was not capable of telling right from wrong because he had been under the influence of drugs, for which he needed treatment, not incarceration with hardened criminals.

Clean-shaven and with hair cut short, wearing slacks and a sports shirt, Willie looked like the model kid on the block. It seemed incomprehensible that such a quiet, well-spoken young man could have committed an act of violence as gross as that with which he was charged. He was placed on probation and enrolled in a drug program. The newspaper clippings ended with his trial.

Sylvia turned to the back of the folder where additional information was noted as acquired. There, in Craig's strong handwriting, she found Willie's full name — William Stanley Alexander Stoneham — followed by two addresses, the first crossed out, and a short list of the jobs he had held. She closed the folder and put it back in the cabinet. If Joe Parsons wanted information from the file, he would have to get it from David.

She switched off the lamp and went upstairs. David was sound asleep on his stomach, one arm hanging over the edge of the bed. She opened the window, thinking it was almost spring and before they knew it the pool would be open and the flowers would be blooming in the garden.

Parsons phoned David at nine sharp the next morning. When David arrived at the office at ten-thirty his message was lying on top of the pile with URGENT printed across it in capital letters. Always co-operative with the press, David phoned back immediately. Joe answered immediately. David guessed, correctly, that he had been sitting by the phone waiting for the call.

As he had done with Sylvia, Parsons started off with Jim Henry. Like Sylvia, David was surprised. 'How did you know Kevin McGregor was Jim Henry?'

Joe told him about the photographs.

'How many people have you told?'

Feeling defensive without quite knowing why, Joe said, 'No one. Outside of the family.'

'Does Mary know?'

'Yes. And one of the guards at Kingston. But I didn't tell him. Henry did. He wrote to him after he got settled. They were pretty close.'

David swore under his breath. Joe felt guilty, as though he had done something wrong. To right the balance, he said, 'That committee that was working for him . . . they knew, didn't they?'

'Yes, damn it. But we agreed to keep it quiet to protect Mary and the children. Now she's got nothing left. Not even a decent memory.' David's voice was bitter.

'The committee, is it still together?'

'We still see each other, if that's what you mean,' David snapped. 'We spent a lot of time together. We cared about Jim. We'd like to see whoever did this caught.'

'So would I,' Joe assured him. It was true, although he didn't care two pins about Jim Henry. He wanted the story, the break in the case. In an effort to mollify David who was obviously annoyed with him for having spoken to Mary, he outlined his trips to Ottawa and Kingston.

David listened, then said, 'It doesn't look good, does it?'

'That's what I thought, too. Until last night.' He dangled the bait. David bit. 'You've got a suspect?'

'No. But I've got the next best thing.'

David waited. When Joe said nothing he prompted: 'What is it, for God's sake?'

'No one's come up with a motive for McGregor's death. So the motive had to have something to do with Jim Henry. Right?'

'Maybe.'

'The other day a kid was killed here in Toronto. He had pencils in his eyes.'

He could hear David breathing in short, heavy gasps. 'The Clown Killer!' His voice crackled with excitement. 'You think there's a connection?'

'I don't know. But it's a weird coincidence.'

'Have you talked to anyone about this?'

'No. I want to do a little more checking first. It sounds so crazy no one will believe it unless there's something a little more solid to go on.'

'Aside from the pencils, are there other similarities?'

'That's why I wanted to talk to you. Can you tell me where the original murder took place? And when?'

'Near London. In Myron, I think. And it was, let's see, three or four years ago.'

'Okay. That's all I need.' Joe hung up the phone. It rang back before he had time to check his M drawer.

'What are you going to do?' David asked.

'Check my files.'

'We'll have to get more information on the boy. Some of the details.' Joe noticed that David had counted himself in.

'Well, there's the pencils. The make-up. And the hair. I've got a couple of contacts downtown checking to see if there's anything else.'

'I have an "in" with Homicide,' David added. 'I'll give him a call. He owes me.'

David called back shortly before lunch. He was jubilant. 'I've got it. Everything. Even a couple of things no one knows except Homicide.'

'Such as?'

'Listen,' David said, 'We can't do this properly on the phone. Why don't we get together and compare notes? Did you find your file?'

'Yes. It's the same kid all right.'

'How about bringing what you've got out to the house?'

'Sure. If you've got time.' Joe knew David was one of the busiest lawyers in the city. The suggestion came as a surprise.

'I'll *make* the time.'

David arrived at the house with just enough time to give Sylvia an idea of what was happening. She said she was sorry she had arranged to meet Anne downtown. She would have enjoyed sitting in with them; it all sounded very exciting. David promised to fill her in later if they came up with anything significant. He was unusually animated. She thought how boyish he could be when he was caught up in something he was really interested in.

He went directly to the study and when Parsons drove up a few minutes later Sylvia let him in and got him settled with David. She asked if she could bring them anything before she left and when they said no she closed the door quietly and went off to meet Anne.

David had pulled his Myron file and Joe spread his material out next to it for easy comparison. Aside from a few early local clippings that Joe had managed to get through friends on out-of-town papers the material was basically the same. Joe did not have the post-trial information Craig had supplied, but he had everything else. When they had checked through both folders, Joe asked David what he'd learned about the current case.

'It's pretty much as you said. Looks like an exact copy. The make-up. Even the cross on his chest.'

'And the pencils. That's what twigged me.'

'Right. And here's what really ties it up. They were new pencils. The killer had them with him. At least, that's what they think downtown. They were brand new, but they were whittled down and the points were broken off. So whoever did it knew just as much about those pencils as Stoneham did. Probably more, because the kid was really out of it when it all happened with Elsie.'

'If he took the pencils with him. . . .'

David second-guessed him. 'No. They're the kind you can buy anywhere. Not a prayer.'

'Fingerprints?'

David shook his head. 'None aside from Willie's.'

'Nothing left behind? No clues?'

They stared at each other, wheels turning. David was first to break the silence. 'No clues. Chances of that happening are bloody rare. I was just thinking of Jim and Stoneham. Do you think there's a chance the others are tied in?'

'Yes, I do,' Joe said quietly. 'Maybe not all, but some.'

'But who? Why?'

'I don't know. Maybe some kind of vigilante group. Like the block patrols in the States.'

'But Canadians aren't the type.'

'That's changing,' Joe said. 'People are getting fed up. You get guys let out on pass, free to do whatever the hell they like; it doesn't sit too good when they bust somebody in the head and walk away as free as a bird.'

'People are getting together in groups more than they used to,' David said thoughtfully. 'Like that women's group in Vancouver. They're actually busting up porn shops.'

'So we have a bunch of angry people who've decided to take the law into their own hands. To get these guys off the streets.'

'There's more to it than that,' David mused. 'Most of the

killings looked as though they were sexually motivated. Yet the victims weren't homosexual. The police checked and they came up clean. So if we do have a series of duplicate murders on our hands. . . .'

'The victims were involved in some form of violence against women?' Joe looked dubious.

'Exactly. Jim was accused of murdering a little girl. Stoneham killed an old woman because she looked at him when he was spaced out. It adds up.'

'It could be mere chance.'

'It could be. But that's what we're going to find out.'

'Us?' Joe stared at David. 'How?'

'By going through every one of these cases. If the victims have a criminal record, or if sometime in their past they did to someone what was eventually done to them, that's it. We'll know we're on the right track.'

'Why not let Bretz handle it? He's in charge of the investigation.'

'At this point we'd be laughed out of court. If we jump the gun and we're wrong Bretz will make both of us look like fools. Anyway,' he added, 'we'll have a hell of a time.' His black eyes glittered.

They stared at each other, their minds racing. They were near-strangers, two men with only one thing in common. But that single common interest had brought them together as a team.

Anne and Sylvia had lunch at the Silver Rail, across the street from the Eaton Centre. They planned to spend the afternoon shopping at the Centre, a busy, people-packed super mall that Sylvia normally avoided. She had agreed to the trip when Anne assured her that during the week, and off-season with tourists at a minimum, they would practically have the place to themselves. Sylvia doubted it, and was determined to stretch their luncheon as long as possible.

She had a salad and soda water. Anne had the Sea Tangle with gin and tonic.

'You shouldn't drink liquor with seafood,' Sylvia admonished. 'You're liable to fall on the floor in a fit.'

Anne looked stunning. Her short dark hair shone with vitality.

She was wearing a light winter white wool suit and creamy silk blouse with a brilliant yellow and crimson scarf. Her smooth skin was deeply tanned from a trip she had just taken with Bill. She ignored the warning about liquor and seafood. Life's little annoyances, allergies included, were not part of her game plan.

'How's Bill?'

'Gorgeous. Like the car people say — the more you see, the more you like.' She grinned. 'How're things with you?'

'Boring.'

'Then you didn't. I didn't think you would.' She sawed at the thick, crusty bread.

'Didn't what?' Sylvia asked.

'Get it on with Craig Faron. You sure as hell wouldn't be bored if you were getting it on with him.'

'You're incorrigible. Don't you ever think about anything else?'

'Not lately,' Anne said. 'How's David?'

'Having the time of his life. I left him at home with a reporter. They're like two kids playing cops-and-robbers.' Sylvia explained about Jim Henry and the phone call the night before and how Parsons and David were going through their files looking for a clue to the recent rash of murders.

'The male strikes?' Anne's grin was wicked. 'They expect to track the killer through a bunch of files? Good luck to them.'

'Well, at least it's given him something to think about besides those clients of his.'

'You're not getting along too well, are you?' Anne's direct gaze was disconcerting.

'As well as anyone who's been married as long as we have. He goes his way. I go mine. It's not a bad arrangement.'

'For Christ's sake, Sylvia, there's a lot more to life than a "not bad arrangement." I saw the way you and that sexy hunk looked at each other. God, if you can't go that route, which is the one I'd recommend, why don't you drag David off for a weekend at that sex farm, Happy Acres, or whatever the hell it's called.'

Sylvia exploded into laughter. The thought of David running around naked in a room full of people engaged in group sex was so comical she laughed until tears streamed down her face. Anne, afraid she would choke, rushed around the table and thumped her on the back. The solicitous head waitress, one of the best in the city according to David, hurried to the table with a pitcher of ice water to refill her glass. Finally, laughed out, Sylvia wiped her eyes and told Anne that the sex farm had been raided and closed down.

'You're kidding. What the hell business is it of the police? Did someone complain?'

'I don't think so. The locals didn't seem to mind. They seemed to feel it upgraded the area.'

'So what were they charged with?'

'Everything but the kitchen sink. Including keeping a common bawdy house.'

'Were the women prostitutes?'

'Oh no. There were some singles, but a lot of married couples, too. And they were doing it for fun, not money. Recreational sex, they called it.'

'You can't have a bawdy house without prostitutes. And you don't have prostitutes unless you have women selling themselves. I don't understand.'

'I don't either. But that's the way it is. And that's what happened.'

'Jesus Christ, this fucking country is getting more hypocritical every day.' Anne finished her drink and waved for a refill. 'Whatever happened to that large L liberal sentiment that consenting adults are free to do whatever they like in private?'

'I guess this just wasn't private enough.'

Disgusted, Anne said, 'The whole goddamned thing is out of whack. The cops are paid to protect people. The city is full of hoodlums and vandals. And people minding their own business, bothering no one, get it in the neck.'

'We're a very moral society, Mrs. Campbell.' Sylvia's grey eyes sparkled with amusement. 'I heard David say once that there's an old law, still on the books, that only the missionary position is legal in Canada.'

'What the hell position is that?'

'Flat on your back, of course.'

'God.' Anne speared a hunk of crust and chewed savagely. 'Okay. So the sex farm is out. What about a marriage counselor?'

'Anne, for heaven's sake, we're fine. We don't need anything like that.'

'You're almost like strangers. I remember how close you were. I envied you.'

'People change. It's true I don't feel the same way. I used to think David was the most wonderful person in the world. I had a tremendous amount of respect for him. For his integrity, his ideals.'

'And now you haven't?'

'It's not the same. It's not David's fault. It's just the way things are.'

'You're not making sense, Syl.'

'I thought it was terrific that David wanted to be a lawyer. I was really proud of him. Remember the woman up north that killed her husband? David got her off.'

'He's still getting people off,' Anne said dryly.

'I know. That's what bothers me. He's getting a lot of people off who should be locked up.'

'But Syl, that's his job.'

'It just doesn't seem right. It almost makes him an accomplice.'

'Have you discussed this with him?'

'Not lately. I know what he'd say: "Our courts function on the adversary system. Every man is entitled to the best possible defense. We are all innocent until proven guilty. Better a hundred guilty men should go free than that one who is innocent be made to suffer. The judicial process may not be perfect but it is the best we have to work with." And on and on, ad infinitum. I've heard it all a hundred times.'

'But it's all true.'

'But it isn't true. It's bunk. We've been sold a bill of goods. We're so programed that we accept these clichés without even thinking about them.'

'I know it's a stinking mess, Syl. But you can't hold David responsible.'

'Why not? He's a part of it. Did I ever tell you about Andy Fisk?'

Fisk was a young auto mechanic who had two interests in life: cars and rape. He was first accused of indecent assault when he molested a child he was baby-sitting. Being a juvenile, he was released into the custody of his family. By the time he was twenty he had been accused of rape by five different girls. All of the charges were withdrawn when the girls were made to realize that they would be subjected to more judicial and public pressure than the accused. It wasn't until Fisk raped a young mother in her home, in front of her children, that he was actually brought to trial. His family engaged David to handle the defense.

Anne listened intently, her dark eyes flat and beady.

'They came to the house. I don't know why. David would never allow it now. We were living in the Beaches.'

'That skinny old house with the creepy attic?'

'Yes. David had an office in the basement. Right under the living room. They were on the same heat register. And I could hear every word. They all knew he was guilty. His parents. David. He actually sat there and told David about the other girls. And he said there were a couple of dozen others that hadn't complained. He laughed. I couldn't believe how cocky he was.

'David said to forget about the others — they weren't relevant. His mother was afraid that if one of the girls came forward it would make it bad, but David said that wouldn't happen; all they had to worry about was the case at hand. Would you believe he told him what to wear? How to act. Said his attitude would carry as much weight with the jury as the actual testimony, for God's sake not to be arrogant or smart-alecky. I couldn't believe it.'

'What happened?'

'He was acquitted. On a legal technicality. Something that had nothing to do with the fact that he had beaten the woman to a pulp, traumatized the children and ruined the marriage. The woman's husband eventually divorced her. He said he couldn't get the memory of it out of his mind.'

'The lousy sonofabitch.'

'Well anyway, I've never felt quite the same way about David. I was naive enough to think that a lawyer has a debt to society as well as to his client. Innocent until proven guilty. I took that seriously. I still do.'

'But David believes that too.'

'No. To David, "proven guilty" means proven in a court of law. It has nothing to do with guilt or innocence. The whole thing is a game. It's worse than a game. It's a bad joke on all of us.'

'So what do you think David should do? Refuse to handle someone like Fisk? That wouldn't change anything.'

'I expect him to show as much concern for society as he does for the people who pay him. Andy Fisk is a good example. He should have been sent somewhere for treatment, not put back on the street. And he should have received some type of punishment. Can you imagine what would happen in a family if one child knew he could bully and terrorize the others as much as he wanted to? Never reprimanded? Just given carte blanche to do whatever he wanted to do, whenever he wanted to do it? It would be sheer hell.'

'I don't think men look at it that way, Syl. Women tend to see society as an extension of the family. I think men see the family as a unit of society. A completely different point of view.'

'Then we need more women out there making decisions.'

Anne sniffed. 'A lot of good that would do. Women at the top tend to join the system, not fight it. And remember, Syl, some of the best rape lawyers *are* women. They're probably making a killing.'

'In more ways than one,' Sylvia said in a tight, hard voice.

'Maybe you should get involved, Syl, instead of spending so much time at home, just letting it all go by.'

Sylvia's smoky eyes were the color of cold gray slate. 'I'm as involved as I want to be, Annie. Come on. Let's go shopping.'

They jaywalked through traffic and stepped into wall-to-wall people in the Centre. Anne selected some items in Eaton's designer shops and Sylvia, determined to buy something, picked up a bathing suit in the South Shop and an expensive set of coordinates in Jaeger's. When they finished their personal shopping, Anne dragged Sylvia off to the chocolate shop where she spent a small fortune on chocolates for Bill.

Sylvia was exhausted, but Anne had one more stop to make. She took Sylvia's arm and led her to an ice-cream shop, explaining, 'I never leave here without a sundae. They're the best in the city.'

Worn to a frazzle, Sylvia welcomed the opportunity to sit down for a few minutes, away from the shoving crowds in the mall. She was not an ice-cream buff, had never been in the shop that Anne described as one of her favorites. She had a scoop of vanilla ice-cream and Anne had a towering sundae smothered in three different syrups and mounds of fresh fruit.

She spooned a maraschino cherry from the crest of whipped cream. 'This is terrific,' she said. Then, so deliberately casual that Sylvia knew it was the reason behind the ice-cream stop, 'Tell me about Craig Faron, Sylvia.'

Sylvia knew the question was prompted by concern, not prurient curiosity. 'Anne, he's a friend of David's. He travels a lot. He bird-dogs for David occasionally. What else can I say?'

'Do you see a lot of him?'

'More than I used to.' Anne brightened. Sylvia hastened to explain. 'We're working on David's files. You know how much stuff he's got. He's decided to put it all on computer. He'll decide what's going to go in but he can't do that until we've got the records in shape.'

'I hope it's going to take a long time. A bit of excitement will do you good.'

'Excitement? Filing?'

'I wasn't thinking of the filing,' Anne said pointedly. 'You should let your hair down. David doesn't have to know. He probably wouldn't even care as long as his friends didn't find out. Times have changed, Syl. Chastity belts are out of style.'

'You don't understand.'

'I do understand. I understand that you're letting the best years of your life slip away because of some goofy idea of morality that no one else gives two hoots about. You need a damn good shaking.' She stopped, out of breath.

Sylvia picked up the check. 'I think it's time to go.' She didn't try to explain, didn't try to tell Anne that she did live by a code of ethics, as did Craig Faron, but that code had nothing to do with the standards imposed by society. More important than the moral climate that adapted, chameleon-like, to the majority view was the small inner voice, the inward monitor that set her course.

She did not think of herself as either moral or immoral. And neither, she knew, did Craig Faron.

10

March 1985

Joe transferred the required files to a portable case and drove back to the Jennings' house the next morning. He and David set up a master work plan, with sub sheets in duplicate for each of the victims. The names on the sheets were Arthur Maitland, Jay Smith, Roly Burns, Nat Berger (the married man with three daughters), Robert Willard aka Bottle Bob, Buddy Thompson, Keith Hallworth, Willie Stoneham and Kevin McGregor aka Jim Henry. The task seemed formidable.

'This is going to take a helluva long time,' Joe complained.

'Depends. We know about Willie and Jim. That just leaves seven. If we were a month down the road all we'd have to do is punch it up on the computer.' He told Joe about the Prime while he pulled out the files he needed. Joe was interested, but more concerned about the task at hand. He looked at the twin stacks of files, his at one end of the desk and David's at the other, and said, 'There's something about this that bothers me. If we're right, how come Bretz hasn't got it figured? They must know all there is to know about these guys.'

David shrugged. 'They've been up to their necks. They could be so busy trying to keep up with what's happening now that they haven't had time to dig into the past. And don't forget, if it hadn't been for the Clown and Jim Henry, the combination, you wouldn't have thought of it, either. Jim was killed in St. Catharines. Bretz is strictly Metro.'

'But good God, David, the man knows what's going on. It doesn't make sense.'

David shoved a set of duplicates across the desk and said, 'Maybe you're right. But let's take a run at it, anyway.'

They worked quietly, each checking his own files, making notes on their work sheets. It took less time than they had anticipated. When they finished they shoved the files to one side and compared what they had. David called off the names from the master sheet:

'Jim Henry.' He put a check mark beside the name.

'Willie Stoneham.' Another check mark.

'Jay Smith.' Joe had nothing on him. David's file contained a report from Craig: 'A juvenile. No record. Questioned in the death of a seventeen-year-old student, bludgeoned with a fence post. Smith a prime suspect. No charges laid because of insufficient evidence.' A check mark for Jay.

'Roly Burns.' Joe contributed: 'Guilty of second degree murder in the death by strangulation of a prostitute. Sentenced to life imprisonment.'

David added, 'Served twelve years. Released on parole. Considered rehabilitated.' Another check mark.

'Nat Berger.' Neither had a file on Mr. Berger. No check mark.

'Robert Willard.' From Joe's file: 'Guilty of second degree murder for the sex slaying of a ten-year-old girl. Sentenced to life.' From David's file: 'A history of child molesting revealed at trial. No previous charges. Served ten years. On parole.' A tick for Bottle Bob.

'Arthur Maitland.' Nothing from Joe. David didn't have a file on Maitland, either. He thought of mentioning the rape case, decided the acquittal made it irrelevant. No check mark.

'Buddy Thompson.' Again, Joe had nothing. But David had a complete report, compiled by Craig: 'Sentenced to life for armed robbery. Spent first two years in and out of solitary. Released on mandatory supervision after seven years.'

'Armed robbery, hell,' Joe said.

David held up his hand. 'There's more. After his release he was picked up for questioning in a murder. A young woman who was found in a field after being picked up in a bar by Buddy. It was the night after he was released. He wasn't charged. They still haven't found her killer. P.S.' — he paused for effect — 'Her throat was slashed from ear to ear.' Another tick.

'Keith Hallworth.' They looked at each other, puzzled. Neither had files on Hallworth. Both felt it inconceivable that he had ever been in trouble with the law.

David picked up the list and studied it. 'How does it shape up?' Joe asked.

'They all check out but Hallworth and Maitland.'

'And Smith and Thompson — maybe, maybe not. It's not exactly conclusive.'

'But it could be. And this also explains why no one else seems to have come up with the copycat theory. Neither Smith nor Thompson was actually charged with murder. No way of Bretz knowing.'

'Hallworth's the monkey wrench,' Joe said. 'That scene was right off the wall. I still can't figure it. I think if we could tie in Maitland and Hallworth we'd have it together.'

'All right. Suppose you take Hallworth and I take Maitland. We dig around. See what we can come up with. And if we find anything, even a whisper, we turn it over.'

'And I write my story.'

'Agreed.'

The Maitlands still lived in Stratford, where Arthur had grown up and attended school. When David called and asked if he could drop in for a visit they agreed readily, saying their home would always be open to the man who had done such a fine job of defending their son.

They were an attractive couple, still in shock over Arthur's death. 'He never should have left home,' Mrs. Maitland confided, tears brimming. 'He was our only child. We wanted to do so much for him. Dad was heartbroken when he decided not to go on to university.'

Dad, a mild-mannered man who sat beside his wife as quietly as a well-behaved child, said nothing.

'Did he have many friends?'

'Not too many. He wasn't like some young people, willing to take up with anyone. He was very choosy about the people he associated with.'

'Did he have many girl friends?'

'He could have had any girl he wanted. They threw themselves at him. But he could see them for what they were. Ready to go to bed with the first man who asked. Girls aren't what they were in my day.'

'Was there anyone he seemed to like more than the others?'

'No one he really cared about. Oh, they'd phone and pester him and he'd go out on a couple of dates sometimes, but he was wise to them. Always cut it off before it got too serious. First thing we'd know they'd stop coming around and we'd never hear from them again.'

'What about older women?'

'There was Selma May,' Mr Maitland said. David had almost forgotten he was in the room. Mrs. Maitland turned a dark red. 'They hardly knew each other,' she said in a quick, it's-not-worth-mentioning voice.

'He spent a lot of time at her house. She was very good to him.'

Mrs. Maitland smoothed her skirt with nervous, fluttering hands.

'Perhaps I could talk to her,' David ventured.

Mrs. Maitland looked at her husband, then at David. 'That's not possible.' She turned back to Mr. Maitland. 'Dad, why don't you fix us a nice pot of tea?'

He rose obediently and started toward the kitchen. He paused in the doorway and without turning around, as though speaking to someone in the kitchen rather than the living room, he said in a very quiet, even voice, 'Selma May is dead.'

David stared at the kitchen door. Mrs. Maitland fidgeted. When she realized the subject was there, it wouldn't go away, she said, 'It was horrible. The poor woman. I told Arthur she was loose. She would come to a bad end. All those young men who used to hang around her house. Like a Queen Bee, she was.'

Mr. Maitland appeared with the tea tray. 'She was all right, Mother,' he said mildly. 'I always liked Selma May. Lonely she was, after her husband died. Just lonely. And friendly, is all.'

'What happened to her?'

'Had her throat slit.' The mildness of his voice made it sound as though she'd had her appendix out or a tooth filled.

Mrs. Maitland's voice wasn't the least bit mild. 'Our poor baby. He took it very hard. He left home not long after. I'll always blame Selma May for that.'

'Do they know who did it?' David's throat was so dry he could hardly get the words out.

'Oh yes. It was one of the boys who was always over there. They caught him the next day. On his way to Calgary, he was. Everybody knew he did it.'

David shifted to the edge of his chair. 'Did he confess?'

'Of course not. You wouldn't expect him to admit it. They never do, do they?'

'Where is he now?'

'In Kingston. Ray Foster. Always was a wild one. Broken home, and all.'

For the rest of the visit David felt like a runner held at the starting gate. While they drank their tea, Mrs. Maitland produced photographs of Arthur that she kept in a large cardboard box. Arthur as a baby in his crib. Arthur as a first-grader in a bright yellow raincoat with a hood. Arthur as a teenager in tennis shorts and sneakers. Mrs. Maitland was not in the pictures; her hand had held the camera. But the feel of her was there, as though she stood in the background, just out of focus.

David was anxious to get away but she insisted he see Arthur's room before leaving. It was still furnished as it was on the day he left home. There was a poster of the Beatles on one wall and a framed photo of Arthur and his father on a fishing trip. It felt as though whoever lived in the room would be back any minute. It was a bright, sunny room atrophied by death.

David was glad to get out of the house and away from Mrs. Maitland. He wondered if Arthur had felt the same sense of freedom the day he set out to start a new life in the city. He had intended to be home before dark but as he neared the city he decided to stay on the highway and drive straight through to Kingston. He called Sylvia and the office and picked up some coffee and pre-fab sandwiches to eat in the car. It was late and he was very tired by the time he got to Kingston.

As he got ready for bed he thought about Sylvia and hoped she would be all right.

Sylvia felt a twinge of annoyance that David hadn't told her earlier he intended to be out of town overnight. She replaced the phone and was trying to decide whether or not she should telephone Anne when Joe Parsons called. When she told him David was out of town, he said he needed a piece of information, hesitated, then asked if it would be an inconvenience if he came over to check the files. Glad of the company, knowing he would busy himself in the study and be no bother, she told him he was free to come if he wished.

He arrived a couple of hours later, rumpled and untidy, and she thought what a strange pair he and David made: David always meticulous about his appearance, Joe in a perpetual state of disarray. He went directly to the den and Sylvia settled down to watch TV.

It was after ten when the phone rang. Sylvia expected it to be David, calling to say he had arrived safely. It wasn't David. It was the voice. A voice she had heard a number of times over the past few weeks. A voice that always asked the same question. 'Is Mr. Jenning at home?' Always before, he had been. She had answered in the affirmative. The caller had hung up. Automatically, the answer simultaneous with the flash of recognition, she said, 'I'm sorry. He's out of town.' She could have kicked herself the moment she said it.

'Really?' The voice was smooth, polite. 'You don't remember me, do you Sylvia?'

The sudden familiarity caught her off guard. He mentioned a name that was unfamiliar to her, said they had met at a party and they had mutual friends. He was sorry she didn't remember him because he had enjoyed her company so much; he had felt a special rapport between them. She thought back, tried to remember, drew a blank. His voice became lower, smoother. It took on a strange rhythm, an almost hypnotic intonation. 'I'm part Indian, you know. Most people don't realize it, but I am. You like Indians. You told me so. You feel Indians have had a hard time in Canada. I like that. It shows you care.'

It was true. She did empathize with Canada's native people, felt a pang of guilt over the shabby treatment they received. But the only Indian she could think of was the soft-eyed young boy who worked in the shop where she bought her fruit and vegetables. He spoke only in monosyllables, bashful and tongue-tied.

The voice was a steady chant in her ear. 'I like blonds, Sylvia. I like white women with blonde hair.' A quickening of cadence. Sibilant. Soughing. 'Do you know what I do to white women with blond hair? Tell me, Sylvia. Tell me what you think I do to white women. Women like you.'

Cold, icy fear gripped her body. She wanted to stop listening, to hang up the phone and run from the house, but she couldn't move. The hand holding the phone began to tremble. The voice echoed, re-echoed in her ear. 'Indians scalp pretty blond women like you, Sylvia. I will scalp your cunt and show it to my friends. I will. . . . ' Sylvia screamed then, and dropped the phone. Parsons came running from the den. Sylvia stared at him in mute terror. She had forgotten he was in the house.

He saw her eyes, saw the dangling phone, guessed what had happened. He poured whiskey straight from the bottle he had brought with him, stood with his arm around her while she drank it. He waited until the trembling stopped, then asked her what the caller had said. When she finished he said, 'Do you think it's true that you met him somewhere?'

'No. Not the way he said. I would have remembered.' She told him about the boy in the vegetable shop. A nice boy. He was the only Indian she had met in Toronto. It wasn't him. It couldn't be.

'I wouldn't worry about it,' Joe said finally. She knew he was trying to reassure her. He continued, 'People who make phone calls don't usually get up to much. They're upsetting but pretty harmless.'

She started shaking again. Joe moved over beside her and put his arm around her awkwardly. 'Could you stay here tonight?' Sylvia asked.

'Sure. I don't have to be anywhere. I planned to work here for quite awhile, anyway.'

Joe stayed with her until she told him there was no longer any need. Later she went upstairs and got pillows and blankets. She fixed a couch for him on one side of the living room and another for herself in front of the fireplace. They both slept with their clothes on. In the morning they were stiff and cramped.

Sylvia, who had slept fitfully, got up first. After showering she plugged in the coffee pot, then shook Joe awake. He, too, had a shower. When he came downstairs he looked just as untidy as he had when he went up.

Over breakfast of bacon and eggs, Sylvia apologized for acting like a neurotic spinster. Joe, who had treated the situation lightly the night before in an effort to calm her down, now told her the call should be reported to the police.

'Do you think it was an Indian?' he asked.

'No. I knew a lot of Indians up north. They may fight among themselves but I've never known them to do something like this. It's too cold-blooded. Too premeditated.'

Joe agreed with her. He had friends in the Six Nations, and had done a series of articles on reserves in B.C. He felt Canada's Indians had been underdogs too long to be capable of the indiscriminate violence endemic to whites and blacks.

To change the subject Sylvia asked, 'How are you doing with your investigation?'

'Too soon to tell. But I think we're on the right track.'

'David's in Kingston.'

'Oh? I thought he was in Stratford.'

'He was. But he phoned and said he was going on and would be home today.'

Joe looked puzzled. 'I wonder why. He's working on Maitland, the good-looking kid that had his throat slit.'

Sylvia's stomach tightened at the mention of Arthur's name. 'He *was* a nice looking young man,' she said. She couldn't think of anything else to say.

'Not when they found him. He was a mess.'

Sylvia changed the subject, not wanting to hear the details. They finished breakfast, chatting about the world in general and nothing in particular. She was surprised to find that Parsons, in spite of his rough edges and pushiness, was a sincere, likable man. But she also realized that, like David, once committed he would let nothing stand in his way.

He helped her with the dishes and left the house with a brown envelope of clippings. When he was gone, Sylvia drove round to 21 Division and reported the phone call. The officer on duty asked what she wanted him to do about it. She ignored the sarcasm in his voice. 'He gave me his name,' she lied, desperate for some kind of action, 'I'd like you to keep it on record, that's all. Then if something does happen to me you'll have some idea of where to look.'

'Lady, he wouldn't give you his right name.' He looked at her as though she were an imbecile let loose on a day pass.

'I know that. But it could give you a clue to his real name.'

The officer was working on a report. Without looking up, he said, 'These calls go on all the time. Report it to the Bell.'

'But he *threatened* me. I think he meant it.'

'Look, lady, we can't do anything until he does something. I'm sorry, but that's the way it is.'

Sylvia thought about smash-and-grab raids on Toronto's gay steambaths, the closing of the sex farm, the costly R.I.D.E.

program that deployed cruisers throughout the city to net drunk drivers.

She had asked for help. She was told to go tell it to a utility company. She left the station, frustrated and angry. And more than a little frightened.

Ray Foster was a tall, heavyset twenty-one-year-old with reddish blond hair and dark, deep-set eyes. He lumbered into the visiting room apprehensively, as though so accustomed to misfortune that anything out of the ordinary could only mean more bad news.

David explained who he was.

Foster said he knew him by reputation; he had heard some of the fellows talk about him. 'If I'd had you, Mr. Jenning, I wouldn't be in this fix.'

'That's what I wanted to talk to you about. Tell me about Selma May Roberts.'

Foster's face twitched. 'She was a friend. A good friend. I never would have hurt her.'

'Do you know who did?'

'I've thought about it a lot. I can't think who would want to. Not anybody who knew her.'

'She had a lot of boyfriends, didn't she?'

'Not that I know. People used to talk about her because she let a lot of the guys hang out there. But the things they said weren't true. She was like a mother to us. Stuff we couldn't talk about at home, we could talk to Selma May about.'

'What about Arthur Maitland?'

Foster looked blank. 'What about him?'

'Could he have been involved?'

'In Selma's death? I don't think so. He was a real mama's boy.'

'You didn't think much of him?'

'I didn't think about him at all. He was always hanging around, but he didn't say much.'

'Did you kill her, Ray?' The question was deliberately blunt, designed to circumvent a glib answer.

'I swear to God I didn't.'

David relaxed. 'I believe you. Did you know Maitland is dead? It happened last summer. He was found nude, with his throat slit.'

'Wow. Who did it?'

'That's what we're trying to find out. We think there's a connection between his death and Selma's.'

Foster frowned, thinking hard.

'I defended him in a rape case.'

'Arthur Maitland?' His expression registered total disbelief. David nodded.

Foster scratched his nose with his thumbnail. 'He was strange,' he said at last, 'but I wouldn't have pegged him for anything like that. He was like a puppy. Trailed behind Selma everywhere. He . . . .' A strange look came over his face.

David felt he had hit on something significant. 'You just thought of something?' he prompted.

'There was once. . . . '

'Go on.'

'Well, he was kind of jealous. Not like you'd be with a girl-friend or anything. More like he felt he owned her. And this one night, when all the guys were there and we were having a ball, I noticed he was sitting there looking funny. Kind of out of it. His eyes were glazed and weird. He was just staring. Right at Selma. Never said a word. But it sure was creepy.'

It was enough. Not conclusive, but enough. David looked at the boy, felt a rush of pity. 'Do you have a lawyer, Ray?' He hadn't felt this way since he was first starting out, when he took clients on the basis of need rather than ability to pay.

Foster shrugged. 'No. Not anymore.'

'Well you have now.'

'You?' He was close to tears. 'Mr. Jenning, I couldn't afford it.'

'Don't worry about it. One of my associates will be in touch.'

David was glad to get out of the cramped room, away from the heavy clanging doors. He knew Foster was innocent. He also knew that Arthur Maitland had killed Selma May. He wouldn't be able to prove it, but that didn't matter. The pattern was taking shape. One to go, and then they'd know.

Keith Hallworth was so well known, so much had been written about him, that Joe assumed his life would be an open book. But tracing his past turned out to be a much more difficult task than he had expected.

Hallworth had made a lot of money in a comparatively short period of time. Checking through the newspaper morgue, Joe found reams of information on his business activities and community projects. None of the items dealt with his early life. He had no criminal record. The family was not accessible. The organizations with which he had been associated refused to discuss him with a reporter. Joe was about to write him off as a negative when David provided a vital lead.

David was back from Kingston and had just finished telling Joe about his conversation with Foster. Joe admitted that he was about to throw in the towel on Hallworth. David commiserated, then asked, almost as an afterthought, if he had talked to Sylvia. Puzzled, Joe asked why.

'He came from Sudbury. I think at one time he worked for Inco.'

'I didn't come across that in any of the stuff I read.'

'It wasn't common knowledge. But it wasn't a secret, either. I guess it just wasn't as newsworthy as his later years.'

'Did Sylvia know him?'

'No. I didn't either. But I remember once when he was in the news she said something about him being a hometown boy who'd made good. I hadn't even known he was from Sudbury until then.'

David was right. Sylvia hadn't known Hallworth. All she could tell them was that he had some kind of foreign name which he had traded in for something a bit more Wasp-ish. She didn't know the family name but she felt it shouldn't be too difficult to trace.

The next morning Joe caught a plane to Sudbury. He took a cab from the airport and asked the driver if he'd ever heard of Keith Hallworth. The driver said no. Joe told him to take the shortest route to the *Sudbury Star*.

The *Star* staff was helpful. One of the girls from the front desk took him back to the morgue and he spent the entire morning going through microfilm. Nothing. He turned off the projector and rubbed his eyes. They were smarting from the fine print.

'Find what you want?' The librarian had been on her coffee break when he arrived. He was so deeply engrossed on her return that she had taken care not to disturb him. 'Did you find what you want?' she asked a second time.

'No.'

'Mary said she gave you everything we have on Mr. Hallworth.' Mary obviously was the girl at the front desk. 'What it is you're looking for?'

'His real name,' Joe said wearily.

'John Kolinski.' She said it as though it were common knowledge.

'My God.' Joe looked at her as though he didn't know whether to hug her or kick her. 'Why didn't you say so?'

'You didn't ask. Mary said you wanted everything we have on Hallworth. That's what you got.'

'Does the family still live here?'

'They do.'

'Do you have the address?'

She dug under a pile of papers on her desk and came up with a phone book. 'In here. Under K: Stephen Kolinski. They live somewhere in the Donovan.'

Joe had no idea what the Donovan was, but he found the address in the phone book and scribbled it on a piece of paper. After thanking her he hurried out of the building. There was a taxi stand on the corner. He grabbed a cab and gave the driver the address. A few minutes later he was there.

The house was a small frame bungalow with a glass porch at street level and a slope that fell away at the back. It looked deserted.

He handed the cabbie a bill telling him to wait in case there was no one at home. He knocked on the front door. A dog barked in the backyard. He continued to knock until, after what seemed a long time, the curtain was pulled aside and a wizened face peered through the edge of lace. He waved at the driver to leave and waited for the door to open. He thought of his trip to the Hollanders. Door-knocking was becoming something of an avocation.

Eventually the door inched open and a beady eye peered at him through the crack.

'Mrs. Kolinski?'

The eye stared at him suspiciously.

'I'd like to talk to you about your son.' It was the wrong thing to say. She tried to close the door. He pushed back, fingers curled around the edge. If she had enough strength to slam it shut she'd crush his fingers.

Unable to close the door, unwilling to open it, she said, 'Me no speak English.' It was her magic wand, the words that turned away salesmen, made communication impossible. But Joe Parsons was not a salesman.

'I want to talk about John.' He enunciated each word clearly, as though he were speaking to the deaf.

She relaxed her grip and he eased the door inward until there was enough space to sidle through. He stood over her, looking down into the dark, wrinkled face. She had a babushka tied round her head and knotted under her chin. Her dark, high-collared dress reached to her ankles and most of it was hidden under a huge white apron so stiff with starch that it crackled when she moved.

'I would like to talk to you about John,' he said again.

He stepped from the enclosed porch into a small, drab parlor. She darted ahead of him, feet hidden under the long skirt. 'Like a battery-operated Granny doll,' Joe thought. 'If I pull the string she'll say, "Me no speak English" and show me to the door.' He fought back an urge to laugh, to break out in mad, maniacal guffaws. The impulse, goofy and irrational, unnerved him. There was nothing funny about the situation.

Mrs. Kolinski's gutteral voice snapped him back. 'John gone,' she muttered.

Joe took three giant steps through the living room into the kitchen. It was brighter than the sunless parlor, the linoleum floor scrubbed and spotless, plants filling the windows that overlooked the sloping backyard.

Mrs. Kolinski's mechanical toy feet carried her past him in a smooth glide. She called out the back door and a stoop-shouldered figure stepped out of the shed in one corner of the yard. She beckoned and the man started toward the house, climbing laboriously up the crude steps hacked into the ravine-like slope.

'That bastard Hallworth,' Joe thought. 'He lived like a king. Probably never set foot in this house after he left.'

Mr. Kolinski came into the kitchen, and his wife spoke to him in a language Joe didn't understand. The man nodded. Watching him, Joe felt he must have been handsome when he was young. Even now, after years of back-breaking labor underground, his face showed a craggy, attractive strength.

'You know John?' His English was much better than his wife's.

'Yes. I wondered if you could tell me what he was like before . . . .'

Mr. Kolinski interrupted him. 'John was good boy.' He pointed to a built-in dishwasher next to the sink. It looked as though it had never been used. 'He send money. He buy big presents.'

The old woman stamped her foot and let loose a torrent of words. 'He give things. But he no come home,' Mr. Kolinski said.

'My son dead,' Mrs. Kolinski said. 'Twenty years my son dead. No more John.'

Mr. Kolinski was edging Joe back toward the door. In spite of the miner's stoop, he was big and muscular.

'Did he have any friends here? Is there anyone I can talk to?'

Mr. Kolinski continued his advance, forcing Joe back through the parlor, the sun porch, on to the street. The door slammed shut. Closed out, Joe stood on the walk wondering what to do next.

As he stood there, trying to decide which direction to take to find a public telephone, a plump woman with her arms full of groceries came up the street and turned into the house next door. She balanced one of the bags precariously on her knee while she fumbled for her keys. Sensing an opportunity, Joe walked over to her and offered to hold the bags. Her smile as she handed them to him was friendly.

'Have you lived here long?'

'Since I was married.'

'Do you know the Kolinskis?'

'Since I was married.'

'Did you know their son?'

'Since he was born.' She had the door open and was reaching for her groceries.

'I'll take them in,' Joe said quickly. He kept his fingers crossed while he waited for her to make up her mind. He breathed a sigh of relief when she stepped inside, leaving him to follow.

'What was he like?' He set the bags down on the kitchen counter.

'Very smart. Always into things. Couldn't sit still a minute. He always said he was going to be rich when he grew up. He was, you know, a very important man.'

'Did he ever come back to see his folks?'

'Once. Not long after he left. He was all dressed up. He had a big car. A Cadillac. Parked it right out there. Right in front of the house.'

'Mrs. Kolinski said he died twenty years ago.'

She laughed mirthlessly. 'She didn't mean he was *dead* dead. He changed his name. She never spoke to him again. As far as she was concerned, he *was* dead.'

'And now he is,' Joe said grimly.

'I know.' She looked sad.

'How old was he when he left?'

'Maybe twenty-two, twenty-three. He was working in the mine already.'

'Was he popular? With girls, I mean.'

'They were crazy about him. Always.'

'Was he ever in trouble over girls?'

'Oh no. A little bit wild. But always a real gentleman. My daughter went out with him once.' She sounded proud.

Joe felt he was headed nowhere.

'Would you like a glass of wine?' It was the best suggestion he'd heard all day.

She went down into the basement and came back with a bottle of homemade red. He took a sip and felt it warm, burning, all the way down.

'Do you have much trouble here? Violence, people getting beat up, that kind of thing?'

'Same as other places. Paydays it used to be bad. A lot of fights.'

'What about for women? Is it dangerous to be out alone at night?'

'Same as other places.'

'Would you remember maybe twenty, thirty years ago, a girl getting murdered? Her head beaten in?'

'We've had some like that. Mostly family fights.'

'This girl would have been raped. And gagged. With her underwear.'

'Maybe you mean little Pearl. The Bertrand girl. They found her up in the rocks. That one?'

Joe's heart pounded against his ribs. 'Can you tell me exactly what happened?'

'Little Pearlie.' She went back over it in her mind, staring into the glass of wine as though it were a crystal ball. 'She was a pretty little girl. My daughter knew her. Lived just a few streets over. She was working at Kresge's to earn enough money to go back to school and learn something better.'

'Yes?' Joe prompted.

'She was walking home from work and that's the last anyone seen of her.'

'Did they ever catch the man who did it?'

'No. They said it must of been some old tramp. They used to go up in the rocks and drink cheap wine. Never did catch anyone as I remember.'

Joe thanked her for the wine. He went back to the *Star* and asked the librarian for whatever she had on Pearl Bertrand. She remembered the murder, and the year it happened. He left with copies of the stories reporting the girl's death and the discovery of her body.

At the airport, waiting for his plane to load, he phoned David. 'We've got another one,' he said. 'Keith Hallworth used to be John Kolinski. I think he killed a girl with a tire iron, stuffed her panties in her mouth, and raped the body.'

The flight back was short and he slept all the way. He was light-headed from the wine and the good feeling of a mission accomplished.

That evening David and Joe were jubilant. The last two pieces of the puzzle were in place. Joe had taken a limousine from the airport and he and David were relaxing in the living room with a bottle of Scotch between them. Sylvia was with them, anxious to hear what Joe had found out about Hallworth. She listened as he told them about the Kolinskis, their neighbor, and little Pearl.

'But there's nothing to indicate Hallworth was responsible,' she pointed out.

'That's not the point, Syl. He was there. He must have known the girl. We're not trying to make a case against him. We're concerned with the possibility, not the probability.'

'David's right. It's *his* murder we're interested in, not Pearl's.'

'If you're right,' Sylvia said coldly, 'Pearl was the real victim, not Hallworth.'

Joe hadn't seen Sylvia since the night he stayed over. He

turned to her now and asked, 'Did you tell your husband about that phone call?'

David held his finger to his lips, warning Joe not to continue the conversation.

'He's called three times this week.' Sylvia said. 'Used to be maybe once or twice a month.'

'We've asked the phone company to install one of those gadgets,' David said. 'We'll get him.'

'As long as he doesn't get me first,' Sylvia said coolly.

Joe was surprised by her composure. Her terror the night of the call had been stark and overwhelming.

'That reminds me, David. What did you do with the gun?'

'You said you didn't want it around. I put it in the safe.'

'I've been thinking about it. It probably is a good idea, having it upstairs.'

She is worried, Joe thought. It doesn't show, but it's there.

Sylvia returned to the phone calls. 'As long as I tell him David is here, he hangs up.'

'Then so long as you keep on saying he's here, there shouldn't be a problem.' He looked relieved.

David did not want to discuss the phone calls in front of Sylvia. 'I think we're ready to go to the Attorney General, Joe.'

Persistent, Sylvia asked, 'And then what? They've been investigating these cases for months. What difference is it going to make?'

'The difference,' David said, relishing each word, 'is that now they can stop running around like chickens with their heads off and start looking for someone who has access to old records.'

'Do you think it's the same sort of thing as the Zebra murders in the States?'

Joe hadn't expected Sylvia to know about the Zebra killings. Aside from a wifely interest in David's career he would have imagined her to be more the food-and-fashion type. The Zebra slayings occurred in San Francisco during the early 1970's: twenty-three known assaults and murders in a six-month period. The victims were white. The perpetrators were black. White and black. Black and white. Zebra.

'I don't think so,' Joe said. 'That was a religious cult.'

'Kill nine white men, five women, or four children. Win your wings as an Angel of Death.' Sylvia recited it as though it were a children's nursery rhyme. Her lips curved in a strange half-smile, her gray eyes were a dark smoky slate.

Joe's skin prickled. David ignored her. 'I'm glad it's over,' he said. He turned to Sylvia. 'Now that we're finished with the files you and Craig will be able to get together with Gilbert and start coding.' Gilbert was the computer analyst. He had completed the space allotment for the office programs and had been kept on hold until David and Joe completed their search.

'If we ever have to do this again,' Joe said, 'it will be a breeze. All we'll have to do is punch buttons.'

'Don't expect miracles,' Sylvia warned. 'A system is only as current as its back-up. Before a computer can tell *you*, someone has to tell *it*. Isn't that true, David?'

Joe wrote his story the following morning. It appeared in the afternoon edition. The headline was a screamer:

MOTIVE IN MYSTERY MURDERS

and directly underneath, in bold type: by Joe Parsons, *Toronto Star*.

The front page story spilled over onto the second page of the first section. It listed the victims, gave their backgrounds, included information from both sets of files and credited David Jenning's records with providing key information, not listed in official reports, that helped provide the necessary link between some of the victims and crimes with which they had not been charged but of which they might have had knowledge.

Reaction to the article was immediate and pronounced. It caused a furor in the Ontario Legislature, sent the Police Commission into a spin and muddied the reputation of the Task Force. The media made much of the fact that a lawyer and reporter had accomplished more in a week than Bretz and his men had in eight months.

David was spending the afternoon at home to finalize the subheads and cross-indexed topic files that would make up the data base for his private material. He and Craig were with Gilbert discussing the amount of space required for the op system when the doorbell rang. Sylvia opened the door and found Superintendent Bretz and two companions on the step, faces grim, backs ramrod stiff. Even if she hadn't known Bretz she would have recognized all three as plainclothesmen.

'We called your husband's office and his secretary said he was at home. May we speak with him, Mrs. Jenning?'

She was amused by his attitude. Instead of simply asking for David, he had made a point of letting her know that he knew David was at home. She stepped back from the door. 'Come in. I'll see if he's free.'

They filed into the living room, with Bretz in the lead.

No, Bretz said, she needn't take their coats. And no, they wouldn't sit down, they preferred to stand. She left them in the middle of the living room, stiff and straight, and told David of their arrival, asking whether he would see them now, or should she try to get rid of them?

He replied that after Joe's story he'd been expecting a visit from Bretz, and he might as well get it over with.

He left her with Craig and Gilbert. A few moments later he called out to Craig and Sylvia to join them.

'The Superintendent is interested in our files,' he said. His eyes were twinkling and there was a smile in his voice.

'Oh no,' Craig said. The three men looked at him, faces set with determination.

Sylvia knew he was thinking of the neat rows of files being thrown back into disorder.

'Is there a problem?' Bretz asked. He was staring at Craig, his eyes, magnified by the heavy lenses, as large and round as those of an owl.

'Yes, there is,' Craig said curtly.

Bretz stiffened. He hadn't expected co-operation. Troublemakers, he thought. Ready to raise hell but not about to lift a finger to help.

David was enjoying the whole scene. He knew what an effort it must have been for Bretz to have to come to him, David Jenning, for information. The Superintendent looked cool, but he must be burning up inside.

Bretz turned from Craig to David. 'Do you have any objection, Mr. Jenning?' He was courteous. Meticulously polite. But each word was frosted with ice.

David didn't mind at all. He had, in fact, been looking forward to this moment. He was about to tell them so when Gilbert, a file in each hand, appeared in the doorway.

'Mr. Jenning,' he said, 'these two files aren't compatible. Do you intend to include victims as well as felons?'

Sylvia recognized the folders immediately.

Craig, with his back to Gilbert, knew intuitively what they were. He had intended to remove them from the files, to destroy them. He moved to Gilbert, reaching for the folders.

Puzzled, David said, 'What are they?'

'One is for a girl called Bertrand. The other is a Selma May Roberts. We're set up for felons. If you want victims too we'll have to go into another system. What it means . . . ' He kept talking, unaware of the effect he was having.

David was flabbergasted.

Craig was ashen.

Bretz and his men were attentive, not yet aware of the full implication of what Gilbert was saying but sensing its significance.

'On the other hand,' Gilbert continued, 'if we forget about Bertrand and Roberts and enter Maitland and Kolinski instead there'll be no problem.'

Craig reached him and seized the folders.

Bretz turned to David and said, 'Mr. Jenning, if you had this information on file, why didn't you come to us sooner? And why did Parsons make such a big thing of going to Sudbury, tracking the Kolinskis down, if you knew it all beforehand?'

David ignored the question. Dazed, speaking to no one in particular, he said, 'I don't understand. When we checked the other day, there was nothing there.'

And then he remembered that they had looked under Maitland and Hallworth. They hadn't even known about Selma May and Pearl until a few days ago.

11

Late March 1985

'Craig has been arrested.' David blew into the room like a whirlwind.

Sylvia looked up from the book she was reading, struggling to comprehend. The words didn't register. They were disconnected and senseless. Gibberish. Fugitives from a lunatic crossword puzzle.

'Sylvia, they're holding Craig downtown. They think he's responsible for the murders.' He was shaking her, trying to force comprehension.

The words came together. Formed phrases. Became a sentence. She felt struck out of the blue, like a victim of an earthquake or flood.

The phone was ringing. David was talking, shouting at someone. She came to her feet, felt dizzy, grasped the back of a chair for support. The room spun, tilted at crazy angles, closed in like a suffocating box. And then she passed through the turmoil into the quiet place, the long white room in her mind that was a vacuum, the eye at the heart of the hurricane.

David stormed back into the room, saw her unaffected, and misread her composure for shock. He poured a glass of brandy, gulped it down, refilled it and offered it to her. She pushed it away.

'I have to go,' he said distractedly.

'I'll come with you.'

'You know that's impossible.'

'I want to come with you.'

'You know that's impossible.'

'They can't keep him locked up. He'll go crazy.'

He was too busy stuffing papers into his briefcase to respond. She thought of Ciba the day she had put him in the cage: bleeding nails torn, eyes smoldering with a desperate need to be free. But Craig wasn't a mere cat. He was not even a run-of-the-mill, pedestrian human being. He was an act of nature. As well try to dam the ocean or screen the sun. She blocked David's path as he tried to leave. 'What happened? Has he been charged?'

'Sylvia, I don't know. All I know is they've picked him up. He left a message with Henny.' Thank God for Miss Henderson, the loyal secretary. 'They have him in interrogation. I have to get down there. Expect me when you see me. And don't discuss this with *anyone*. I don't care who it is. Not Joe Parsons. Not anyone.' He talked in short, sharp bursts. This was not the professional David, the calm, cool, collected David. He skirted her.

She heard the door slam, heard the squeal of tyres as he backed out of the drive, gunned the motor into instant high. The house, drained of his frenetic presence, was cold and still.

She went into the kitchen and made a pot of strong coffee. Poured it, thick as syrup, and drank it black. Thought of Bretz in the living room. Holding the folders. Looking at the information. The clippings. The typed notes. Heard David: 'I didn't know they were there.' Bretz: 'Then how did they get here?' Craig: 'I'm in charge of Mr. Jenning's files.' Herself, explaining that David sometimes used the files for reference but it was years since he'd worked on them, contributed anything; that Craig occasionally did investigative work, handled special assignments, but knew nothing about the files. They had ignored her, intent on the business at hand.

Later that evening they arrived with a search warrant. They were highly selective. They did not take all of the files, choosing only eight. They knew in advance which folders they wanted.

David was not surprised by their selectivity. The list, he assumed, was culled from Joe's newspaper article. But he was surprised when they asked for Nat Berger. There had been other murders during the past year. Why only Berger?

Sylvia made a second pot of coffee, drank it slowly as her mind sorted events, impressions, voices. David questioning Craig about the files. Sylvia telling him she had set them up months ago, forgotten about them; they had nothing to do with Craig.

Craig explaining how he had stumbled on the Hallworth story while he was up north. He was in Sudbury, he said. There for a week arranging supplies. Getting building materials and renting skidoos for the cabin. He was having a beer at the Frood Hotel.

There were men there who remembered Kolinski, who didn't like him. He had gone into minute detail until David, confused, had not known what to believe. And now, because of those files — it had to be because of those files, what else was there? — Craig was under arrest.

She heard a scrabbling at the door, followed by a sharp, imperious cry. It was Ciba, body humped on splayed legs. He had never before asked to be let in. She opened the door and picked him up. His green eyes were watchful, menacing, as though he sensed her concern. She held him close, feeling the warmth of his massive body. He growled, a low steady rumble that was more comforting than a contented purr.

'Don't worry,' she murmured. 'Everything is going to be all right.'

David expected to find Craig in a disheveled state. Instead, he looked as fresh as though he had just risen from a full night's sleep. In sharp contrast, the interrogation team looked as though they had lived in their clothes for days. Having picked Craig up late the previous evening and questioned him in relays throughout the night, they were rumpled, crumpled, bleary-eyed and snappish.

David was furious. 'Why in hell didn't you call me?' he roared.

The room was crawling with people. Alfred Bretz, who had made the arrest personally, snapped back, 'Ask him. . . . ' His head jerked toward Craig.

'I didn't want to disturb you, David,' Craig said quietly. 'What difference can a few hours make?'

'A hell of a lot of difference,' David grated. Slamming his briefcase on the table he thundered at Bretz, 'You know better than to pull a stunt like this.'

'We read him his rights. He could have called you. We told him he had the right to counsel.'

'I'm glad to hear it,' David said coldly. Then, sweeping the room with an icy stare, 'I'd like to speak with my client. Now. Alone.'

The Superintendent shrugged. He did not underestimate David's ability, but he despised the use of that ability. And Faron, that bastard, wasn't much better. Hours of grilling and they were no further ahead than when they picked him up. The arrogant sonofabitch. He was guilty as hell. Bretz knew it. His subordinates knew it.

Jenning or no Jenning, Craig Faron didn't have a snowball's chance in hell.

Joe Parsons heard the news sitting on the edge of his bed, one shoe off and one shoe on. He hobbled to the phone and called the newspaper. The city editor corroborated the story.

Although he didn't know Faron well, he found it difficult to believe he was the killer. He might act openly and take the consequences, Joe felt, but he didn't seem to be the type that would sneak around in the dead of night. He gave the impression of living by an inner code that, in times of conflict, would take precedence.

On the other hand, he was a handsome bugger. It was possible he was playing both sides of the street. Maybe he and David were out in left field. Maybe revenge wasn't the motive, after all. Maybe the rumors of gay bashing were on target. Homo-cide instead of homicide? Blackmail? Either way, you had to hand it to him. He was smooth as silk. Joe knew the boys-in-blue were far from infallible. Even if Faron was innocent, he was in one helluva spot. Bretz was a bulldog. His department was under siege, his neck was on the block. He had to have someone to clear the slate.

Sylvia changed into leotards and went downstairs to the gym. Ciba followed, tail thrashing. Under the deck, Prinnie peered through the basement window – almost invisible against the snow. Prinnie. Ciba. Ciba. Prinnie. Lares and penates. *Anima mundi. Bene, Benedicite, Benedictus*.

David was exasperated. 'They can't hold you without charging you,' he said again. He was beginning to sound like a broken record. 'Either they lay it out, or we walk.'

'David, you're not listening. I'm going to make a statement. I would have done it earlier but I wanted you to be here. It's important for you to be here.'

'A statement? You must be out of your mind. They haven't

even got enough to hold you and you're talking about making a statement. What in hell's been going on here? What have you told them?'

'Nothing.'

David breathed a sigh of relief. 'Then there's no problem.' He held up his hand, silencing Craig, who was about to speak. 'I don't want you to worry. Whatever they think they have, it's garbage. If they thought they could charge you, they would have done it by now. I'll put a man on every one of those dates. We'll prove you weren't around.' He shuffled through papers in his briefcase, pulled out the master list he and Joe had worked on. 'Buddy Thompson,' he said triumphantly. 'Right off the top, there's Thompson.'

'What about Thompson?' Craig's face was emotionless.

'That was the weekend you spent at the cabin. You wanted me and Sylvia to go with you.'

'David, leave it alone.' There was a sudden weariness in Craig's voice. 'The sooner Bretz gets what he wants, the easier it will be.'

'Easier?' David exploded. 'Easier for who? For you? They'll put you away for life. And for what?'

Craig shrugged it off. 'What's life? With time off for good behavior — a breeze.'

'If they nail you for this they'll throw away the key. I won't help you destroy yourself. I can't.'

Craig knew David well enough to know he was close to tears. The mocking grin faded. 'David, leave it alone. I know what I'm doing. It has to be this way.'

Their eyes locked, glinting blue steel against soft fathomless brown. Finally, his voice low, David said, 'You're my best friend. I care about you. Don't you think you owe me an explanation?'

The clock ticked, each tick, like dripping water, louder than the one before. Craig sat still as death. David waited. After a long, long time, Craig said, 'Bretz is convinced your files are involved.'

David relaxed, the worry lines smoothed into a smile. 'Is that all? Man, you had me worried. He's got his ass in a sling because we were one up on him.'

'Maybe it started out that way. But it's serious, David. You remember the two files you didn't know about?' He paused. 'It has something to do with them. I don't know what. But they found something that convinced them.'

'I don't give a goddamn what they think they found. If they wanted to arrest someone, why didn't they arrest me? They haven't a hope of making this stick.'

'That's right. So we're not going to fight it. You see, David, whatever it is they've got, they're convinced the killer was working from your files. If it wasn't me there's just one other person.'

Perspiration broke out on David's forehead. He felt sweat in his armpits, on the palms of his hands. When he could trust his voice he said, 'If you mean Sylvia, that's preposterous.' His mind raced back to the directionless spring and early summer. Anne's and Bill's references to Arthur Maitland, the subtle shift in attitude as the summer wore on, the times he had arrived home and found her out, times when he had not asked for an explanation and she had not offered one. As much for his benefit as for Craig's, he repeated, 'That's preposterous. They'd be laughed out of court.'

'*We* may think it's preposterous, but would you want her here? In this position? With Bretz pounding at her? He's not going to let up, David. He needs a conviction and he's going to get one.'

David sat with his head bowed while the clock ticked away the minutes. Craig knew he was hurting and he felt helpless in the face of that hurt, like a parent unable to offer comfort to a stricken child. When David spoke at last it was a whisper, barely audible. 'Let me think about it. Perhaps there's another way.'

And Craig's answer, decisive and final. 'There is no other way, David. This is how it has to be.'

Bretz was jubilant. Jenning must be slipping. The little fart was losing his grip. It was *ipso facto* that a Jenning client never confessed. Yet no sooner was he out of the room than the know-it-all s.o.b. spilled his gut. And he hadn't even had to spring his ace, the blank shipping tag stuck in the Bertrand folder. True, it was a common enough tag, the kind you could pick up anywhere. It was all circumstantial. They wouldn't even get past the preliminary with what they had; it would take months of investigating before they had enough for a true verdict, enough to get the bastard sent up to trial. And just like that, it was all wrapped up.

Detective-Sergeant Hagen, his second in command, wasn't so sure. He suspected a trick. 'Jenning is up to something,' he warned.

But Bretz, waving the statement over his head, had come back with, 'Tough. It's all here. Places, times, dates, the whole shebang. We've got him right by the balls.'

Sylvia went through her regular exercise routine, then repeated it three more times. Ciba lay flat on one corner of the padded mat and watched. Anne phoned five times and got no answer. Henny Henderson called once, looking for David, and after ten rings decided no one was at home.

David did not bother to phone the office to say he wouldn't be back. When he left Craig he got in the car and drove north, foot flat on the floorboard. The car hurtled down the center lane like a jet-fired missile. When the three-lane highway narrowed to a single lane he looped through the cloverleaf and headed south. He ran the sixty mile course, up and back, twice. At the end of the 240-mile run he had it sorted out in his head. It was not a good plan, but it was the best he could think of under the circumstances.

Craig did not know whether or not David would accept his decision to plead guilty. If not, he would simply dismiss him and hire another lawyer. Having made up his mind he wanted the entire affair over and done with as quickly as possible. He did not want to be out on bail. That would merely delay the trial, prolong the waiting. But he did want David as counsel-of-record. An over-zealous attorney – determined to prove his innocence, probing his confession for soft spots in an attempt to discredit it – would be a disaster.

He had tried to make this clear to David. He was not sure he had succeeded.

Hagen went home for a quick shower and a change of clothes. Standing in the tub with hot water pelting against his skin he thought about Faron. He was a tough cookie, all right. Hard as nails. Hadn't said a word all night. Didn't even seem to be listening. Not until Bretz brought up that business about Jenning and his files. That registered. Most people wouldn't have noticed. But if you'd been through as many interrogations as he had, you picked up on the little things. With Faron there'd been a quick muscle spasm, a fleeting expression in the eye. Still it was weird. Cool as a cucumber. Then, bingo. Right out of the blue he sang like a canary. After he'd talked to that shifty little shyster, Jenning. Thick as thieves and just as slick, he thought. They're up to something, sure.

David got home at the usual time, exhausted from his day on the road. Sylvia had dinner ready. Aside from being quieter than usual she behaved as though nothing had happened.

David watched her when she wasn't looking, trying to see her as a stranger would. It was difficult. He hadn't really looked at her for years. He had seen her, but he hadn't looked at her. She was not ordinary. No one could consider her ordinary. She was too tall for a woman. Slim to the point of being thin. She was not voluptuous, as some men felt a proper woman should be, yet the austere body emitted an animal grace, a controlled sexuality that was powerful, almost intimidating. Compared to his wife's spare clean lines, boobs-and-ass were over-lush and vulgar.

She passed the salad bowl and he took it from her, eyes fixed on her hands. They were long and slender, wrists narrow, fingers tapering. Fragile enough to be crushed in a strong handclasp. Yet once he had seen her smash through a piece of plywood, splitting the board cleanly in two. He had been shocked, his concern forbidding her to indulge in parlor-game theatrics. 'Breaking boards with your bare hands,' he'd said. 'You'll do yourself an injury.' She had laughed and said, 'David, you don't break boards with your hands. You do it with your mind.' He had not mentioned the incident again, and she had not repeated it.

They ate in silence. David left Sylvia to clear the table while he watched the six o'clock news. The major story was Faron's confession. He had half expected it and yet it caught him in the stomach like a physical blow. Sylvia came into the room in time to see Bretz talking affably into a barrage of microphones.

At the end of the item Sylvia switched off the set and faced David. 'The man is a fool,' she said contemptuously.

'Craig?' He sank back, overcome by weariness. He was not yet ready to discuss it.

'Not Craig. Bretz. An incompetent imbecile.'

She did not mention the confession. Did not ask if he had been party to the sorry business. No emotion, no expression showed in her face. But he noticed, for the first time, the hint of cruelty in her still gray eyes.

Craig lay on the narrow cot and stared at the ceiling. He did not think about his surroundings. He lived in a universe held captive between his ears, safe and inviolate. He could be where he wanted to be. On the craggy shoreline at the island. On a peak in the Rockies. On his balcony, high over the city.

Hands behind his head, long legs trailing over the end of the bed, he fell into a deep dreamless sleep.

David sat across from Craig, his face haggard from a sleepless night but his manner once again that of the cool, utterly professional lawyer. Without preamble he said, 'You made the statement.'

'Yes.' No elaboration. No further explanation.

'You can retract it.'

'No.'

'All right. Here's what I suggest. The first thing is to get you out of here.'

Craig shook his head. 'We do it now and get it over with.' Then, with a smile, 'I take it you've decided to represent me?'

'Yes. If you can call it that.' He looked down at his hands, avoided Craig's glance. 'The options are limited. We can go for insanity. . . .'

'No. That's out of the question.'

'There's nothing else. That way the confession stands but we get a not guilty verdict. We can't plead provocation, self-defense or accidental death. So we're left with delusion, automatism, or insanity. Delusion and automatism are out. All we've got is insanity. And I can make that stick.'

'You know what that would mean, David? If we were in the

States, maybe, but here? I'd be locked up with a bunch of crazies for God knows how long. I might never get out. It would be worse.'

David knew he was right, but when he thought of the alternative his body broke out in cold, drenching sweat.

'You realize we're looking at first degree. Twenty-five years with no parole. With remission, if you're lucky, you'll be out in twenty-two years. It's the rest of your life.'

'Then so be it.'

David looked up, his face tight with resolve. 'All we can do is go for a deal. If they'll go for second degree instead of first you'll be out, with luck, in seven years.'

'They'll never go for it. Bretz intends to go right down to the wire.'

'It's not up to him. It's the Crown's decision.' Craig hesitated. David prompted, 'Either you agree, or you get yourself another lawyer.'

The answer, slow in coming, was a concession. 'All right, David. But you're wasting your time.'

David phoned Flaherty when he got back to the office. When he mentioned the Faron case the Crown Attorney agreed to a meeting that afternoon. When he arrived he found Bretz and Hagen also in attendance. Bretz looked smugly confident. Hagen looked wary. Flaherty looked sober and thoughtful.

David ignored Bretz and Hagen. Speaking directly to Flaherty he said, 'My client is anxious to go to trial as quickly as possible. I'm sure you agree that with the unfavorable publicity this case has generated'— he threw a scornful look at Bretz and Hagen —'a speedy trial will be in everyone's best interest.'

'A trial?' Bretz sputtered. 'Forget the trial. He plans to plead guilty.'

Damn, David thought. He didn't tell me he'd told them that. Aloud, he said, 'That was before he had benefit of counsel. He will not plead guilty. Not unless. . . .' he paused for effect, his eyes on Flaherty.

'Unless what?' Bretz roared. Flaherty said, 'Please, Alf.' And to David, an echo of Bretz, 'Unless what?'

'Unless you reduce the charge. Second degree and there'll be no contest.'

'Go to hell,' Bretz yelled. 'Ten murders. All premeditated. We've got the sonofabitch all wrapped up and you. . . .'

'You have nothing wrapped up,' David said. 'You have a confession. We retract that and you're right back where you started.' He was bluffing. There was no way Craig would withdraw the statement. Nor, David had decided, did he want him to. To Flaherty, 'Think about it. A hearing now, neat and simple, or we go into court and it costs the taxpayers a bundle. And drags on for months. And you, Superintendent, will be back on the street, working your ass off, trying to come up with some hard evidence that you're going to need to get a conviction — if you couldn't come up with anything before you're not going to come up with it now. You can charge him with first degree. But you're not going to make it stick.'

He reached into his briefcase and pulled out his copy of Craig's statement. Carefully he tore it in half and tossed it on the desk. 'Let me know what you decide,' he said. 'My secretary will know where I am.'

It was late that afternoon when Flaherty called back with the news David wanted to hear. The hearing, a mere formality, would be held as quickly as possible. Possibly sometime within the following week.

He drove home slowly, wondering how best to break the news to Sylvia. He realized, with a start, that he no longer knew her well enough to anticipate her reaction. She might do as she so often did — lapse into silence. Or she might refuse to accept Craig's guilt, embark on a crusade to prove him innocent. It would be safer, he decided, to say as little as possible beforehand. And when it was over they would take the vacation postponed in January. Visit relatives in England. See the Continent.

The house was dark when he pulled into the driveway. Sylvia was waiting for him in the living room. She switched on the lamp, called him to join her. He paused on his way upstairs. 'Not tonight, Sylvia. I'm tired.'

'David, I have to know what's happening. Is Craig still in custody?'

'Yes,' he said, wanting to get away.

'Are you arranging bail?'

'We'll talk about it tomorrow.' He started up the stairs.

She came to the bottom of the stairway. Called up, 'David, there's something I have to tell you.'

He turned on the landing, looked down at her figure dark against the light with Millie at her side and said, 'I don't want to hear it, Sylvia.' And then, impulsively, something he hadn't said for a long time, 'I love you. Whatever happens I just want you to know, I love you very much.'

He undressed quickly, tossing his clothes on a chair, and got into bed. It was eight o'clock, and he was asleep by five after. It was the earliest he had gone to bed in years.

12

April 1985

Sylvia didn't know how long the phone had been ringing. The luminous digits on the alarm radio blinked one a.m. Half asleep, she reached across David for the phone, recognized the tear-filled voice as that of David's sister. She knew something was wrong, guessed correctly that it was David's mother.

She shook him awake and handed him the telephone. He listened, asked 'When?' then 'How bad?' and replaced the instrument and threw back the covers.

'Mother's had a stroke.'

'David, I'm sorry. Is she. . . . ?'

'No. She's in intensive care. They don't know how bad it is. Syl, will you pack some things for me?'

'David, you can't go now. It's the middle of the night. You're not going to drive?'

'It's the only way to get there.'

'But it will be just as fast if you wait till morning and fly. You're tired. And the road will be bad.'

'I've been asleep since eight o'clock. I'll be there by the time the planes start flying. If I wait I may be too late.'

She packed while he showered, offered to go with him, made a large thermos of coffee he could drink in the car. Not until after he left did she think of Craig, and the effect on him of David's sudden departure. She did not know that the arrangements had been made, the plea established. Nor was she overly concerned. Nothing could possibly happen to Craig. David wouldn't allow it. And failing David, she wouldn't allow it. It was unthinkable that Craig Faron should be locked away, buried in damp gray stone with the world of sun and wind and rain forever out of reach.

The next morning she called the hospital in Sudbury and was told that Mrs. Jenning was doing as well as could be expected. The standard response told her nothing about Mrs. Jenning's condition, but it did tell her that she was still alive.

Later that morning David called and said the crisis appeared to be over; there would be some damage, a slight paralysis, but they were assured of at least partial recovery. He would be home by the end of the week: he had told Miss Henderson how to get in touch with him if she needed him. When Sylvia asked about Craig he said everything was under control, there was no need to worry. She assumed that meant one of his assistants was arranging bail and the preliminaries that are part of any court action were being attended to.

The day was clear and bright, the air cold but not frigid. Sylvia pulled on a heavy ski sweater and coaxed Millie out onto the deck. Ciba jumped the fence and joined them. They sat there side by side on the top step, watching the squirrels and pigeons wage war over the peanut feeder. Later Sylvia called Anne, hoping she'd consent to stay with her until David got back. There was no answer. She tried Bill at the office. He was holding a three-day seminar for his salesmen in one of the downtown hotels and was incommunicado. Obviously, wherever Anne was, she was not with him.

Sylvia fed Millie and Ciba and thought about spending the night at a hotel. She tried Anne once more, letting the phone ring interminably. She replaced the receiver and was about to call the Valhalla for a room when there was a knock at the door. Millie, safe behind the sofa, gave a feeble growl. 'A lot of good you'd be,' Sylvia said affectionately. Millie's tail thumped on the soft carpet.

There was a young policeman on the porch, tall and trim in his immaculate uniform. Her first thought was that something had happened to David.

She opened the door and when the officer asked, 'Mrs. Jenning?' she nodded, unable to speak.

'Your husband called from out of town and asked us to keep an eye on the house while he's away.'

Weak with relief, Sylvia stepped aside and invited him in.

'No thank you, ma'am. I just wanted you to know that there's no need to worry. We'll come by every half hour. Just make sure your doors and windows are locked.'

He got back in the car and Sylvia, taking his advice, locked and bolted the door. Then, although it was still early, she went through the house, checking the remaining doors and windows. She was touched that David had taken time to think of her in the midst of what must be a trying situation in Sudbury. It didn't occur to her that this was the first time he had requested police surveillance during an absence from home.

Reassured by the guarantee of protection, she dismissed the idea of a hotel. She was not a nervous type by nature. She had always moved through the city freely and without fear. And always, until recently, she had felt a sublime sense of confidence at home. Nothing, she had believed, could ever invade the privacy of this quiet house on this quiet street in the city's west end. If it weren't for that damned phone. . . .

She resented the easy access afforded by the telephone. Anyone, anywhere, could gain entrance simply by dialing the correct number. There were no locks, no bolts, no guards that could prevent a crazy from spilling poison into an unsuspecting ear.

For a moment she considered taking the phone off the hook. She resisted the impulse, determined not to give in to a fear both neurotic and irrational. 'Sticks and stones,' she reminded herself.

The evening was uneventful. At one point she happened to glance out of the window as the patrol car went by. It paused briefly in front of the house. Knowing they were there, Sylvia felt no worry, no tension. She read for awhile. Watched television. Tried not to think of Craig.

Blessedly, the phone didn't ring.

It was just before midnight when she went to bed. She had a shower, checked to make sure the gun was back in place, then, because the room was stuffy, she opened the window a few inches. Cool air puffed through the screen and she got into bed quickly, pulling the blankets up to her chin.

The sun was streaming through the windows when she awoke. It was after eight; she had slept well and late. Ciba was clinging to the edge of the window sill, perched precariously in the skinny branches of the lilac tree, yowling for food.

Sylvia stretched. She felt good. She threw back the covers and got out of bed. The day had begun.

She finished the few household chores quickly and then called

Henny to see if there was anything new on Craig, and could she speak with whoever had been assigned to fill in while David was away. Henny said as far as she knew David was handling Mr. Faron's case personally, and to the best of her knowledge there were no new developments. She then called 51 Division and asked where Craig Faron was being held. The desk sergeant said he would let her speak to an inspector. The inspector said he was not at liberty to give out that information.

Frustrated, she dialed Anne's number. After last night she knew she could manage just fine by herself. She didn't need Anne for reassurance, but she'd enjoy her company. Like the day before, there was no answer. She wondered if something could have happened. Anne would have told her if she planned to be away. She decided to give it another couple of hours and then, if she still couldn't rouse her, she would call the police and have them check.

An hour later she called again. The relief she felt when the phone was picked up on the second ring was like a three-martini high. 'Anne?'

'Anne isn't here. This is her mother. Is there any message?'

'No. That is . . . I've been worried about her. Is there anything wrong?'

'Goodness, no. Not that I'm aware. She'll be back some time after dinner.'

'Will you be seeing her?'

'No, but I can leave a message. Would you like her to call you?'

Sylvia left her number and Anne's mother said she would put it on the message board near the phone where Anne would be sure to find it when she came in.

Satisfied, Sylvia went out to pick up some fresh vegetables and a newspaper. As she pulled back into the driveway the patrol car went by. The driver blew the horn and waved. Sylvia smiled and waved back.

She made a pitcher of iced tea and took it into the living room with the paper. The late afternoon sun shone warm through the window, the pale rays magnified by the heavy plate glass. The house was quiet. The paper slipped to the floor. Drowsy and relaxed, she drifted off into a light dreamless sleep.

She awoke with a start. The room was pitch black. Confused and disoriented, she didn't know where she was. Then, coming awake, she switched on the lamp and looked at her watch. It was after nine o'clock. She'd been asleep for hours. Millie, lying near her empty bowl in the kitchen, looked at her reproachfully. She fed the animals and got a glass of milk for herself.

The paper was scattered on the floor in the living room. She folded it neatly and rinsed out the few dishes that had accumulated. Working in the brightly-lit, glass enclosed kitchen she felt exposed, like an object in a fishbowl, prey to any passing eye. She switched off the light and looked out. The dimly lit street looked deserted. She checked the back. With the pool still under cover, it was too dark to see anything beyond the circle of light from the windows. She felt she was being watched, her every move noted and registered by sly, unseen eyes.

The phone rang, the sound so piercing she almost screamed. Then she remembered. Anne. She had left a message for Anne. Thank God. In her rush to reach the instrument before Anne hung up, she tripped over Millie, triggering an indignant yelp.

She reached the phone. Picked it up. 'Hi. Am I glad you called.'

'Mrs. Jenning?' The voice was polite, cordial, unfamiliar. It was not 'the' voice. 'Is Mr. Jenning there?'

Caught off guard she said, 'No. I'm sorry.'

'Will he be home later?'

Cautious now, she said, 'Yes, he will. But I suggest you call him at his office.'

'They don't expect him until later in the week, Mrs. Jenning.' The voice was pleasant. Friendly. It held the hint of a smile. He hung up. So did Sylvia.

It was not the same man. He had said nothing improper. Still, it was disturbing. She stared at the phone as though it were a snake coiled to strike. She picked it up and made one more call to Anne. No answer. She broke the connection, then took the receiver off the hook and placed it carefully on the kitchen counter. There would be no more calls for the rest of the night.

Not wanting to switch the kitchen light back on, she groped under the sink for the flashlight and used it to check the doors and windows. Closing the front wall drapes in the living room, she blocked out the view from the street. The rear wall, overlooking the deck and backyard, was solid glass – centered by a sliding glass door between the living and dining rooms. David had wanted to install floor-to-ceiling drapes along the full length of the house. When she had objected, prizing airiness and light above privacy, they had compromised on filmy sheers that were the next best thing to nothing. She was sorry now that David hadn't been more firm.

The sheers ran in panels on a single track stretching from wall to wall. To prevent blocking off the sliding door, they were never fully closed. She tried the door to make sure it was secured, then inserted the contraption David had brought back from New York. Wedged in the runner, the device was a much more effective lock than the flimsy snib. As she knelt to adjust the bar, she noticed a flicker of light at the bottom of the yard. Crouching, she watched it weave back and forth through the shrubbery. It was so quiet she could hear her own breathing.

The light came closer. Huddled, still as death, she watched. Her spine tingled. Every sense was alert. She was not frightened. She had never been frightened of danger perceived. This she could cope with. It was the unseen that unnerved her: a faceless telephone call, the threat of sudden and unexpected violence, of being taken by surprise, trapped in a situation without control. Deprived of initiative and cast as prey, Sylvia's assurance gave way to panic-tinged fear.

She waited until the light neared the far corner of the house. Shielded from view she moved into the unlit kitchen with quiet, cat-like grace. If she circled the house and approached from the rear she would have the advantage.

She unlocked the door without making a sound. The knob turned easily and she eased the door open. Making no sound, she unhooked the aluminium storm door. It was free of the catch, partly ajar, when the huge black figure stepped up on to the porch. In the pale backlight of the streetlamp, the faceless silhouette towered larger than life.

Quickly she pulled the door shut and clicked on the outside light.

'Mrs. Jenning?' It was the young officer, eyes blinking in the sudden glare, hand on holster.

Tension drained, Sylvia smiled weakly and stood back for him to enter. 'You surprised me.'

'Is everything all right? We saw a flashlight in the kitchen.'

'That was me. I felt a bit nervous with the light on.'

'Did you hear something? Notice anyone around the house?'

She was about to tell him about the prowler in the backyard when the second officer came around the garage, flashlight in hand.

'Nothing back there,' he reported.

Limp, Sylvia leaned against the counter for support. 'I thought you were prowlers,' she explained.

'What made you feel nervous?'

'I don't know. Yes, I do know. There was a phone call.'

'Obscene?'

'No.'

'What kind of call?'

'Just a call, that's all. Someone who asked for my husband.' She felt foolish, like a neurotic spinster obsessed by fantasies. The young constables looked at each other. It was a knowing, here-we-go-again glance.

Embarrassed, Sylvia explained about the feeling of being watched. They were polite and attentive.

'Would you like us to check out the house?' They were humoring her, she felt. Determined to do their duty regardless of how unnecessary it seemed.

'No. No thank you. I feel better now. I'm sure everything is fine.'

They walked down the drive, chatting to each other in low voices. She felt they were talking about her, perhaps joking about the inordinate vanity that made some women think all men were after their bodies. The two young officers were not talking about Sylvia; they were deciding where they would stop for coffee.

Millie ambled into the kitchen and asked for a fresh bowl of water. Sylvia refilled the dish and added a handful of ice cubes. As she set the dish down beside the basement door, she heard a grating noise downstairs. Millie, slurping water, heard nothing.

Determined not to give way to fear for a second time, Sylvia flicked the main switch to the basement and descended the stairs cautiously. Every sense was alert, her body as smoothly reactive as a precision instrument.

The utility room was undisturbed, the above-ground windows securely fastened. The large family room was also in order, everything set in its proper place. She checked behind the bar and looked behind the lounge, sofa and club chairs. The room had the lifeless, vacant air of living space seldom used. Nor was there anything unusual in the gym. As she left each room she pulled the door shut behind her, leaving no openings in her wake as she walked along the narrow passageway to the furnace room at the far end of the hall.

This was the only room in the house that Sylvia consciously avoided. It made her claustrophobic, dominated by a gas furnace that she half expected would blow up if approached too closely. She pulled the chain and the light bulb, set high in the ceiling, threw a harsh glare over the box-like room. It, too, was empty.

She was about to leave when she felt a draft and looked up. The window was partly open. She reached up to close it and discovered the screen was missing. David had hired a handyman to replace a cracked pane in the window earlier in the month. He had obviously been careless. She made a mental note to phone the agency and complain about their shoddy service. Luckily he had picked the best room in the house to be slipshod. The furnace room door was the only inside door with an outside bolt.

She closed and bolted the door, then checked the storage cupboard and pantry on her way back to the stairs. In the pantry she found her old tin tea caddy had toppled off the shelf. That was probably the sound she had heard. She picked it up, hoping they weren't about to undergo another invasion of field mice.

As she passed the family room she noticed that the door she had closed had slipped open. She pulled it shut again, making sure the latch clicked into place.

Millie was sprawled in the middle of the kitchen, waiting for her. She gave her a biscuit, then put her out the back door for her last trip of the night. When she returned, Sylvia locked the door and replaced the bar in the runner.

A friend had told her there was no way on God's green earth a sliding door could be made safe. 'You don't open one of these doors,' he'd told her, 'you remove it. Give me a blunt knife and I'll have that door right out of the frame in five minutes.' She hadn't believed him until she saw a woman on TV whose home had been vandalized while she slept. She was standing in the hole in the wall where the door had been. The door was lying in a flower bed, as good as new. The woman was crying.

The memory of that crying woman brought back the feeling of apprehension. Sylvia felt as though the house harbored a strange, unwanted guest; as though eyes followed her every movement. Determined not to be undone she forced herself to think of other things as she switched off lights and mounted the stairs for bed.

She undressed and adjusted the water in the shower. A bath would have been easier; the shower was her way of proving to herself there was nothing to fear. She settled Millie on the bathmat, and stepped into the tub pulling the shower curtain snug to prevent drips.

Isolated behind the translucent curtain, cut off from sound by the rush of water, it was hard not to think of the classic scene in *Psycho*. Often, when she was showering with no one else in the house, the Hitchcock sequence flashed through her mind like a series of sharp stills: the blurred shape, the hand clutching, the blood gurgling into the drain. Graphic violence could not equal the mind-bending terror evoked by the suggestion of evil, the allusion to deeds dark and dreadful.

Sylvia showered quickly and pulled on her heavy terry robe. Millie waddled down the hall behind her and collapsed for the night in her usual spot between the wall and the bed. Her back to the open door, Sylvia picked up the spray deodorant from the dresser under the window. As she did so, there was a soft, shuffling sound behind her. Millie raised her head and growled. Sylvia tensed. She knew she was not alone.

Slowly, her body rigid, she turned and saw him. He was standing in the doorway, poised on the balls of his feet. Their eyes met. They stared at each other. Silent. Tense. Frozen in space and time. She knew the face. Recognized the long, unkempt hair and fierce blazing eyes. The boy who had stolen the purse. The boy she had tripped, then beaten. The boy who had stared at her in the courtroom, burning with rage. He was wearing a soiled T-shirt and skin-tight jeans. One hand held a thin-bladed knife. It looked razor sharp.

Half-crouching, arms held wide, he moved forward. She stood, transfixed, watching him inch forward, his body swiveling in slow motion, blocking escape.

He stopped just beyond arm's length, mouth open, breath coming in shallow gasps. Sylvia measured the distance between them. She was no longer afraid. She had passed through fear into a place in her mind beyond fear.

There was a game she played with Ciba. A game Ciba had initiated. He would drop his toy mouse at her feet. When she tried to pick it up, he struck at her. It was a game he always won until she learned to stop looking at the mouse and watch him instead. There was always something that gave him away. A tensing of muscles. An expression in the eyes. She became so proficient that he eventually abandoned the game. She watched the boy as she had watched Ciba. The cat had taught her well.

He made a sudden short lunge. Testing. Expecting Sylvia to jump out of range. When she didn't move he relaxed, grinning. He had seen women, even men, paralyzed by fear. The shoe was on the other foot. Lou was right. This would be a piece of cake.

Knife poised, he took a step forward and grabbed at her robe. Lightning fast, Sylvia whipped her arm from behind her back and shot a spray of deodorant into his face. He dropped the knife and staggered back. Gagging. Rubbing frantically at his eyes. Sylvia stepped forward and struck him under the nose with the edge of her hand. He screamed as the cartilage tore. His nose was mashed out of shape, the nostrils tilted up, blood seeping into his gaping mouth. He mouthed a name. 'Lou. Lou.'

He forced his eyes open, tried desperately to get them in focus. They were blood-red and streaming with tears. He groped for the door in an effort to reach the hall. Sylvia grasped his belt and pulled him back into the room. Terrified, he spun around and lunged towards her. She stepped back and swung sideways from the shoulder, catching him on the bridge of the nose, shattering the bone. He collapsed against the dresser and she struck him once more, a deliberate, lethal blow across the temple. He slid to the floor, lifeless, blood oozing into the thick gray carpet. She prodded him with her toe, then leaned over to feel for a pulse. She knew, without checking, that the boy was dead.

It seemed as though hours had gone by. It was actually only a few minutes. She picked up the phone to call the police. There was no dial tone. She remembered that the phone in the kitchen was off the hook. The call would have to be made from downstairs.

The hands closed around her throat as she turned to leave.

Stunned, unable to comprehend where this second person had come from, she stood frozen. It had not occurred to her that the boy was not alone. This man was older — his face round and stubbled under a bowl haircut, his eyes murky and deep-set in hollowed sockets. She recognized him. Had seen him in the courtroom, his features twisted in a vindictive leer. Lou. Lou Germaine. Sibling to the body, now lifeless, lying at her feet.

For a split second they stared at each other, their faces inches apart. Then Sylvia moved, bringing both arms up between his, levering to break his grip. She stepped back, out of reach, and the man looked from her to the body on the floor.

His face twisted with rage. 'You bitch,' he hissed. He saw the knife, picked it up.

Sylvia backed away. Her foot struck something soft and she tripped over the corpse. Before she could regain her balance he was on top of her, holding the knife at her throat, punching her head and face. She fell across the bed and he stood over her, calmer, the blinding fury under control.

He tossed the knife on the floor, feeling no need of it. 'Is Mr. Jenning at home?' he asked mockingly. It was the voice. Recognizing it, she felt the same sick dread it had bred, disembodied, over the phone.

She tried to sit up and he smashed her across the face with the back of his hand. Pain pounded through her head. She tried to focus her good eye but it was like swimming underwater. Everything was blurred and out of perspective.

She knew he was going to kill her. They had come intending to kill her. Young Germaine must have known she would be able to identify him. He had known and hadn't cared. He made a point of accosting her openly, as though he wanted her to be aware of what was happening and who was responsible. Which could mean only one thing. He did not intend to have her testify against him a second time.

Cowering behind the bed, Millie emitted a low, agonized whimper. Momentarily distracted, Germaine moved out of her line of vision. Reacting automatically, she rolled over. Reached David's drawer. Tugged it open. Felt frantically for the gun. The drawer was empty. The gun wasn't there. And then he was on top of her, slamming the drawer shut on her wrist, and pain was shooting up her arm in ribbons of fire.

Millie slunk from the room with her tail between her legs. Realizing she was not a threat, Lou ignored her, rising instead to drag Sylvia over and up to a half-sitting position. 'Is this what you're looking for, Mrs. Jenning?' He pulled the gun from his back pocket. 'You didn't think we'd be so careless, did you?' He laughed softly, crazily.

Sylvia knew about death. She had seen it in Arthur Maitland's eyes as the knife laid his throat open. She had heard it gurgle in Keith Hallworth's throat, she had felt the life flow out of Buddy Thompson and Jim Henry. She knew about death in all its slow, agonizing forms. She knew that this was her turn, that she was about to die, that it would take an excruciatingly long time, that she was not ready, and did not want to go.

Bruised and bloody, she struck out with her one good hand. Enraged, Germaine grabbed her by the throat, dug his thumbs into her windpipe.

Gasping for air, fighting to free herself of his weight, she heard the sound of metal tearing, like the rasp of sandpaper on rusty nails. It was remote, far away, disconnected to what was happening in the room.

The light faded. Her eardrums roared as though they were about to burst. Scenes from the past began flashing through her mind. She felt herself slipping down a long, dark, spiraling tunnel. And as she was slipping down, a blood-curdling scream was rising, piercing the air with inhuman frenzy. And following the scream — part of it — a huge black shape that hurtled through space.

She felt the hands go loose, the weight on top of her give way. She lay there, gulping for air, vaguely aware of violent turmoil at the foot of the bed.

The scream, high-pitched and primeval, seeped into every corner of the room. And now the man was screaming too, his voice a minor counterpoint to the unearthly banshee wails.

Sylvia tried desperately to see what was happening. It was difficult to concentrate, almost impossible for her eye to follow the feverish, flailing activity. With superhuman effort she rolled to the edge of the bed and swung her legs over the side. One foot landed on the dead man's chest. It heaved under the pressure and she jerked her foot away.

Her head felt like pulp and her right arm hung uselessly at her side. She wiped her face with the corner of her robe. It came away soggy with blood.

Slowly the vision in her undamaged eye cleared. The room looked as though it had been ripped apart by a tornado. The screen over the window was torn loose and objects from the dresser underneath were scattered across the floor. Chairs were overturned. The wardrobe mirror was shattered and dagger-sharp shards of glass littered the floor. There was blood on the rug, the bedspread, splattered on the walls. And on his knees, in the middle of the wreckage, Lou Germaine hunched unmoving. His arms were torn open, his face was scored and raw. On his head, clinging to the lacerated skull with each claw sunk to its sheath, was Ciba.

Pulling herself to her feet, she stumbled over to the blubbering, terrified form. The knife was lying on the floor where he had tossed it earlier. In easy reach. He could pick it up without moving from where he sat rooted, but he was too petrified to stretch out his hand.

Sylvia looked at the knife and shuddered. She wanted to remove it, but she did not want to touch it. Reaching into her pocket for a wad of Kleenex she dropped it on top of the weapon and scooped it up. She opened the nearest drawer and shoved it under a stack of neatly folded lingerie. Out of sight, out of reach.

She stretched a hand toward Ciba. He growled. The green eyes were steady and unwavering; the heavy body, blown almost double in size, was tense. Cautiously, afraid he might turn on her, she stroked his head. He arched his neck to her touch, and the great shoulder muscles relaxed. She picked him up carefully, one hand under the coiled body, the other unhooking his claws from the torn flesh.

Lou remained on his knees, sobbing convulsively. He did not know what had happened. He was in terrible pain, but worse than the pain was the sheer, overwhelming terror. He had been attacked from behind by a raging fury. He would remain where he was until someone led him away.

Sylvia left him there and limped out of the room. It took a long time to get from the bedroom to the kitchen. Ciba followed her down the stairs, stopping when she paused to rest, treading slowly when she moved. Millie trailed behind.

She reached the phone as the patrol car came down the street, red light flashing. She flicked the outside light and the car stopped, then pulled into the drive. She managed to get the door open just as the young officer came up the steps.

'My God,' he said. 'What happened?'

'I killed a man,' Sylvia whispered, and fainted in his arms.

13

May 1985

It was early May, but the air was as warm and pleasant as a day in June. Sylvia was sunning at one end of the deck; David and Joe were talking quietly at the other. Prinnie was lying in the grass, her long coat whiter than usual against the green. Millie drowsed on the top step. Ciba, flat on his back with sturdy legs outstretched, was sound asleep under Sylvia's lounge. It was a quiet, peaceful scene and Sylvia was content.

Except for a wrist that ached when it rained, Sylvia was completely recovered from the beating she had suffered. Lou Germaine, the man who had attacked her, was out on bail awaiting trial. His face was permanently scarred, he had developed a nervous tic in his right eyelid and a fear of the dark. Ciba was now one of the family. Because of the viciousness of his attack on Germaine, the authorities had ordered him destroyed. It had taken all of David's skill to save the cat and Sylvia was grateful, but she also found it ironic that he had done a better job for Ciba than he had for Craig.

She tried not to think of Faron. It was Joe, not David, who had told her about the hearing and immediate disposition. Twenty years in Canada's oldest and most fearsome jail: Kingston Penitentiary. She had lain in the hospital with the scene vivid in her mind. Craig, standing before the judge while the charges were read. Ten charges. Ten admissions of guilt. Craig in handcuffs being driven through a blinding blizzard to the stone fortress overlooking Lake Ontario. Craig walking through the dungeon-like entrance, across the frozen yard, into the admissions building where his name became a number and his life became a nightmare in hell. She understood then why David had refused to discuss it. Understood, also, that if she allowed herself to think about it she would go mad.

She could not hear — was not interested in — the conversation taking place at the other end of the deck. Brought together by their brief collaboration, David and Joe continued to see each other. David enjoyed Joe's company but he was made uneasy whenever mention was made of Faron and the copycat deaths. Joe sensed this and tried not to talk about Craig but there were aspects of the case he still did not understand. Now, encouraged by the warmth and sunshine and easy ambience, he tried again. Why had Craig offered no contest? Why had he refused to discuss the missing body number 2 when he was so candid about the others? Why had he numbered them in the first place?

David knew the answers to some of his questions, but not to all. Craig had not discussed the missing body because he knew nothing about it. A body could lie hidden for months, years even forever. There was no significance to number 2 other than the fact it was missing. As for the numbering itself, he did not know, but he guessed that it was meant as a message, the killer's way of saying the victims were cut from the same piece of cloth and, in the end, justice had been done.

And why no contest? He looked at Sylvia, silken body languid in the sun, eyes closed, lips curved in a gentle half smile. He had loved her from the first moment he saw her, standing in the schoolyard, laughing, face upturned, hair gleaming in the sun. He had always loved her. But in the last few weeks, inexplicably and beyond reason, he had fallen *in* love with her. He felt about her now as he had not felt since the time, before they were married, when he was obsessed by the thought of owning her.

He had been afraid to tell her about Craig. When Joe told her he had braced himself and, expecting some form of violent reaction, had hurriedly suggested a trip abroad. Was resigned when she refused to leave the city. And disconcerted, too, by her complete indifference. She never mentioned Faron, asked no questions, made no comment; it was as though Craig Faron had never existed.

He did not blame her for what happened; he blamed himself. He had left her alone too often, been away too much. But he would not make the same mistake again. Except for one quick trip out of town, when he made arrangements with Joe to stay overnight, he had spent every evening at home. He would watch her, take care of her, and when he did have to travel she would go with him.

Joe was still talking about Faron, still looking for answers. 'Joe,' he said, trying to smile, 'I don't know any more about it than you do. He said he did it. Beyond that, he refused to discuss it.'

Sylvia stretched luxuriously, feeling wonderfully vibrant and alive. The first few days had been traumatic. When she returned home from the hospital, over the objections of David and her doctor, she had been cushioned by shock. The first thing she had done was go upstairs to the bedroom. She knew if she didn't do it immediately she would never feel safe in the room again. Although she had only been away for a few days, the room looked much as it had before the attack. The screen had been replaced; so had the wardrobe mirror. David had hired a woman to clean up and she had done a good job. Even the bloodstains in the carpet had been removed.

It wasn't until Sylvia opened the drawer and found the knife, wrapped in Kleenex, that the violence of that night came alive again. She slammed the drawer shut and turned back to the window with its peaceful view of the backyard. As she turned her eye caught a glint of light under the dresser. She leaned over and retrieved a needle-thin splinter of mirror, too fine for the vacuum to have picked up. There was blood along one edge, and glued to the blood, strands of hair. She picked it up carefully and was about to drop it in the wastebasket when she thought of Craig. She removed the hair and added it to the Kleenex-wrapped bundle in the drawer.

The sound of church bells drifted up from the Lakeshore. Ciba stirred restlessly. Millie raised her head and gave a perfunctory bark. And Anne came through the side gate as she had that other spring day almost a year before, shattering the quiet. She was pale, breathless, with a Sunday copy of *The Sun* held overhead like a banner. Her arrival was so noisy, so unexpected, that David and Joe jumped to their feet. Sylvia didn't move.

Anne bounded up the steps and shoved the paper at David. 'It wasn't Faron,' she said, her voice one decibel short of a banshee's. 'He's innocent. It wasn't him.'

Joe grabbed the paper from David. 'My God, there's been another murder. The guy they suspected in the telephone repairman attacks.'

David looked at Sylvia. 'There's probably no connection.'

'There is,' Anne insisted. 'They're positive. It has something to do with a label. A tag. I don't know exactly. Whatever it is, only the real killer knew about it. They're calling this murder 11, and they have all kinds of clues. A knife with fingerprints. Even some hair under his fingernails. He must have put up a real fight.'

David's skin was sickly green. 'A fingerprint is useless unless they can match it up.' His voice lacked the usual timbre.

'But they can. They have,' Anne prattled. 'They say an arrest is imminent. That must mean they have it on file. They'll have to let Craig go, won't they?'

'That depends.' David, eyes fixed on Sylvia, was turning from pale green to cadaver white.

'Of course they will,' Sylvia said placidly. 'It doesn't even require an appeal, does it, David? The Cabinet has full pardon power. A stroke of the pen.'

'I have to call the paper,' Joe said, furious with himself for having missed out on the story.

'I'd better get in touch with Flaherty.' David moved heavily, like an automaton. As an afterthought, he added, 'See if you can get a lead on the suspect. Someone down there might know who it is.'

Calm in the midst of pandemonium, Sylvia unwound from the lounge and said pleasantly, 'I think I'll make breakfast. David, why don't you pour us a drink?'

Busying herself in the kitchen, she didn't hear David ask Joe if he had stayed that night or hear Joe explain that he had wanted to, but Sylvia had made arrangements to stay with the Simmonds.

Joe picked up the phone and David, waiting to call Flaherty at home, poured three tall glasses of Scotch and carried them out to the deck. A few moments later he bounded back into the kitchen, ruddy complexion restored and eyes gleaming with relief. 'They've got an ID. You'll never guess. I'll let Joe tell you about it.'

She stood in the doorway, waiting for Joe to complete his call.

When he finally signed off he turned to them and said, 'You're damned lucky, Sylvia. It's that Germaine character. They've matched the print and they've got a round-the-clock on him till they get a warrant. You needn't call Flaherty, David. It seems he's away for the weekend.'

Anne's glance grazed Joe and came to rest on Sylvia. 'He killed all those people. Syl, it's a miracle he didn't get you too.' Her mouth made an 'O' as round as her eyes.

'The whole police department looking for him, and you're the one who caught him. You should get a medal.'

'Ciba,' Sylvia corrected. 'If it weren't for him. . . . It can wait till tomorrow,' she added lazily. 'You can't do much on a Sunday anyway.'

Standing apart from the others she seemed remote. Untouched. 'I have to run down to Min-a-Mart. I'll just be a few minutes.'

David half rose, intending to accompany her. She held up her hand. 'I won't be long,' she promised. He searched her face, was about to insist, thought better of it and said, 'Take my car if you like.'

More amused than pleased by what to him was a major concession, she shook her head. 'Mine is in the driveway.' On the Lakeshore she picked up a loaf of cheese bread warm from the oven and a dozen croissants. Then she crossed the street to a phone booth on the corner of the service station lot. Rummaging in the lining of her handbag, she pulled out a crumpled piece of paper. Most of the names on the paper were stroked off. Only three names were left. These she struck off, too. Low on the list, they were not worth worrying about.

Lou Germaine's name and telephone number were inked in at the bottom of the sheet. Using the lighter she still carried in spite of having stopped smoking months before, she burned the scrap of paper on the narrow shelf in the booth, scattering the ashes over the tarmac.

She checked her watch. The time was right. His wife would be at work. Lou would be alone. She dialed the number, covered the mouthpiece with the end of her scarf, and when he answered she said, 'Mr Germaine – is your wife at home?' This was the third time she had called him and each time she sensed a deepening of terror at the other end of the line. Now there was a quick intake of air, followed by a pregnant silence. Smiling, she hung up without waiting for a reply.

Back home once more, she made a fresh pot of coffee and served thick slices of cheese bread dripping with butter, and croissants with homemade strawberry jam. Later she opened the bottle of champagne that had been kept on ice for just such an occasion. The four of them sat on the deck in the sunshine and drank a toast to the end of winter and the beginning of spring.

Sylvia, languid on the lounge, said she was looking forward to a long, lazy summer.

Epilogue

With the arrest of Lou Germaine, the wave of numbered murders came to an end. The final killing occurred while Craig Faron was incarcerated in Kingston's sombre jail. Although no proof of his innocence – copycat deaths could themselves be subject to copycat spin-off – the evidence against Germaine was conclusive. His fingerprint was found on the knife beside the repairman's body. The strands of hair snagged under the fingernails of the *corpus delecti* matched Lou's with twenty matching characteristics. But even these affirmations of guilt paled beside the discovery of the map. Discovered by Bretz in the toe of a winter boot stashed for the summer in the basement of the Germaines' frame bungalow, the city map bore numbered locations of each of the metropolitan crime sites. There had been so much publicity that anyone interested in crime could have laid out a similar blueprint, a point which might well have been successfully argued by even the modestly competent defense team, were it not for the numbered crosses. Only numbers three and nine were missing, both deaths having taken place outside the city. But the others, including the missing number 2, were there. The X, inked on a ravine in the city's east end, led investigators to a carcass scavenged by animals. With only a few bones to work with, identification was impossible. The body had been located, but the erstwhile owner of that body remained a mystery.

Despite his frenzied claims of innocence and his stubborn refusal to admit the map as his, Lou Germaine was declared guilty of first-degree murder on eleven counts. The verdict was not surprising – the disposition was. Instead of eleven life terms to be served concurrently – judiciary temperence that limited the penalty for any number of murders to the level of one – the Germaine sentence broke with tradition and was levied consecutively. The indications were that Lou Germaine would remain behind bars for the rest of his life. Those concerned about the victim rather than the perpetrator hoped that this departure would set a new course for justice, a wish further heightened when a private member's bill was brought before the House introducing a tightening of the Criminal Code and abolition of automatic remission and mandatory supervision.

Craig Faron was back on his island in the north. Released by Cabinet Order initiated by the Minister of Justice following a deposition by David, he refused to discuss the matter, declaring it a chapter closed.

David wrote his book on crime and criminals, assisted by Sylvia, who typed up the transcript, edited and proofread the manuscript.

Ciba grew fat and lazy and relaxed into the role of pampered house pet. He had fought his last battle — won his last war.